Josie King

Planet Fran − Population One
& Just a Little Unstable

Josie King

This book is dedicated to
Tony, Laura, Jack and Danny with much love.

And...is in loving memory of my good friend

Philippa 'Richards' Humphreys

who set me out on the eventing path.

Acknowledgements and Author's Note

There are a number of people to whom I owe a debt of thanks. To my good friends who took the time to read my early drafts, offered valuable feedback and helped me to shape the story into a workable book, thank you all: Mandy, Gill, Nicky, Laura, Amy, Danny, Joan and Emma.

Amy has listened to me prattle on about this book over many a climb at the local wall, whilst Laura has listened to me trying out funnies for the book over endless horsebox trips. To Jack, thank you for the endless cups of weak, milky tea whilst I was poring over what to write next!

The characters in the book are all fictional, although, I have been furnished with much material, on which to base some of Fran's exploits, over my years on livery yards with my instructors and my riding buddies. Much like Fran, I was a late starter to riding and was introduced to eventing by my good friend, Phil. She taught me and my daughter, Laura, to ride and introduced me to eventing. When she later moved to the USA, where she sadly later died doing the sport she loved so much, that mantle was picked up expertly by Tuffy Tilley, then Tracy Garside and Dee Hankey with much help from my good friend Shane Sullivan. The instructor, Gabby, in the book draws on the characters of all of my instructors who have each been instrumental in making me a halfway competent rider and who continue to see my daughter excel at this super sport.

Huge thanks go to my editor, Danielle Wrate (www.wrateseditingservices.co.uk), for her structural help to get the book into shape and to Pumbaa Goess-Saurau for her proofreading.

Lastly, and by no means least, special thanks goes to my long-suffering husband, Tony, and he is indeed long (at least six feet) and suffering, having put up with me for so many years! He's been by my side through all of my ventures and I suspect (and hope) he'll be there through the rest to come.

This is my first full-length novel and I've loved writing it. I really hope you enjoy reading it and that it puts a smile on your face.

Fran Rides Again is now in progress. If you'd like to keep in touch, give me feedback and register for my progress updates, please drop me an email at josiekingbooks@gmail.com. I'd love to hear from you.

Here I am, warmed up, all my show best on, ready to go into the arena. My heart is beating ten-to-the-dozen, as they say. After all, there's more to this than just winning a competition. Staying on, in fact, would be a good start given my relative immaturity at this whole horsey malarkey. I've seen it said (on a horsey greetings card, I think), that the art of riding is keeping the horse between you and the ground. That is surprisingly more difficult than you might think when you're thirty-eight, single by choice (although not my choice), sporting false teeth, are just slightly overweight and are learning to ride for the first time in your life. And under considerable sufferance, I might add.

The teeth are an important detail. I lost most of them when I was quite young and now I have a full top and partial bottom plate. Over the years, they have caused me all sorts of grief. For example, there's the time I vomited them down the toilet and had to fish them back out before flushing, after having drunk a shedload of Prosecco. There's the time I lost them in my sleep – God knows how, though, after another shedload of Prosecco. I found them stuck to the bottom of my pillow. There's the time my brother Paul's dog was wandering the house with them in her mouth. It's no mean feat to scrub a set of dentures to the point it's acceptable to put them back in your mouth, I can tell you. But each time, with no appropriate backup if they broke or went missing, I've rescued them. So, when riding I find I have to be so careful with them.

I tend to think a little differently to other people, too. I don't think in straight lines and if there's an alternative way to take something, you can be sure that I'll be the one that interprets it that way. Sometimes that's a gift and other times it just makes me look like a bit of a muppet. I can give you an example. I needed some footballs for a team-building day at work. Off I tootled to the shopping centre and the biggest toyshop I could find. I was approached by a young man who attentively asked if he could help.

'Yes, if you have big balls?' I said with a wry smile.

I like to think I'm a bit of a comedian, you know, got that funny bone in me, and that line between what's appropriate and what's not is sometimes not quite as it should be. Clearly this poor young man wasn't on my wavelength and I had to apologise profusely to him as he looked visibly shaken.

As I said, here I am, the sun is shining, although we're now into autumn, I'm at Bears Grove College, near York and the place is heaving with end-of-season competitors. I was hoping for a quiet day, not so many entries so I will have a better shot at the prize I must win. And, indeed, less people to watch, laugh and mock. I could kill Richard for putting me in this position but it's done, so I need to stop bellyaching and just crack on. Three simple phases and I'll be finished, then I can get off this creature, although to be fair I've kind of grown to like him, and get on with what I set out to do.

How did I get here? Well, that's a long story, so grab yourself a bottle of Prosecco (or a cup of tea, if you're so inclined) and I'll tell you how it came to be that I'm sat waiting to go into the arena to do a dressage test in only my third ever eventing competition, after just ten months in the saddle and having an inherent disinterest in horses. Oh boy does this result matter!

It all started with a business idea...

Chapter 1

Tuesday nights I'd tend to meet Sue for an early-doors drink in the village. It's something to look forward to on a Monday, when the last weekend has just finished and the next weekend seems like a lifetime away. I didn't work on Wednesdays or Fridays so I could afford a drink or two without worrying about getting into the office the next day. Sue and I have been friends for around ten years now. We met when she started work with me in Allpro Power PLC as an IT trainer. We became good friends quickly. She worked to pay for her hobby, which is her horse riding. I never quite understood that – not my thing, but it was most definitely hers. She'd tell me her horse, Robbie, had new shoes every six weeks. The shoes would cost seventy pounds a set. OK, so I'd get the fact that they have four feet, not just two, but for heaven's sake, seventy-bloody-pounds! So Sue was bound to her job to pay her mortgage and pay for her horse.

She'd always been into horses, having ridden since she was a child, but when she and her husband separated three years ago she took the plunge and bought her own. I hear all about him (the horse, I mean, not the ex-husband, although I'd hear a good bit about him too on occasion and it was not usually complimentary) and I'd smile and nod in the right places. I'd do this because Sue is a good friend. I'd avoid at all costs getting myself positioned in muddy, pooey, wet and smelly locations and that most certainly included being within fifteen metres of a horse. So with that in mind, I'd not actually met Robbie in person, although I had seen lots of photos of him. In fact, every time Sue went out somewhere on him, like jumping and stuff (I say it like that because I'm not sure what the other stuff actually is), she seemed to pay God-knows-how-much for these professional photos which, whilst they're very nice and very, well, professional, they did get just a bit samey. I didn't understand why she didn't just save her money and go buy herself some new (even possibly Jimmy Choo) shoes to go with the extortionately priced shoes she'd buy for Robbie. Sue insisted that each of these competition photos look completely different. I personally didn't see it. To me they were either jumping a jump or running along the ground. One of each would do, in my mind, and it would be money in the bank for Sue. It really wasn't rocket science. I'd given up trying to make her see sense, so I looked at the photos and say: 'Wow, that's fabulous!' every time. And that seemed to please Sue.

She'd invited me to her stable yard periodically to meet her horse but I successfully managed to decline on every occasion. I was quite simply not interested in the four-legged creature, had no desire to be close to one and emphatically didn't like them.

Sue had been my saviour when my long-term relationship with George had ended. Although never married, we'd lived together for eight long years. He was an IT manager – another mind-numbingly boring profession, to go with my own. At least, it was when he was talking to me about it. Ultimately, he wanted marriage and kids and I wanted a super yacht. He felt my *dreaming* was getting in the way of real life and that I should just grow up. In the end, he had a fling with a project manager that worked in his IT department. I found out, threw him out and that, really, was that. I imagined their riveting conversations about screen resolutions and disk space in gigabytes and decided they were welcome to each other. He thought I'd forgive him, that we'd work it out. I didn't and we didn't. I actually felt a touch liberated. Free to pursue my dreams of riches unhindered by his small mind.

Sue was there to see I was OK and I was very grateful for her support. No matter how liberated you feel when a relationship ends, it's still never easy and there are rough times to deal with. She's one of the best type of friends.

I was particularly looking forward to tonight as my progress in finding cash for my venture had hit every brick wall going, indeed, it had also fallen down a few additional ditches and been run over by the odd car to add further insult. There was just no investment to be had.

These people out there who seem to land on their feet with business deals don't represent the everyday entrepreneur, that's for sure. A full bottle of Prosecco was in order I felt, rather than the usual glass. I try to keep my mid-week ventures into bubbling wine territory in the single glass arena lest I appear (or indeed become) slightly dependent. Alcohol is never the answer, unless, of course, the question is 'Why were you only just conscious on the kitchen floor humming "Three Blind Mice" and slurping up the remainder of the cat's meat?' Then, alcohol is absolutely the answer.

There first, I took an armchair by the log fire, pulled my wedgied trousers out of my backside – surreptitiously of course, so no-one saw me. This was an unfortunate recurrent side effect of being just slightly overweight but not accepting said additional (even though, in my mind, small) bulk enough to warrant buying some trousers that actually fit! I slouched down, getting comfortable in my miserableness over the lack of sufficient funding that had just been doubled by the reminder that my diet had, yet again, been delayed.

I didn't have too long to wallow in my self-absorbedness before Suet breezed into the pub in her usual effervescent way, with her smart riding trousers, figure-hugging top and flare of thick, red, shoulder-length hair pulled back into a sleek ponytail. Typical horsey girl.

I waved her over and she joined me.

'How's things?' she asked.

After what felt like a lifetime of friendship, I was comfortable with skipping out the pleasantries of small talk. What even is the purpose of small talk, anyway? I don't get it when people sit down together and talk about the weather! 'Isn't it hot for the time of year?' 'Haven't we had such a lot of rain?' 'Wasn't it pleasant with the sun out today?' Unless it's the difference between a bikini or a coat, who even cares?

'Bloody awful,' I answered, slightly petulantly, if I'm honest.

'I know what you mean. The bloody rain today – would you believe it for the time of year!'

Sure she could actually read my mind I chose to ignore the weather comment.

'That horse of mine, too, has decided he's taken a dislike to cows – nearly had me off on a hack.'

I was quite sure that Sue was seriously overreacting. I mean, really? A horse deciding it doesn't like cows? How does it even know what a cow is? It could be looking in the mirror (four legs, tail and a long face) for all it knows. But, of course, when she comes out with crap like that about her horse and all of its personality traits, I just humour her with one of my sweet I'm-really-listening-to-you smiles, and let her babble.

'Oh really? That's not very clever of him,' I cooed supportively. I was glad the four-legged presence in my house extended to only Tarquin, my Scottish Fold and slightly special needs cat.

'What's wrong with cows, anyway?' I asked rhetorically, but realising Sue was gearing up to give me the benefit of her view on what's really wrong with cows from the perspective of a horse, I jumped in and quickly changed the subject.

'I'm struggling, you know. I can't believe how difficult it can be to get some simple funding. I mean, you've got to admit, it's the best business idea I've ever had. Who wouldn't want a business mobile app for the cost of a new laptop? It's simply a genius idea.' It seemed my light at the end of the tunnel had gone out due to lack of funding.

'You do know that if you make a success of your business you will actually have to become a bit more sociable and be nice to the general human race?' Her tone was bordering on sarcastic.

'I can be nice...when I need to be.' In fact, although I tended to take each day as it came, living in the moment, they say you should live each day as if it's your last but with my inherent dislike of people in general, the body count would be staggering.

'Have you tried one of the supermarket banks? Are they not easier?'

'Honestly, I've tried everywhere. No-one will back me. I've got no real security, a rented house counts for nothing, and I don't have much I can put in myself, so I'm quite scuppered really. Seems a bank will only lend money to you if you can prove you don't actually need it!' I took a sip of my Prosecco. I like Prosecco very much, perhaps a little too much, but hey; it's my only vice. Well, outside of too much caffeine and spending too much instead of saving, but a girl needs a bit of a release from the working grind.

When my next big idea goes stratospheric I'll be able to swan about in complete luxury. I might even tidy my image up and look like a proper girl for once, with nice, expensive, designer clothes (that actually fit) and makeup that I actually apply to my face, as opposed to leaving it in my makeup bag. I'll buy a super yacht, called *Liberty*, and travel the world whilst I expand my business empire. I'll have a team of helpers to look after my every whim as we sail the seas.

In fact, life for me seemed to be full of lots of little challenges; like putting my underwear on the right way out or putting my jumper on with the label at the back. Left and right posed a particular problem for me and to be honest it would always be a fifty-fifty chance of getting it right but I'd say ninety per cent of the time I get it wrong. I've even tried to trick myself into getting it right by going for the other choice – even that doesn't seem to work, so having paid help could only work in my favour.

Maybe that's why I'd remained single, not counting Tarquin that is. It's more a case of not being sufficiently coordinated for a serious relationship, even though I've tried and failed on numerous occasions.

'Fran,' said Sue, sternly, bringing me back into the room, from *Liberty* the yacht and my general human-being failings, with a jolt. I was immediately on high alert though. Whenever Sue used my name with this tone there was usually something serious about to erupt from her mouth. 'Do you not think you should get yourself an interest? I mean, an interest outside of your obsession with becoming super rich?'

'Like what, exactly?'

'I don't know, but there must be something out there that can capture your imagination. With an IQ like yours you could pick any hobby you like and excel at it. It would give you something a bit more normal to focus on.'

I thought about it briefly but whilst sporting a suitably high IQ, I find myself liberally under-blessed with both common sense and bodily coordination. Coming up with a business or product idea would come easy to me, but dancing and, indeed, finding my way from A to B (even with a satnav) continued to be endlessly challenging. In fact, when I've been somewhere new in the country, I often surprise myself by turning up back at home. When I finished my undergraduate degree, all I hoped for really was to be able to make my living out of what I loved the most. But since there was no real market for Prosecco-drinking chocolate eaters, I had to fall back on my information technology abilities and this saw me ending up doing more study and going for a masters. I liked the idea of letters after my name, plus I was brainy enough. That equated to approximately one year, seven months and five days procrastinating about what to do, interspersed with lots of nights out with friends. Four months and two days actually doing something productive. And then one month realising I was going to fail miserably through lack of interest. At the beginning there was a short time when I thought my destiny might actually be in academia. After all, I loved discovery and finding things out. What I actually found out though, was that I was more money motivated than I was altruistic, so academia was not for me. I needed the commercial world (although I'm not so sure the commercial world needed me).

'But, Sue, I am focussed. I don't need some waste-of-time hobby to take my mind off my business ideas,' I said, just a touch defensively.

'OK, OK. I worry about you sometimes just working all the time. You need down time, too. I am just thinking of you.'

'I know you are, and I really do appreciate it. But, I've got a business to make a success of. That's number one priority for me. Anyway,' I said, gesturing around the pub with my glass of Prosecco, 'what's this if it's not down time?'

'Oh Fran, you'll never change,' she said with a smile. 'Well, actually, I've been thinking, and there is one more option,' Sue said cautiously.

I looked quizzically at her. 'Oh?'

'There's a guy, called Richard, at my yard – you know where I stable Robbie. Well, actually, he owns the whole farm. He's pretty damn loaded and he's a nice guy too. I bet he would loan or maybe invest. What you want would be small change for him. It would be worth asking. I'll see him tomorrow.'

I liked the idea. I liked the idea very much. I had nothing to lose (or so I thought). 'Would you do that for me? Would you sound him out and see if he'll meet me?'

'Sure, leave it with me.'

I went home positively excited. All thoughts of cows were banished. Pinning my hopes very highly on the Richard possibility, I was feeling a sense of good things coming. I think that particular sense, along with many of my other personal attributes, is actually quite lacking in accuracy.

Chapter 2

After another boring day at work I'd managed to sneak away early. I slouched in front of the television – the best way to spend a January winter's evening. Tarquin joined me. I love him to bits but it's a bit hit and miss as to whether he likes me at any one point in time. I tentatively patted him gently and the outcome was positive – he didn't try to bite or claw me, so that was good.

I was flicking through the channels, looking for something to watch for half an hour before getting back up to make myself some tea when my phone rang. It was my baby brother, Paul. I hadn't heard from him in, what, three months maybe? This was a pretty good sign he wanted something and I wasn't mistaken. He made no illusion of getting straight to the point.

'Sis, I need a place to crash for a bit.'

'You and Mike fallen out again?'

'Something like...'

'What did you do this time?'

'Why do you always assume it's me that's at fault?'

'Because it always is!'

'Can I come over? I can be there by eight. I'll bring takeaway.'

'I guess I can't really say no, can I?'

'No, I guess you can't. See you at later. Oh and by the way, I need to bring Portia too. Mike's parting words to me were "take that bloody dog with you!" '

Before I could scream down the phone that *NO dog*, let alone a super-hyper, naughty eighteen-month-old pug was gracing my home, he'd hung up. Oh joy. Tarquin would be delighted – not. Whilst he's very photogenic and looks just the image of cat perfection in a photo, when you see him in the flesh he's just a little bit wrong. His feet turn out, he's got an ingrowing claw that, even though it's clipped regularly, gives him a most unusual tiptoeing type gait and his head is just a touch too big for his scrawny body. All of this means that Tarquin is just a bit crap at being a cat and he doesn't suffer dogs easily. Last time Paul stayed he'd fallen out with his better half and he stayed for six weeks, but that was also pre-Portia. I've been subjected to one weekend with Portia and that was enough. I have to say, I'm not sure I can cope with a six-week-type stay again. I quite like my little house the way it is. Palatial it's not, but I have it comfortable and Paul and Portia were about to disrupt that. I definitely fancied takeaway though, along with the energy saving of not having to cook my own supper.

The suspected chaos ensued as soon as Paul and Portia walked through the door. The pug bounced around in excitement. To be fair, based on its last stay here, it seemed unusually excited at most events in life, even the uninteresting ones: pick up the food bowl, it got excited. Open a bag of crisps, it got excited. Get up to head for bed, it got excited.

Right now, Portia was super pleased to see Tarquin. Tarquin was less pleased to see Portia and was scowling, his little ears flat to his head. I sensed tears coming at some point and I suspected they wouldn't be Tarquin's.

Paul and I unpacked the Chinese takeaway, opened a bottle of Prosecco and sat down at the kitchen table. I didn't realise how hungry I was until the smell of Chicken

Chow Mein filled the kitchen. As we ate, we ignored the mayhem of Portia chasing Tarquin, hissing, yapping and general commotion. Food and wine were far more important.

'He thinks I cheated on him,' said Paul.

'And, did you?' I asked through a mouthful of chicken and noodles.

He looked indignant. 'Of course not! How could you even think that of me?'

'Because you're a flirt and you like the attention.'

'I'm wounded by that,' he said in his most effeminate voice. 'Well, I didn't. I promise. He just needs to wake up and realise that.'

'I'm sure he will. He's a good guy and you don't need to lose him.'

'Well, I'm a good guy too and he needs to appreciate me.'

I left it alone at that and went back to my Chinese and wine. I told Paul all about my business idea and my lack of investment. He ate quietly and listened.

'Haven't you ever just thought about sticking with your regular job and giving up on all this get-rich-quick rubbish?'

'I'm the one that's wounded now! How can you say that? It's my life's dream.'

'But it's just not happening. You've been trying for years.'

'You sound like Mum. Just because it hasn't happened, doesn't mean it won't. You can't just give up on things when they don't work out first time.'

'First, second, tenth time, in your case. What about the party messaging software or the universal pen lid product or the reversible trouser design? I mean, who's going to wear a pair of smart trousers to work then turn them inside out to go to the pub after work? How much did you waste on that venture? Thousands? Thousands that you couldn't afford to waste.'

'I've told you a trillion times not to exaggerate!' The sarcasm, however, was lost on him. 'They were good ideas. People just didn't get them; I was years ahead of my time. That's all the more reason to keep going. I will do this. It will happen. You'll see.'

I wasn't so sure I felt quite as confident as I sounded but I knew I wouldn't give up until that super yacht was in my possession and I was sitting on its deck, on the shores of Capri, drinking champagne (I'd upgrade from Prosecco when I became super rich). They say that money doesn't bring you happiness but I say neither does being broke.

I did, however, wish that for once in my life I might find just one member of my family who was right behind me, instead of trying to constantly derail me. It can be soul destroying you know, to have the ones you love constantly up against you. I'm sure they do it for all the correct reasons, but that still doesn't make it right. Support is what family and friends are all about. If you can't give that unconditionally, then in my book you are neither.

I fell asleep that night to the vision of my wealthy future. Little did I know that the new venture in my life wouldn't be my super yacht but a four-legged creature of which I had no knowledge and, indeed, had no desire to have knowledge of.

Chapter 3

My phone rang and I answered it to hear Sue's bright voice.

'He'll see you,' said Sue. I was feeling less bright, having polished off two bottles of Prosecco with my brother after supper last night.

'Who?' Having almost forgotten our conversation in the pub two nights ago, the penny was more sinking into a pretty thick consistency of custard rather than actually dropping.

'Richard! Richard, at my yard. The rich one!' Her words sunk in and I started to join the dots.

'Oh my God, Sue, that's brilliant,' I screeched at her. I wanted to jump around for joy but that was a touch too much strenuous effort at the moment given the presiding hangover, so I resigned myself to a brief triumphant fist pump.

'Can you come over after work, this evening? Meet at the yard at six pm?'

'Yes, definitely.' I couldn't hide my enthusiasm. 'Text me the postcode and I'll see you later. And Sue...thank you!'

I was all of a dither (not much new there, to be honest) and keen to do my prep properly. I had this vision of presenting myself as a competent business person that could take his money and make something of it with my new app system. How to dress though? A business suit was the first outfit that sprung to mind but heels and horse crap don't really work well together – in my mind at least. Business suit and wellies? Firstly, I wasn't even sure that I owned a pair of wellies and secondly, whilst not vain in any way, even I wasn't loving the potential for that look.

I decided on jeans and boots. Casual but mud-cope-withable. That would have to do.

As I was getting ready Paul's dog was busying herself downstairs with a nice little surprise for me: twelve rolls of loo roll, pack opened, chewed and the kitchen newly decorated in a kind of Christmassy toilet-tissue way. Tarquin was sat watching with interest. Added to that, being the greedy dog she is, Portia clearly thinks that watering the kitchen carpet will encourage it to grow more food as she's now taken to tipping the water bowl over. I think she's reached her teenage years early.

I left that mess for Paul to sort out.

I set off in plenty of time, parked up, texted Sue to say I'd arrived and waited for Sue to come and find me. I didn't fancy wandering around the place in case I ran into a horse. They scare me! Big and with a mind of their own; I don't trust them at all. Plus, I had actually no idea what Richard looked like.

Five minutes later Sue knocked on my car window with her usual wide smile. My breath clouded in the cold air as I got out.

'Sorry, I was just untacking,' she said, brightly. 'Come on, Richard's waiting.'

She led me round the yard to a stable block at the back. There were eight stables, four on each side. As we walked in a rather pleasing-looking guy was walking out. My eyes followed him for a moment and Sue smiled.

'That's Gary,' she whispered into my ear. 'He's in your age range!'

'Oh,' I said, trying to sound disinterested. There was no room for distraction here. The last thing on my mind was any complication, including a man at the moment.

Richard was busy in a stable brushing his horse. Great, big, red beast it was. I bet dressed in a business suit he would probably look close to halfway normal, however, standing there grooming his horse in a pair of tight jodhpurs that were moulded to his middle-aged ass, in a way that can only kindly be described as decidedly unflattering, he looked just a touch more like Humpty Dumpty than he maybe should, his balding head the convincing finishing touch. To be fair he wasn't that, shall we say, rotund, but the skinny legs accentuated his slightly well-made upper half. I suddenly wanted to laugh. I imagined this slightly slimmer version of Humpty Dumpty sat on the ginger horse, with little skinny legs flapping in the wind. I struggled to maintain control.

'So you're Fran then.'

With his eyes on me, I felt a little like I was back in the headmaster's office in my school days again (I frequented that office often), although Mr Browne's office didn't quite smell this...equine.

'Yes, that would be me,' I said with a smile.

'Sue tells me you have a good business idea that needs some cash behind it.'

My heart fluttered. I was getting nervous.

'It's a great idea,' I blurted out.

'And how much does this great idea need to come to market?' he asked, still gently grooming the horse.

'Well, I reckon on about seventy-five thousand pounds.' When I said it aloud like that, it sounded like such a lot of money. And then, I just couldn't stop babbling!

'I know it's a lot but the app system is just so innovative and I know there's a huge market out there and I'm just the best person to get this out there. You'd make so much back and we could look at a proper exit strategy...'

'Whoa for a second. Take a breath.' He laughed.

I stopped, looked down at my boots and did indeed take a long breath.

'Seventy-five thousand pounds – that's what I need.' Then I shut up and let the silence do the persuading.

'And the headline of what it's about?'

'Well, it's a smartphone app system that lets businesses create their own mobile app. I...'

'Slow down there again. That's enough, I get the idea. I like it and I think I'd like to be involved. I miss being in business full-time so this could be good for both of us.'

'Don't you want to hear more about it?' I heard myself say. *What the hell are you doing, you stupid woman?* I screamed in my head. Don't talk him out of it! How could a man I've never met talk to me for all of ten minutes and then choose to invest a serious amount of money in me? It seemed too good to be true, but it was also too good an opportunity to walk away from. I felt that there must be a catch somewhere.

'I'm assuming this is a new start-up? You've done your feasibility study to make sure your product is viable?'

'I sure have and it sure is.'

'Good. I'm a risk-taker. That's why I love riding. Putting my money into your business will be a little like doing the lottery for me but there will be a condition.' He raised a mischievous eyebrow.

'A condition? What sort of condition would that be?' From the look in his eye, I actually wasn't sure I quite wanted to know the answer.

'I'll get to that in a moment. Do you ride?'

'Erm, that's a big fat no. Not ever.'

'And, do you like horses?'

'Well, I like all animals – from a distance.'

'From a distance?' he asked. I felt a sense of mocking.

'Yes, they smell and make a mess. Horses are big and, well, dangerous and I'm small-ish and fragile. At least physically!' I didn't want him thinking I was some sort of psychotic, hormonal female who would fall apart and break down in tears at the first sight of trouble.

'And are you active? Exercise?'

'I do four body-rolls every day. I know it may not sound like much, but there's only so many times you can hit the snooze button!' I chuckled a little, thinking myself quite funny. He looked less amused!

'I see. Bit of a comedienne too,' he said. He stopped grooming the horse and came out of the stable. 'Well, here's the deal. Seventy-five thousand pounds is yours to develop your idea into a profitable business. You can have twenty-five thousand pounds to get you going and the rest of the money will be available to you in a few months' time. In the intervening period I need to know you've got the staying power to make the investment work and make the business a success, you know, when the going gets tough, as they say. I want forty per cent of the company BUT, and I must stress that this is non-negotiable, you must first compete in a horse competition of my choice and win.'

His words hung in the air a moment as my little brain processed what he'd just said and if I was just slightly shorter than my five feet two inches, my lower jaw might actually have broken on the concrete I was standing on. Clearly the man was a raving lunatic. He was mad!

'You what?' I exclaimed.

'I'll sort out the horse for you and it will stay here. You'll learn how to look after it, ride it and drive it out and about in a lorry. You'll need to do some small competitions to prepare for the main one. And it will all be at my expense, so that's one less worry for you.'

'But I work!'

'Sue tells me you work with her, that you work three days a week and that outside of work you don't have anything else major that takes up your time. So, you're well placed with free time for you to devote to my little challenge. Although a horse is a full-time responsibility, so he'll still need caring for on the days you are working.'

I was speechless, but I felt if I didn't say something remotely useful quite quickly, this turn of events would go permanently in a direction I had less and less control over and, indeed, was liking less and less by each spoken word. In fact, if I wasn't very careful, I could find myself committed to riding an actual horse and riding it competitively (I think, attached to my name, that might potentially be what you'd call diametric – which means it's not EVEN possible in the real world!). Perhaps emitting the persona of a psychotic, hormonal bitch might not be such a bad idea, after all.

'Do you want the money?'

'Yes!' There was no hesitation in that.

'Are you prepared to show your grit to get it? This really is a very generous offer.'

'Ride? Go to competitions? Drive a lorry? All in a matter of months?'

'Not just any competition, a proper British Event.'

'But I don't know what one of those is and I'm not convinced I want to. Do I need to understand it to make my decision?'

'Nope, just understand it won't be easy and you will have to learn to jump - successfully.'

'Forgive me for labouring the point but I need to be really, REALLY clear here: you give me a horse, I learn to ride it, I learn to drive a horsebox and I have to win at the chosen competition - then, I get the money?'

'Yep, all of that and not a penny of cost for you. Aren't you the lucky one?' Lucky wasn't quite the word I had in mind, at this point.

'For your amusement?'

'Like I say, I'm a risk-taker but I'm also an all-round fun guy and I just love a bit of sport. I like to make money though. Are you up for the challenge?'

'Can I think about it?'

'Yep. Until ten a.m. tomorrow. Here's my card,' he said, handing me a glossy little business card from the back pocket of his riding trousers. 'Call me with your answer.'

He returned to his stable and started to put a big blanket thing on his horse.

'Ten a.m. at the latest but earlier is better,' he called as I walked to the barn door. I couldn't help feeling that there was a village somewhere that was currently being deprived of its idiot!

I found Sue waiting in the tea room. She walked to the car with me.

'So what's the outcome?' she asked.

'I can have the money.'

'That's great,' she said. Then added, when she saw my face, 'That's not great?'

When I explained, she burst out laughing.

'It's really not that funny. It's really not funny at all.' I think I might have sounded a little like a spoilt child throwing a bit of a paddy. That's actually just how I felt at that point in time.

'Don't worry, I'll help,' she said, still chuckling. 'The months will pass in no time at all.'

I doubted that very, very much indeed.

Chapter 4

Sleep was very slow in coming that night and when I did drift off, I jolted awake when I fell off my new horse and splatted, face first on the ground with a thud.

Mind whirring, I got up and headed for the kitchen to get some water. I do hate it when I get up in the night to get a quick drink of water and then accidentally eat a whole pack of Custard Creams. I do, though, tell myself it's important to live life to its fullest even if that does mean eating everything in the fridge. Still, if I wasn't careful, I'd end up having to dig out my fat pants again, rather than squeezing into the skinny jeans that I hoped would become part of my regular set of daily clothes.

So, the options? Carry on working in a job I really don't like which realistically offered earnings limited to what I could go out and bring in myself or try and find funding with, shall we say, less strings, or rather reins, attached? I've tried that with no joy.

That was it, decision made. All I had to do was get my head in the space of accepting Richard's ridiculous challenge. I'm determined, I'm capable and, if I put my mind to something, I tend to make it happen.

So yes, bring it on, I told myself. First thing tomorrow, I'd make that call. I could start my business straight away. In just a few months time I'd have the rest of the money, and in a year I'd be wealthy. I had a feeling I already knew which direction my 'get rich or die trying' decision was heading.

Making the decision helped me fall sound asleep. It wasn't the prospect of the challenge, it was the prospect that my business was now just a horse-hair's breadth away from becoming a reality.

Six-thirty a.m. felt a reasonably early time to wake the crazy bastard up and tell him the 'good' news. I set my alarm especially.

'Richard, it's Fran. I'll do it. I accept your challenge.'

I could almost hear him grinning on the other end of the phone (clearly six in the morning wasn't early enough to catch him off guard). It made me nervous.

'Excellent news. I'll make all the arrangements. As soon as it arrives, I'll let you know, but be prepared to get going quickly. Welcome to the yard!'

Quickly? I actually hoped it would take time to get the beast ordered and delivered, if that is in fact what happened when you acquired a horse. It wasn't actually something I'd ever really considered in the past. Then, I started to think about what it would look like, how tall it would be. Would it be fat or thin, a boy or a girl? Is a boy horse better than a girl horse? So many questions. How the hell was I going to look after it? I didn't have the slightest idea on what to do with such a big four-legged creature!

I told myself to stop panicking and over-thinking this. I'd had a dog in the past and I have Tarquin. Just how difficult could this be? It's just on a bigger scale, I told myself. The crap just takes a shovel and a wheelbarrow rather than a poop-scoop to get rid of. The feed is in buckets rather than bowls.

The 'yard' obviously had a grapevine (thank God, since I love wine), and Sue was on the phone before nine.

'I hear you went for it! You'll be joining as a yard livery. Is it going to be a mare or a gelding?' she chattered cheerfully.

'Talk in English, woman,' I replied.

'Fran, you've heard me using all of this terminology before! Don't play ignorant now.'

'Yeah, well I'm not convinced I was actually ever listening properly – just to the horsey terminology I mean, just the terminology. Everything else you say, well, I hang on every word, you know that.'

'I saw Richard this morning. I popped up to his house at the back of the yard for a quick coffee. He told me the good news. Your horse will be living at our livery yard – it's what it's called. A mare is a female and a gelding is a male. I'm sure you must know that. You're going to have to get up to speed on your horse-related lingo.'

And so, even before it had started, it was already getting worse. Bad enough that I'd been working in the acronym universe, known as the utilities industry. Now I had a whole new niche language to learn.

Since I was being put in such, shall we say, an unusual position, I asked Sue to tell me what she knew about Richard. I'd looked him up on the internet and it was clear he was very successful, having built a massive recycling business, but I wanted the low-down on him as a person; the real Richard. Whilst incredibly grateful for the opportunity for investment that I had struggled to get from any other source, I was less enthused at his idea of me proving myself.

So, we met at the pub and chatted.

'Well, he's rich, he owns the whole farm and built the equestrian yard ten years ago. He rides, of a fashion. His wife died eight years ago and, to be honest, I think he's a bit lonely. He sold his recycling business five years ago and since then has spent his time around the yard, effectively in early retirement. When I landed there, I was moved quickly into his block of stables. He's picky who's allowed to be stabled next to him. You'll be in there too, so you're honoured.'

'You don't think he's...you know, after more than just the investment opportunity?' I asked.

'Hell no. He's a nice guy and, given his money, he has enough attention, although he never seems really interested in anything long term. There's been a few on the yard who've thought he'd make a good catch but he's confided in me in the past that he's only really interested in *the one*, whenever she comes along.' Sue then turned her attention to the yard occupants. 'I'd watch out for Bridgett, who runs the yard. Not to influence you in any way but she's an out-and-out bitch.' I found myself immediately influenced. 'You'll like Marcus, though. He's Richard's personal groom and assistant. I do like Richard, you know, he's a good guy and we've become good friends. I trust him so I think he'd be a good business partner for you too.'

If Sue liked him, he was okay in my view. As my best friend in the world, outside of Tarquin (and, given his deviant feline behaviour at times, that could be in doubt anyway), I'd always trust her judgement.

I intended to make the most of my freedom before the creature arrived to take over my life. A relaxing weekend followed by a night away with work was on the cards and I was going to enjoy every minute of it.

Chapter 5

Saturday morning saw coffee in Costa in Otley town centre with Richard. He wanted to do the business side of the investment away from the yard and any potential 'prying eyes'.

I sipped my extra-hot and extra sweet latte. The café was busy and there was a buzz of conversation in the air.

'Tell me a little bit about yourself - I hear you studied for a masters. What was your subject?' he said, drawing out his tablet and placing it on the table in front of him.

He'd clearly done his homework on me. My eyes were firmly fixed on the screen as he navigated the browser to his business banking site. This was my pass into my new business. I was more interested in getting the first twenty-five thousand pounds than I was about discussing my life history, but right now I'd humour him.

'It was a research masters rather than a taught one. My subject was computational and psycho-linguistics. I used a back propagation neural network to recognise stressed syllables within the English speech signals to identify islands of reliability for speech recognition algorithms.' It was a well-practised response as I'd been asked many times, but since he was giving me such a hard time, I went a bit further.

'Whilst the supervised connectionist approach was the principal learning mechanism in my thesis, I looked at heuristic and unsupervised algorithms too.'

Richard's face had taken on a familiar glaze of that's-stupid-boring-rubbish but that was okay because he'd passed me his pen and a piece of paper.

'And jobs?'

'I've worked in a few. The one I'm in now is in the IT training department in a large utility provider. Pretty boring stuff really, but it pays the bills, as they say.'

'There must be something you like about it?'

'Sometimes, people have birthdays and there's free cake. I've always wanted to work for myself, I've thought of going in for one of those make-eight-thousand-pounds-a-month-working-from-home jobs you see advertised around the place but then I wondered why anyone in their right mind would take the more difficult job of nailing those signs to lampposts all over town, so I decided to give it a miss.'

He smiled.

'Still the comedienne,' he said. 'You keep that sense of humour active. You'll be needing it very soon.'

I smiled lamely, as he continued: 'And do you think you have the passion then to build your own business and grow my investment?' He emphasised the word passion. 'And...to do this challenge?'

'Anyone who thinks I don't have passion hasn't seen me with a glass of Prosecco and a fruit Yorkie bar.' I raised my eyebrows in an I-see-you're-getting-me kind of way.

He ignored my last remark. I was only trying to lift the mood a little. It crossed my mind that his personality was temporarily out of order and he needed to lighten up a little. Pretending to be this nice was actually proving exhausting. I might definitely need some medicinal Prosecco to compensate.

'And,' I said, 'can I ask a little about you?'

He looked up, almost startled.

'Sure, fire away,' he said, eyeing me closely.

36

'Well I am, of course, extremely grateful for the opportunity, but why would you invest in me and my business? I mean, you don't know me from Adam.'

'That's a good question Fran, and the fact that you've asked it gives me confidence that this is a good investment to make. As I'm sure you know I'm widowed. I've been semi-retired for a few years now and, to be brutally honest, I'm just a little bored. Your business is an opportunity for me to be involved in a new venture and one that's outside of my current comfort zone. Like I'm setting the challenge for you, I'm relishing the chance for a challenge too. Sue speaks very highly of you and that says a lot to me.'

I appreciated his frankness. It still seemed a lot of money to hand over on a whim to someone he didn't know though, but I wasn't complaining.

'And I understand that you own the farm that Sue keeps Robbie, her horse, at. There must be plenty of people already there that would be first in the queue to take advantage of a decent "investment".'

'Yes, I own Meadowgrove Farm and its Livery Yard. You're right, there probably would. When you think about it, who would turn down an easy investment? You, however, have a business idea, are keen and come recommended, so you were already streets ahead. Having built my money in working very hard and building a recycling operation, I'm now happy to sit in the background and enjoy watching another business build. So, do my credentials stack up?'

'I never really questioned them, but they do indeed. I just needed to ask the questions. Please sign me up right now!' I said, jovially.

'That's what we're here to do. Bank details, please.'

I was just about close to drooling now and had to clamp my mouth shut to avoid any inappropriate dribbling juices exiting my face at this crucial moment in public, I pulled out my purse and wrote down my bank details, then slid the piece of paper back across the table to him.

'I've got to say I'm impressed with your qualifications. You're quite clever then?' he asked. I gave my best 'yup smile' but my attention was focussed on his tablet and my bank details.

'You should find my challenge nice and easy then. Just apply a little of that sharp brainpower you have.'

That I knew would be easier said than done. If I could coordinate my body and my common sense like I do my intellect, I would be a very capable lady indeed. As it is, I can't and I'm not.

'There are two additional conditions.' He looked at me gravely. My heart sank. For heaven's sake, it was bad enough as it was. What else on God's good green earth could he impose on me?

'Oh?' I said, meekly, eyebrows raised. 'More than the whole life-changing requirement to get to grips with a horse?'

'Yes, more than that,' he said. 'The first is that you need to get your business to the stage that the app is developed and ready to go before the rest of the investment will be made available to you. This means I want to see and approve a solid business plan, marketing plan and a working prototype of the app system.'

'That's OK,' I said. That wasn't too bad a condition.

'And perhaps a little more importantly, the last condition is that I don't want people thinking I'm a soft touch for money. With that in mind, no-one, and I mean NO-ONE must know about our deal.'

'But people already know. Sue...'

'Sue's the only one. Your new instructor, Gabriella, she'll know too, as will my groom Marcus, and that will be it. There will be plenty on the yard at my farm that will be interested in where you've come from. Horsey people tend to be inquisitive, so be prepared. If anyone finds out, the deal is very definitely OFF.'

'My brother, he's staying, I talk to him...'

'He's family, so that's OK with me. Otherwise, no-one.'

'But what do I tell people?'

'You make up a good story – that you decided you want to learn to ride. It's been on your bucket list for a while. You woke up and had an epiphany and you just had to learn to ride. I don't really mind nor care, provided no-one realises I'm involved.'

'I'll try my best.'

'No, try means you won't do it. You need to say you WILL do it. Be positive from the start.'

'OK, I'll do it.'

He tapped a button on his screen.

'That's it. The first instalment of the investment money is in your account.'

I resisted the temptation to throw myself across the table and kiss his almost-bald head in gratitude and instead said a simple thank you before draining my slightly cooler coffee in quiet celebration.

So this was how my life was going to be structured, at least for the next few months: work three days a week in my day-job, sort my new horse, seven days a week and develop my new business in every single free moment of time I could find. As Meatloaf said, *'two out of three ain't bad,'* and I know which one of the three was just bloody awful!

I met up with Sue when I was done with Richard. She was taking me shopping to get me kitted out to ride. Richard had set a budget and wanted someone knowledgeable to go with me to make sure I got the right stuff. Apparently he'd told Sue to make sure I looked the part.

We went to a store called Forrester Equestrian, not too far away from the yard. We looked at jodhpurs (I could only spell jodhpurs correctly because of the spell check on my laptop - I mean, if you're going to have such a ridiculous name for a pair of riding trousers at least spell it phonetically!). I wasn't so sure I could wear something I was unable to spell. In the end, I didn't buy jodhpurs, I got breeches instead and I can spell that. They look better apparently. I squeezed myself into a thirty-six-inch waist. They took some hauling up and breathing in, but I told myself that, with all the added exercise this challenge is going to involve, I could expect to lose at least half a stone in two weeks without even having to cut out a single caramel custard doughnut. Added to my two pairs of breeches were some tops, a coat, a gilet, boots and gaiters. We got a hat fitted and when we came to the body protectors, I got a touch twitchy.

'And why exactly do I need body armour? Just how dangerous is this horse riding malarkey going to be?'

Sue smiled the smile you'd give a small child.

'It's just added protection for if you fall off. They say a rider has to fall off at least seven times to be a good rider. So expect a few times on the deck as you're learning – it's only natural.'

I'm not sure if I was just choosing not to consider that possibility or if it genuinely hadn't actually crossed my mind, but the thought of falling off and hitting the rather hard and potentially-damage-causing-to-Fran ground was now racing through my significantly concerned mind.

'Well, I don't want to be a good rider, I just need to be a rider, so I'll pass on the seven and go for the zero to none falls, if you don't mind!'

'Good for you! We'll still take the body protector, just in case and add to that an air jacket for extra protection!'

I considered myself suitably kitted out but was quite sure I was going to look a complete idiot when I actually put all this stuff on. Sue dropped me back at home and I went through my new kit, taking off all the labels and stickers. This goes out to the individual who thought up the idea of putting extra sticky stickers on each and every piece of riding equipment I purchased today. Nobody (what I mean is me) likes your idea!

When I got home, Paul had the kettle boiling.

'You've been out for ages. Good day?'

'Exceptional day! My investment is sorted. I have the first instalment. That's me under way.'

'Really, just like that?

'Well, of course not, I have the whole horse thing to deal with but yes, the first instalment is in the bank. I can get cracking. Maybe you'll be working for me sometime soon,' I teased.

'I doubt it. With my architect skills, I'm not sure you could afford me.'

You watch this space Paul McBride, you could be on my payroll before you know it! Who wants to work in a big corporate consultancy anyway? How boring can that be? My offices will be veritable business play-parks compared to your workplace.'

Paul and I drank our tea then I headed off upstairs to try my new gear on. OK, so although just a touch on the slightly plump side, it actually didn't look as bad as I thought it would! *Just half a stone off will do it*, I told myself. It's so damn difficult to get into shape and look good with so many temptations like chocolate, cake and Prosecco around. Caterpillars, well they seem to have it made. They eat a lot, go to sleep, then wake up beautiful. I wished it could work like that for me too.

Chapter 6

So this was the week that things were going to start to happen for me. I'd secured the funding, albeit from a crazy, mad but very rich horseman, who owned his own farm and stable yard, but it was coming as an investment and not a loan either. I just had to make-willing humouring him with this whole horse malarkey and all would be good. I was getting my head around this now. Not knowing the lead time for ordering a new horse and its delivery, I busied myself with my current job and my plans to get my new business off the ground.

I was delivering a training course at one of our remote sites that week. The place was down in Ashford and it's a long drive so the powers-that-be, i.e. Nina, decided I could stay over on expenses. It was nice to have the time away from my usual routine. I would use the time in the evening to do some planning for my enterprise. I left Paul in charge of Tarquin and Portia and Sue was taking care of Batman for me.

I booked myself a Holiday Inn thinking it would be nice to have a night away. I hadn't done that in a while. Knowing my directional handicap and inability to reliably follow a Sat Nav, I printed a map on A3 so I couldn't go wrong.

The drive down was good. I did some serious thinking about my new app system, outlining it in my head and decided I'd have room service, a glass of vino and get my thoughts written up on my laptop that evening. I forgot my phone charger, but hey, I've forgotten worse - at least I had my printed map.

Room service arrived and was extremely nice. I went for the curry so I decided to pop my tray outside the door when I was done so I didn't have to sleep with the residual smell. Warmed by my glass of wine and comfortable in my pink-pig pyjamas (ideal for stays in warm hotel rooms as they're shorts), I opened the door to put my tray on the hallway floor, with my foot strategically placed to stop the door from closing. Unfortunately, my tray wobbled and my wine glass threatened to topple. With my reactions like lightning, I made an impressive full-body move to save the glass and the tray but that move required the use of the strategically placed foot, which I realised, as I heard the door slam, was no longer strategically placed.

So there I was in short, pink piggy pyjamas locked out of my room! Reception it was. Now, how busy do you think a Holiday Inn reception is at nine in the evening? Well I can tell you: it's bloody damn busy. People arriving in business suits, people relaxing in the annexed bar and, do you know what? They ALL noticed. How could they not? When the receptionists stopped laughing, they got a spare key and let me back in.

I ordered a second glass of white as a consolation, so there's always light as they say.

I set off the next morning with an hour to spare (so I thought) ‑ I always leave a little Fran-got-lost extra time. With no charger and a dead phone, the Sat Nav was out of the question, so thank God for the printed map! The map, however, just wasn't making sense. Where I could find road names, I couldn't match them to my map. Knowing my complete inability to understand directions, the best course was to ask a local and what better local than someone in a garage (I could even furnish myself with an express out-of-the-machine coffee).

'I need to get here,' I told the nice man behind the counter as I stabbed my A3-size map with my index finger. He took it from me, scrutinised it for a moment and then looked up at me with a smug expression on his face that I really didn't care for.

'Sweetheart,' he said to me. 'This is Ashford in Kent.' (This I knew.) 'You want to be in Ashford in Middlesex.'

Why is it that there are always a lot of people around to witness my most clueless moments? A whole queue of people had amassed behind me in the interim between me arriving and the smug man pointing out my geographical mistake.

'Just about eighty miles different from here,' he said. I'd clearly made his day, perhaps even his month. I'd be top of his storytelling list about the stupid woman in the wrong county. I found I wanted to kick him in the shin just to make me feel better, but that wasn't happening because a) I'm a grown-up and, more importantly, b) he was behind a counter with a locked door.

No phone to call ahead, I legged it as quick as I could. Hot-footing around the M25 got me there just in time.

When I finally arrived home, it had been an extremely long day and the house was ablaze with lights. Paul was clearly home. If my brother knew there was a light in the oven, I'm sure he'd leave that on too. When I walked through the door late that evening, it was most definitely Prosecco time. Paul was in the kitchen and there was a delightful smell emanating from the oven. He'd cooked. I poured us both a glass of Prosecco.

'Good trip?'

'The training went well. I need to get better at the whole A to B thing.'

'Lost again?'

'Wrong bloody county, never mind lost!'

'How's you? You and Mike any further in the making-up stakes?'

'He's playing hard to get.'

'I guess you're here for a while then.'

'I am. Is that OK?'

'I guess it will have to be.'

'You love having me here, don't pretend you don't.' He was bantering with me.

'I do, actually, Paul. I guess it gets a bit tedious on my own but, that aside, you need to sort this out. You can't live like a nomad every time you and Mike fall out. You're supposed to be getting married in seven months. I'm looking forward to being your bridesmaid.'

'I know. We can talk about that another day.'

'Do you have commitment issues, Paul? Is that what's going on here?"

'No,' he said, perhaps a little too quickly. 'No, I'm happy to commit. I just need to know it's right.'

'Paul, you've been with him for five years now. How much knowing-it's-right do you need?'

'I know what you're saying. I just need a little space to get my head together, that's all. I think things between us have just turned a little stale. I think an architect and an accountant together don't make an exciting combination. I may be just a bit bored.'

There wasn't much more I could say. Dead tired after the long trip, I headed off to bed early. With the excitement to come, I needed all the rest I could get.

Chapter 7

I was up early for work and Richard rang. My horse is called Batman, he has arrived and apparently he's grey. This seemed to cause Richard much amusement - the grey bit, I mean. Must be an in-joke. I was quite sure I'd find out in good time.

Turned out he actually had two names - Batman, not Richard - although there are a few choice additional names I could have used for him. Batman's proper name is Blue Eyed Batman. I mean, really? Can you see me hollering that up the field? I think whoever named Blue Eyed Batman should be banned from naming any more things in this world!

After work, I headed up to the farm to meet him - the horse and probably Richard, too. I got myself dressed in my new gear all ready for the big meeting with my new four-legged friend (or perhaps nemesis).

When I arrived, I was full of trepidation as I headed for the stables.

'Bloody hell, he's a big one,' I said, looking at Batman over his stable door. Richard had parked him in the stable next to his own. Keeping a close eye on his investment, I didn't wonder.

Richard laughed. This seemed to be becoming his default status when dealing with me; full of mirth.

'Big? He's only 15.1 hands high.'

'Well, those hands must be the size of my front door, if you think that's small!'

'Four inches. A hand is four inches.' I was dubious.

He wasn't what I was expecting colour-wise, either. Richard told me he was grey. He looked bloody snow white to me and I told him so.

Yet again Richard laughed. And loudly. Sue, who was already at the yard, heard the raucous laughter and came to see what was so funny.

'She thought he was white!' he said, as if that made perfect sense.

Sue joined the laughter.

'Oh, Fran, you've got such a lot to learn! Grey is what a white horse is known as. There's no such thing as an actual white horse – well, except a Lipizzaner, of course.'

I wanted to beg to differ. There was a bloody great white horse standing in my new stable, but I kept my mouth shut. And, it didn't end there. White isn't the only colour that isn't a colour.

Apparently, a brown horse is called a bay, which is actually something I thought was found at a beach. Bay isn't a general colour, though. So I can't, for example, say I've got bay hair. There is another brown type of horse but not if it has a black mane and tail. An orange horse is a chestnut, which to me is a brown nutty thing that's found on trees and doesn't actually resemble the colour of these so-called chestnut horses. But, within the whole chestnut colour area, there are liver chestnuts and chestnuts. Liver chestnuts kind of look like brown horses. When I heard Sue say that Katie's horse was green, I really thought she was taking the Michael. Even I'm not that thick. Even the least horsey person knows that there is no such thing as a green horse, but apparently that's not really a colour at all, and refers to one that is not experienced. Not sure I'll ever really get to the bottom of this.

And I've got to say that so far, in my limited (about ten minutes to be exact) exposure to them, I've found these horsey types are particularly precious about their colours too. Get it wrong and the reaction you get is like telling a new mother her baby's ugly.

I looked down the block. There were two multi-coloured horses too. I thought I had this now.

'Grey and bay?' I hazarded.

'Now that's just being silly,' said Richard. 'It's a skewbald.'

In my opinion, it was neither skewed nor bald as it had plenty of fur.

'And the black and white one – that's a piebald,' Sue added.

'But you said white? I thought there was no white?'

'I only said it to describe the colours of the piebald to you, not to say it's a black and white horse.'

As a black horse was led past, I sarcastically said: 'What colour's that one then? Charcoal?'

'Doh, of course it isn't – it's black!' said Sue, rolling her eyes. 'You're just making colours up now.'

'Here's a grooming kit. Brush the body with the soft brush, brush the mane and tail with the spikey, round brush and pick his feet out with the metal hookey thing,' said Richard, passing me a blue canvas bag. 'He's all yours. As you have your first instalment of the investment, feel free to crack on and prove I should give you the rest.'

With that, he left.

I looked at Sue and shrugged my shoulders. I actually had not a single inkling of where to start.

'What do I do?'

'Come on, I'll help you groom him.'

Sue spent an hour with me. She taught me how to put on a head collar and, when she saw me double knot his rope round the stable bars, she rapidly untied him and taught me how to tie him up correctly.

'He could hurt himself if you tie him to a fixed rail like that,' she explained. 'Tie him to some rope or bail twine so if he pulls back, it will break and he'll be free.'

'Free? Is a free horse around a stable yard not a bad thing?'

'Better than an injured horse. Take my word for it.'

Sue showed me how to brush him, how to walk around him without fear of being lamped with his feet, and how to get knots out of his tail.

She coached me on how to pick up each of his feet individually. Not that I'd be picking them up more than one at a time of course (he'd fall over), but each was different and where I put my arm to lift the foot really mattered. Lifted incorrectly and there's a risk of a broken arm (or, indeed, much worse) if the horse chooses to exercise its right and kick its leg out. I'm particularly fond of my arms (and, in fact, all of my extremities) being in full and correct working order, so those were instructions I was particularly keen to understand and heed to the full.

Then she taught me how to make his feed, how to muck out his bed, where to throw the muck and then how to fill and tie up a haynet.

So much to learn. But the money was in sight, my business career ready to fly. I just had to knuckle down and get this bit over with and I'd be good-to-go for the rest of my life!

We headed to the tea room – the hub of the yard. Sue needed the loo which was just out the back of the little building. There were two women sitting chatting over a brew.

'Camilla, Flo, this is Fran. She's the new livery you'll have heard about.'

They both said 'hi' to me.

Sue dipped through the back to the loo and I stood, a little like a spare part, waiting for her to come back. My eyes wandered around the little stone tea room but to my further discomfort, there was nothing really of interest to settle my eyes on. A small microwave, a few kitchen cupboards, a kettle and a sink. In fact, Flo and Camilla were positively electrifying in comparative terms but I didn't want to look at them in case they spoke to me some more. Bearing in mind Richard's insistence that I don't come clean about my predicament, that meant I needed to look somewhat both competent and interested in horses.

'You settling OK?' asked Camilla or, indeed, Flo (I wasn't quite sure yet which was which). You could tell, looking at the way she had applied her makeup, that she couldn't have excelled at colouring-in as a kid.

'Yes, thank you.'

'Saw your man earlier. Nice stamp,' said the older Camilla-or-perhaps-Flo.

Rabbit and headlights sprung to mind. What the hell was she actually on about? Man? Stamp? The only man I

51

knew at the yard was Richard and he most certainly wasn't mine! And, stamp? My eyes shifted left and right in an involuntary movement that indicated my poor overloaded brain was trying to find something remotely resembling an appropriate response. The word nice, perhaps indicated a compliment.

'Thank you!' I ventured, struggling to keep the upward question incline out of the statement.

Their expressions indicated that was a good response. I wished to God Sue would hurry up in there. It would be just my luck for her to find herself suffering a touch of constipation right about now.

'Have you got plans for this weekend? Are you showing?' asked the younger of the two.

Showing? SHOWING? What the hell could I possibly be showing? Were these women just deliberately trying to make me look stupid? I decided the best approach was attack so I flew forth with what I thought was a possible good answer.

'Ah, no, unfortunately not this weekend. I'm not sure the world is ready for anything I might have to show yet. Perhaps next week though,' I said confidently.

How was I to know that a show is some kind of organised event where people take their horses and even dogs, cows, pigs and even cakes, photographs and crafts and compete against others for nice rosettes and prizes.

Their mouths dropped just that little bit as they gawped at me like a stick insect in their sticky toffee pudding - that would, indeed, be sticky toffee pudding though! Fortunately, the loo in the back flushed and Sue emerged.

'You all set for home?' she asked me, then turned to Tweedle Dee and Tweedle Dum. 'See you tomorrow, ladies.'

On the way to the car park, I explained the conversation that I'd had and she put me straight. My man is now Batman. He could also be my boy sometimes. Nice stamp doesn't mean he, or I, have a good ability to bash our feet on the ground, it actually means that he's true to his breeding type, but she says most people use it more generally to mean he's pretty well put together. According to Sue, he's an Irish Draught crossed with a thoroughbred. I didn't know what either of those looked like individually, but together clearly they looked like a Batman.

Sue also filled me in on Camilla and Flo. Flo, with her permed set blonde-going-on-grey hair, is the mother and Camilla, the very grown-up, thirty-five-year-old still living at home, daughter. Flo doesn't ride but does spend almost every waking moment at the yard with her nose in everyone else's business. Camilla has a horse that Flo pays for. To me, by the sound of things, the whole situation just seemed wrong. But each to their own, as they say. I guess many would think the whole situation of me with Batman is wrong. To be fair, they'd be bang on right.

Tomorrow, I'd get on him for the first time and the learning to ride would begin. To be fair, I was under-excited, to say the least.

Chapter 8

Tomorrow came waaaaay too quickly. Furnished with strong coffee, I poured myself into my new brown (not bay), posh breeches that were a touch (just a touch though) snug, pulled on my top and got ready to head off to the yard. When I got there, Marcus, was waiting for me. He was not much taller than me, dark skinned and a lovely kind-looking face. I liked him already.

'You must be Fran,' he said, as I entered the stable block, where he was stood drinking a steaming mug of tea.

'Is it that obvious?' I asked and he just smiled.

'Richard has asked me to come and help you get going. I understand you're starting right from scratch – never really done anything with horses?' I shook my head. 'I'll show you how to get tacked up and we'll get you on and moving.'

Tacking up was, to say the least, a challenge in itself. The head thing called the bridle was a mass of leather straps that seemed to have a mind of their own and operated in the same physical sphere as over-cooked spaghetti. I was supposed to, at the same time as persuading the horse to keep his head still and in reach, work out which bit of his head (including some particularly floppy long ears) went through which gap in the vastness of leather straps that were all interconnected AND get a metal bit into his mouth: Houdini in reverse.

Batman thought better of this whole scenario and chose simply to look at the ceiling. He'd clearly done this before and clearly knew I hadn't. Game over, as far as I was concerned! How the hell do you persuade an obstinate horse, doing a pretty good giraffe impression, that he's to put his head down?

Marcus took over, did some secret thing with his hand round the other side of his head and, there it was, his nose came back down! It looked like a bit of black magic to me but who am I to tell. Also, it seemed like Batman was giving me a bit of the eye. You know, the eye that says: *I've got you proper weighed up and I'm in charge here.* I thought he could even be Richard in disguise.

Marcus got the bridle on and we decided tomorrow would be time enough for me to master that skill. Marcus suggested that perhaps taking it off a little later, when I'd finished riding (that's a laugh, riding!) might be a touch easier. I didn't think so but you know me; I'm game for most things.

Marcus led Batman to the indoor arena. He told me it was safe in there – soft and contained so, if I fell off, the landing was forgiving and if Batman tanked off there was nowhere to go. He did give a wry smile so I had an idea he was winding me up. Suitably comforted I was not, however. The arena was huge, like a big warehouse with a sand surface. There was a big wooden wall down one side with stables behind it with sounds from the horses wafting into the arena.

'I'll leg you up,' Marcus told me. I just looked at him. This new venture was providing a whole new category of things proving me to be a completely incompetent human being.

'Think about dumbing this down for a four-year-old and then dumb it down some more so I can understand,' I said.

'Have you never even been on a horse?' I shook my head. 'OK. Stand facing the side of the horse, here.' He physically positioned me so I was facing Batman. 'Hold onto the front of the saddle with your right hand, here,' he put my hand on the saddle, '...and here at the back of the saddle with your left hand.' He stood back. 'Now, lift your left leg at the knee.'

I did as he asked. Or so I thought.

'No,' he said slowly, as if talking to an imbecile (no wisecracks, thank you - in case I haven't already mentioned it, I have an IQ of 160). 'What I mean is, bend your knee so your leg comes out at a right angle. I need to hold it to give you a leg up. I can't do that if you stand like you're doing the Karate Kid stance.'

I did as I was told and he put his hand under my raised shin. 'When I lift, you jump and, when you're high enough, throw your right leg over the saddle and sit down,' he told me. To my mind, this was getting incredibly complicated. He lifted and I jumped, well I tried. I'm not used to doing such acrobatics so, instead of landing gracefully in the saddle looking all horse-ridery, I ended up having belly flopped onto Batman's side, looking all jelly wobbly, arms clinging on for dear life, right leg flailing in thin air for some kind of purchase that just wasn't there (and actually rather close to Marcus's face, he told me later) and Marcus buckling under my (not too heavy, of course) weight.

Feet back on the ground, hands still on the saddle, Marcus suggested we try that again, but a little more successfully this time. The second time, I got my right leg as far as Batman's butt end but not completely over. He seemed to take that as a sign I wanted him to walk away. There I was, stranded half on, half off the damn horse that was no longer static. The movement was just a step too far for me and I plopped to the sand surface, landing on my backside. Who would think even getting on the damn thing would be this difficult? I picked myself up and dusted the sand off my butt. Third time, I managed it. It took a balancing act of my body doing the worm up the side of Batman, Marcus clinging on to my shin with both hands and using all his strength to support me long enough for me to shuffle myself, face-first long ways on Batman and then finally swing my right leg into place. I sat there feeling vaguely pleased with myself. First challenge in the bag.

'I'm on,' I told Marcus, as if he didn't know.

'I know,' he said. 'Let's get going. I know you've got some lessons planned...' this was news to me at this point, but I kept that to myself, '...but for now, let's go through some simple basics.'

He showed me how to hold the reins, told me to squeeze with my legs to go and pull with the reins to stop. 'It's generally a little more complicated than that but, for today, let's just keep it simple.' I sensed he didn't want me stretching his patience any further and was, indeed, very happy to just keep it simple. Marcus attached a rope to Batman's bit and kept hold of us. We walked around the arena and then changed direction and walked the other way.

'Fancy a trot?' he asked me.

Well, I wasn't here to pass the time of day. I had an investment to earn so my philosophy was that I best just crack on.

'Yep, let's go for it.' Walking seemed OK, so I assumed trot would be just a faster version of walk. NOPE! Turned out trot was a bit more like being stuck in a potato rumbler on fast. I was bounced about all over the place in the saddle and was seriously concerned that I was going to be bounced right off the back of him.

I think Marcus could see my predicament.

'Hold onto the front of the saddle,' he shouted up to me as he jogged next to Batman. 'Don't worry, I've got Batman.' I was more worried about my uncontrolled jiggling and didn't give Batman and subsequent control of him a second thought! I did hold onto the front of the saddle but it really didn't help. My lady bits were taking the brunt on a saddle that felt like rock and I was sure I'd struggle to sit down again for days after this. How the hell do real riders actually do this stuff? Trotting torture finally done, I was relieved to hear that my first ride was over and that I had, in Marcus's words, 'done enough'!

Getting off was a damn sight easier than getting on. I slid down the side of Batman and managed to land on both feet at the same time. I was suitably pleased.

The trial wasn't over when we got back to the stable. I remembered the bridle – my turn. It wasn't any easier. Batman saw my arms coming in the general direction of his head and up it went again, nose in the air.

I wanted to kick him swiftly in the front leg shin but I felt that was perhaps an improper response to his behaviour so I restrained myself. Marcus took off his bridle. I guessed we'd tackle that additional skill, also, tomorrow. I realised that sitting on a horse no more makes you a rider than sitting in a cockpit makes you a pilot.

I headed to the tea room, desperate for a brew. It was full and I experienced one of those moments where every head turns to look at you when you walk in a room. The girls (I say girls, there was not one under thirty) were all friendly though and welcomed me in. Introductions then ensued and I had a room full of names to remember. Bridgett, Liv, Sonia, Marcus (although not a girl, he was an honorary girl due to his liking for men), then there was Big Katie (a complete misnomer, as she's five foot one and built like a French fry) and Little Katie (another complete misnomer, as she's five foot eight and built like a well-fed teddy bear). Shortly after, Meg waltzed in with Gary. I did quite like the look of him.

'This is...?' Liv went to introduce me but she'd forgotten my name already. Liv was petite and pretty with short blonde hair. I wished I could look that petite but that would involve some serious food deprivation on my part that I would struggle to put into practice.

'It's Fran but if in doubt, just shout Prosecco and I'm sure to turn round.'

The chatter picked up again and I nipped out back to the loo. Having thin walls, the toilet wasn't very anonymous. I made a mental note to never need to defecate or expel flatulence within this particular toilet, lest the whole yard know what I was up to. There were other arrivals in the tea room, as hi's were said.

The next voice I heard was that of Camilla.

'So, have you seen this new woman ride at all? She looks and acts completely clueless!'

Liv, with her broad Yorkshire accent, wasted no time in piping up in my defence.

'OH MY GOD Camilla, check your face. I think I just found your nose where it doesn't belong; in someone else's business!'

The room erupted in laughter and I chuckled away to myself. Seemed I was going to have to develop a thick skin to get through this. When I came out, Camilla had taken her leave.

'I don't know what the hell she was on about, have you seen Camilla ride, herself?' said Meg.

'Apparently she went to Fieldcliffe Riding School,' said Sue.

'Was it closed?' asked Meg. Everyone laughed.

I didn't know it then, but most of these people were going to become my best friends. It was good to know they were all willing to stick up for me, even though they'd all, with the exception of Sue, just met me. In fact, with my sincere dislike of the general public and socialising with anyone outside my usual circle, it was to be the most friends I'd ever had since my school days when I was part of the not-so-popular crowd. Bridgett, the yard manager Sue had warned me about, was most definitely not included in that group though, she was known as a snake in the grass. However, snakes in the grass are sly and devious, but to be honest Bridgett turned out to be a bit more up front about her dislike of some people on the yard. As I would later find out, the real snake in the grass would turn out to be one of my new-found friends.

Chapter 9

Work today was a welcome relief from all things equine. The normality of the office (I wasn't training today) was heaven-sent and it was good to be amongst the banter. On working days when I'm not training I would use the time in the office to update courses, trying to make them better and better or developing new ones. Well, that's always been my line to the management, mostly I'd look like I'm working but really I'd be up to my own business.

If you asked me how many people work here, I'd say approximately half of them – but that's only on a good day. At least I was still doing something productive.

I've developed particular talents to look like I'm working. So, I might be working on a set of course notes in Microsoft Word. I might also be working on my business plan at the same time. With careful positioning of the two documents on the screen I could flip from one (my business plan) to the other (course notes) if someone even hinted at coming close enough to see the actual contents of my screen. That way, I managed to maximise my time. I'm not so sure my employers would see it that way but I got their job done, and I did it well, so my own little perk was to be able to crack on and do some of my own stuff.

My desk was located conveniently in the corner by the window, with a meeting room directly behind, which helped my cause incredibly. Next to me sat one of the newer trainers in the team, Mark, a senior IT trainer with lots of experience. He seemed OK but my God, did he drive me up the wall. He didn't just type on his keyboard, he bashed the living daylights out of it. If his keyboard was anything but inanimate, it would be considered serial abuse. Not only was it distracting but it was causing me some serious mental grief.   I planned to bide my time and make sure this practice stops. *I have a cunning plan*, as Baldrick would say.

'Fancy a brew,' I asked him. It wasn't that I wanted to make him a cup of tea but it was the done thing to ask colleagues if you were making. I always tried to add a hint of don't-say-yes tone into my question, but it was lost on him.

'Yes, please. Tea, white.'

While in the kitchen stirring the drinks, from nowhere Mark appeared behind me. He leaned over, invading my personal space to reach a teaspoon, placing his other hand in the base of my back. I flinched.

'I forgot to say I take sugar,' he said, adding a spoonful and stirring. He hesitated a moment. 'I was wondering, might you fancy a drink one evening after work?'

'I don't think so. I don't go in for married men,' I said, motioning to his wedding ring.

'Ah...that. I can be discrete.'

'I can't,' I said. Unaffected by my rebuttal, he gave me a wide grin and left, taking his tea with him.

Mentally, I updated my Baldrick cunning-plan to include retribution for his slimy conduct.

In lieu of doing any real work that I was being paid for, I managed to write the first four pages of what I think is actually turning into a pretty good business plan. I've written them before to try and get the cash for my idea but, now with my funding in place, I'm doing it for real and it's coming together well. At one point, whilst I was deep in thought gazing out of the window, I missed it when Nina stood up (she's the Training Manager) and looked remotely like she might head in my direction. Back in the room, I did an internal squeak of fear and quickly clicked my course notes document to bring it to the front. But it was a false alarm so all was good.

We call her Meaner Nina because she is just that; a little bit meaner than anyone else you might know. In fact, she is what you might call a fun sponge.

The main event for today was a conference call. I have a great dislike of any types of meeting, and that includes conference calls. Although, given a choice, the conference call wins in the Fran-preference-stakes any time over a face-to-face meeting. At least I can hide behind a telephone and, with a headset on, I have both hands free allowing me to be up to my own business on my computer at the same time.

I do have to be careful in getting my coordination right when speaking though. There was a time last month when I was working at home and Tarquin decided to join me in the kitchen. He was hungry and when he's hungry he's usually quite vocal about the fact, mewling and yawling loudly to make sure he's got my full attention. To be honest, it's quite off-putting. I found that when joining a conference call and the point comes to record your name, that's not the time to yell at the cat to, and I quote verbatim, 'Shut the hell up, Tarquin!' Imagine my horror when the automated conference call system then announced to at least ten other people on the call that, 'Shut The Hell Up Tarquin has just joined the call!'

In shock, I instinctively hung up immediately and could, in my innermost ear, hear the automated call system subsequently telling everyone that, 'Shut The Hell Up Tarquin has now left the call.'

I had only two strategies open to me: 1) pretend to be sick and not show up at all or 2) redial in and hope that firstly, no-one had recognised my voice (feasible, given the tone I'd taken with Tarquin) and secondly, not everyone had already been on the call so by process of elimination, they couldn't work out it was me!

I tell you, I won't be making that mistake again. Whilst it looked like I got away with it, I'm pretty sure Meaner Nina knew exactly who it was.

The difficult thing, though, with conference calls, particularly when you (i.e. me) prefer to occupy yourself with non-work-related activities that you shouldn't be, it's very, very easy to get a touch confused as to which state the mute setting is currently residing on.

The time to find out that it's not on mute when you thought it was, however, is not when you've just said: 'Christ, this is so damn boring. When will it end?'

Again, as luck would have it, the call was extremely busy and, I was sure it would be difficult for anyone to definitely identify my voice. Thank God for that, is all I can say. This is me, living life on the edge!

Sue, however, knew exactly who it was.

'You moron,' she said, as we had coffee later.

'You knew?'

'Of course, I knew. How could I not recognise that voice? You're lucky no-one else did.' She laughed.

Today's call was to run through the schedule for a series of courses we were running for a department in

Leeds to support their new customer management system. Unfortunately, I was the lead trainer on this and the project manager was Mary Barker. We have an eclectic range of staff from a variety of diverse backgrounds including Liverpool and, unfortunately, Mary speaks with a thick Scouse accent that I have much difficulty deciphering in person never mind on the phone. She spoke and I knew she was addressing me – because she said my name - however, that was where the clarity ended. I couldn't understand another damn word she said. Even though I listened really, really carefully, each time she repeated the question (I think it was a question - it could have been a bloody nursery rhyme for all I could make out), I just couldn't get it. After maxing out on what might be considered a socially acceptable number of times I could ask, 'Can you say that again, please?', I was beginning to think I might just have to feign passing out or losing phone signal.

Fortunately, Sue jumped in and paraphrased what Mary was saying. Clearly she was fluent in Liverpudlian gobbledegook and I was very grateful for that. I made a mental note to buy her an extra large vino next time we were out together. Today had been way too traumatic, in terms of meetings, so I resolved to put that to rights with a glass or two of Prosecco tonight. I might even invite my brother to join me for a glass. In fact, I was finding it quite acceptable having the company at home. I needed someone to tell my horsey exploits to and share business ideas with. Tarquin is fine company but the conversations are particularly one way.

Chapter 10

I'd thought the competition that I'd signed up to was kind of just turn up dressed a bit posh and ride. But it was becoming clear that that was most definitely not the case. I might actually have to put in some serious effort along the way to make this result happen.

'So let me get this right, this competition I have to win is called an event?' I asked Marcus, as we sat in the tea room at the yard.

'Right.'

'Events come in different levels, so the higher the level, the higher the jumps are that you jump?' I took a slurp of my muddy coffee that was a welcome hot and wet relief after riding in the indoor arena.

'Right. See, it's easy.'

'In your opinion, maybe. My level is called BE80? And that's the smallest one I can do?'

'Yes, it's the smallest with jumps around eighty centimetres, hence the name British Eventing 80.'

'That sounds way too damn big to me. Have you seen just how big eighty centimetres actually is?' I stood up and put my hand just below my hip. 'It's right up here Mate, and in my book that's bloody huge!'

'Don't worry, it won't be by the time you're ready to get out there and compete. You'll be well prepared.'

'So, I turn up at this event, and I have to do a dressage test but I've got to learn what all the movements are and I've got to remember them whilst I'm trying to actually ride?'

'Fran, you make it sound so difficult. It's not that difficult. Have you had to remember a set of directions to get somewhere in your car?'

'No, I use a Sat Nav or a map.'

'You're not helping! What about a set of instructions when you're teaching people to use a computer application?'

'Yeah, OK, I get what you mean, but that's stuff I can do. I can't damn well ride, never mind remember a whole load of movements at the same time AND ride them well.'

'You're getting too hung up on technicalities. All we're talking about here is you simply understanding what the competition is all about. Forget about riding it for now.'

'OK, I do the dressage test, I've stayed on, I'm still in one piece. The next thing I have to do is ride a round of show jumps?' The whole magnitude, like the real magnitude of what I'd taken on was properly starting to sink in. This was just impossible. I was struggling to get on, never mind stay on round an entire event.

'And then,' continued Marcus, 'you finish with a round of cross country – that's the best bit. It's the bit that most eventers live for. The freedom of just you and the horse out across the country jumping fences. It's great!'

I wasn't convinced. It felt, actually, like I had just committed to climb Mount Everest on the back of walking up all fifty feet of Almscliffe Crag.

'You can't just head off out there and hope to win a proper event like that, though,' continued Marcus. 'You'll need to enter some smaller, less imposing competitions to get a feel for what it's like and to practise.' This was news to me. So, my one competition had now turned into several competitions. Where would this actually end?

I noticed Marcus looking at me, I could tell something was on his mind. I bided my time rather than prompting him, so took another sip of the hot coffee.

'Can I ask?' he started.

'Ask what?' I ventured.

'Why? Why, when you're not horsey in any way, would you agree to do something like this?'

'You mean the investment, from Richard?'

'Yes, there must be easier ways to make money.'

'You'd think there would be, wouldn't you? But, I've been around the block and back. I could get money at loan-shark rates but I'd go under before I could even get my business up and running. The fact is, I really believe in my idea. I really believe it can work. I kind of had it in my mind that this couldn't really be that difficult but I'm rethinking that now.'

'If you ask me, you need to rethink it.' I looked at him, a little shocked. 'Don't get me wrong, I think you can do this. What I'm saying is that you shouldn't underestimate the task ahead of you. It will be a long road and it won't be easy. That determination you have for your business will need to come into play for you to be ready for this event.'

'So that's what Richard is really testing – my resolve and determination?'

'Looks like it.'

'Well, do you know what? No matter what I face, I'm going to make this happen.' And, when I said it that day to Marcus, I really meant it. Marcus was right. I also had no idea what it would do to my character and my outlook on life. I thought, going into this challenge, that I knew everything there was to know about myself, but I was completely wrong.

Chapter 11

I did laugh so! Tarquin often has what you might call slack bowels - in fact, he's affectionately known in my house as Mr Whippy. So, yesterday morning, Paul picked Tarquin up to assist him down to his litter tray, to avoid an unnecessary *accident* on the stairs and on the way he sloppy-drip-pooed all over Paul's shoes. Given the yelling that came from his general direction this morning, I don't think Paul saw it as a sign of endearment from Tarquin. It was these little moments that really cheered my day up. What are little brothers, who turn up almost unannounced for an inconveniently lengthy stay (with a Pug in tow) for, if not to provide constant amusement at their own misfortune?

These little challenges always seemed to arrive right at the point in time that I needed to crack on quickly, but at least today's minor misfortune fell to Paul to clear up. For me, this particular hour was totally taken up with getting to the yard, getting tacked up and getting on in the arena in time for my lesson. In fact, I was feeling a few little flutterings of something that was sitting about halfway between excitement and a fear of dying in the pit of my stomach at the thought. Today was to be my first proper riding lesson. Richard had organised for his instructor to come to the yard and give me a lesson. Can't say as I was particularly looking forward to it, but needs must!

As I dressed, the doorbell rang. Paul shouted up to me.

'It's for you.'

'I'll be two minutes,' I called back. I hauled on my new breeches. I was glad to have had Sue on hand when I went horsey-clothes shopping. I'm not vain at all, but I wouldn't want to turn up to my first lesson looking like an equestrian refugee. I checked myself out in the bathroom mirror. I was getting more used to this look. Maybe I'd make a horsey girl yet.

Dressed and downstairs, I found Paul in the kitchen drinking coffee with Marcus at the little kitchen table, and, if I wasn't mistaken, flirting!

'So, what do you do, Paul?'

'I'm an architect. I work at a studio in the centre of Leeds,' said Paul. 'Pretty boring stuff really, compared to your horse riding.' Marcus smiled coyly at the compliment.

'And you live with Fran?'

'Just staying for a while. Like to spend a bit of time with my big sis every once in a while,' he lied – or rather didn't quite tell the truth.

Marcus looked up when he noticed me and seeing my surprise explained 'you looked a touch overwhelmed at the whole horse riding and eventing thing yesterday. I thought I'd pop round and help to ease your mind away from the yard. I hope you don't mind.'

'That's really kind,' I said, taking a seat at the table. Paul stood up and made me a coffee, but his eyes were fixed on Marcus.

'I just wanted you to know that I'm right behind you and I'll help in any way I can. Remember that throughout all of this,' Marcus told me.

We chatted some more whilst Marcus finished his coffee, then he left.

'I'll see you at the yard,' he said, then flashing a wide smile at Paul. 'Maybe I'll see you there too?'

'Sure thing,' said Paul. 'I'll be there to support Fran, all the way.'

'DON'T even think about it,' I told Paul, as soon as the door was closed behind Marcus.

'Think about what?' he said, feigning surprise.

'You know exactly what I mean. You're spoken for and I don't need the complication of you getting involved and then falling out with someone I have to rely on at the stables.'

'What makes you think I'm even interested?'

'"I'll be there to support Fran, all the way,"' I mimicked. 'I know you and I saw the way you looked at him. I'm telling you, leave it well alone.'

I wasn't convinced, however, that he would listen to me. I was further not sure if I was keen for him to leave it well alone for my benefit at the yard or for the fact that if Mike found out, Paul would be with me much, much longer.

Chapter 12

'Fran, where are you?' said an unfamiliar voice.

'In here, tacking up,' I called back.

'I'm Gabby, your instructor. Be in the arena in five minutes, please.' She left.

Apparently, she's some bright-spark young rider who does this sport of eventing that I've got to get to grips with. At twenty-four, she's a good deal my junior so my thoughts were that I wouldn't be taking any crap. How little did I know then, young she may have been but a soft-touch, she most definitely wasn't. I was about to learn that on day one.

At that time, tacking up was a bit of a trauma. I'd get reins twisted, stirrups uneven and girth not tight enough, so I was running just a bit late when I rocked up in the indoor arena ready for my lesson. Gabby was there already, talking with Richard in the corner. I wasn't so sure I wanted him there for my first or, indeed, any of my lessons but as he was stumping the bill, I guessed I couldn't complain.

'Let me see what you can do,' she started with as she took her place in the centre of the arena.

Richard found a convenient hay bale in the corner to sit on. His squashed up face was starting to annoy me, the more I saw it. I found myself visualising sinking my fist into it or smothering it with a memory foam pillow.

'Today would be good,' Gabby said, sharply reminding me to be 'in-the-room' or rather the arena, instead of lost in my thoughts. My eyes blazed in defiance but I smiled sweetly and gave Batman a kick with both legs. He pretty much proceeded to ignore me and maintained his spot. I kicked again, harder this time.

'Do you HAVE to do that, Fran? You do know that your arms and your legs are not directly connected, don't you?' The sarcasm was thick.

Seems my legs and arms were, indeed, somehow connected. So kicking also involved an involuntary flap of my arms. I seemed powerless to control this and, as a result, I felt that the whole world had all of a sudden gotten infinitely more difficult to be a part of and, further, my feeling was that it was going to get even more difficult since Gabby had arrived on my horizon.

I'm sure that by the end of the first lesson I actually saw Gabby smile, although I'm not sure if that was because my horse passed wind rather loudly as we headed off up into a very bouncy trot and she thought it was me. I can't say I've ever been more relieved than I was when I got off Batman at the end of that lesson. The ground seemed further down than it was when I'd got on, although, to be fair, I had used a mounting block so I think it genuinely was.

'You did good,' Gabby said, as she walked back to Batman's stable alongside me, with Richard in tow a bit behind us. 'It can't be easy at your age and in your physical condition to get on a horse and learn to ride.' She smiled a wide, cheesy grin. 'But, don't worry, I'm here to help and I'll soon whip you into shape.'

'Can't wait,' I replied, less than enthusiastically. In fact, I wanted to wipe the sanctimonious smug look off her face to be honest, but I didn't think that was a good strategy for future workable relations.

'Richard has booked you in for two lessons a week, so we can really make some headway. I'll see you on Thursday at six – I've already booked the arena,' she paused, 'unless...you have other plans?' It was almost a dare to see if I would defy her. I decided it was best not to irritate one of the natives so early in the game. She was prickly to say the least so I decided the right side of her was the best one to be on and would give me, hopefully, the least painful path through the whole learning-to-ride process. How wrong could I have been?

I think that was the first real time that I questioned my sanity in deciding to take Richard up on his ridiculous offer. It certainly wouldn't be the last time.

'Make sure you brush him off before you put his rug on,' Gabby instructed before turning and leaving.

'Like she said, you did well. I was impressed.' Richard leaned his arms on Batman's stable door.

'Thanks. I was less impressed but I'm sure it can only get better,' I replied, realising how sore my legs were. Again, as things went, that turned out to be a very optimistic view. Getting better in the horse world, it turned out, didn't mean actually just getting better. It meant taking a whole shed-load of knocks and falls, fallings out and trauma to take a few skilful steps forward, but these were life lessons that I was yet to learn. I think if I'd known then what I know now, I would actually have handed Richard the horse back and walked straight down to a loan-shark to get the money. It might have been less painful, in the long run.

'You're right, it will get better. Look, I've got to shoot now. I need to head back up to the house and beautify myself. I'm off out tonight.'

'Someone special?'

'Just a friend, really. I've known her for a long time. I'll maybe see you tomorrow,' and with that, he left.

Infinitely wealthy, it seemed he was never short of female company, even if he was marginally overweight, balding (in a manly kind of way), and just slightly on the uglier side of handsome.

I spent the next ten minutes brushing Batman's sweaty spots before rugging him for the night.

'What do you think, Mate? Are we ready for this?' I asked his long face, but he didn't even move an eye from his haynet to acknowledge my question. It was rhetorical anyway, so what could he say? *Neigh*, perhaps.

Tomorrow would be yet another day and could I wait? I bloody well could wait.

Chapter 13

I ended up taking two impromptu weeks off work. This riding lark was so much more difficult than it ever looked on TV or than I might have imagined. Not only did it take balance to stay on the damn creature but I had to be doing something different with about eight singular parts of my body all at the same time. Now, bearing in mind that I can't even dress myself correctly most of the time, that's a pretty tall order for me. Each hand had to be 'talking' to the horse down the reins, like some sort of special equine Morse Code that I sure as hell didn't understand. My legs had to each be 'on' the horse. Well, given that I was sat on top of the bloody thing, where else would they be? I have an inside leg and an outside leg – I always thought this was used for measuring trousers but apparently, in equine circles, this is not the case and which is which depends on which way round I'm going. My outside leg is nearest to the arena fence and my inside leg is nearest to the middle of the arena. When my left leg is nearest to outside of the arena, I am considered to be on the right rein, and going in the other direction, I'm on the left rein. This is not easy for a simpleton like me to comprehend, in terms of coordination, never mind adhere to. I wanted to gloss over all of this, pretend like I'd got it and just do my own thing, but it soon became very clear that would never in a million years wash with Gabby.

In one lesson Gabby told me to nudge Batman with my left leg, adding further confusion. Lifting my right rein up, Gabby asked what the hell I was doing. I told her I could only work out which leg was my left one by working out which side was my right one and I did that by pretending I'm writing, hence my right hand (and consequently my right rein) waggling in the air. Gabby told me in no uncertain terms that this was just not acceptable for every move to the right or left I was likely to make in a lesson.

'Sort yourself out!' was her final judgement on the matter.

Not quite sure how I was supposed to do that. What I did do was learn how to wiggle my right hand to do the whole pretend-I'm-writing manoeuvre with my hand in situ. If she continued to notice, she didn't say anything, so I guessed that at this level it was acceptable.

My horse, as does any horse, has four paces: walk, trot, canter and gallop. Batman seems to have also developed a whole set of paces all of his own: start, screech to a halt, stumble, stagger and trip me right off.

Trot is proving a difficult pace for me. It's all about timing and I, quite simply, don't have any. I have to go up and down in beat with his legs moving. Sounds simple? Well actually, to me, it doesn't even sound simple. The result is that I'm invariably bounced around all over the shop in the saddle and, I can tell you, that's not a comfortable experience. My butt is screaming for some respite that it's unlikely to see for around six months or more. I was thinking of inventing the first memory foam saddle for riding dullards like me. I would also be learning the art of hacking soon. Hacking, I was led to believe, is apparently good fun and relaxing. Given that it involves leaving the safety of the stable yard to take a four-legged creature onto paths and tracks and even roads with motorised vehicles on, it sounded anything but fun and relaxing. To me, knowing Batman as I did, having spent two weeks with him trying to ride and stay on him, I thought it sounded like a let's-ensure-Fran-ends-up-in-A&E kind of recipe for disaster. But, I guessed I'd reserve judgement until we got out there and gave it a try. One thing I was learning was that I was still bloody keen to stay the course, so to speak, and guarantee my investment. I was pretty sure I would, provided I didn't kill or seriously maim myself along the way which, given my current skill level (or rather lack of it), was looking like a serious possibility.

In between the lessons I'd been learning the ropes of riding with others in the arena. There's always been someone there with me, mostly Sue, and that was reassuring as I still felt very vulnerable on the back of Batman. Liv was a regular rider with me, on her black, heavy set horse that she told me was a cob. Quite a bit smaller than Batman in height, he was lovely with thick hairy legs. I was really getting to like Liv. In her early thirties, she was a bit of a go-getter in the world of event planning.

In our latest riding session together Liv's phone rang. I could only hear one side of the conversation but that was enough.

'Hi.'

'I didn't touch your gym bag. It'll be where you left it.'

'It's not me that's making you late, you're doing that all by yourself.'

'I don't think that's called for.'

'Look, I've got to go; I'm riding. Bye, I'll see...' He'd clearly hung up. *What a dick*, I thought.

She looked over at me.

'That's why I like to spend so much time at the yard,' she said, slipping her phone into her jacket pocket.

'Tough times, eh?'

'Yeah, three years in and it seems like a struggle day in, day out. Mark's just started a new job. He works long days so he's often home late and is mostly tired. I get that, but for marriage to work, it's got to be give and take. Sometimes I think I'd just be better on my own. Running my own business takes a lot of time and effort,' she confided.

'I know exactly what you mean. There's no way I could cope with a man to complicate things.'

'Complicate?'

'Yes, I'm setting up my own business. I've wanted to work for myself for forever and I'm finally doing it. A man would really just get in the way.'

'And a new horse wouldn't?' she asked.

'A girl needs a bit of time out,' I said thinking quickly on my feet (so to speak, as I was actually sat on Batman). 'A horse is definitely easier than a man. I can just stuff him in his stable at the end of the day and go home.'

'You've got that one right,' she said and we laughed.

We finished riding and headed to the tea room to have a brew together. Those two weeks off work were spent, for a good part, riding with Liv and cemented our new friendship. Yes, I liked Liv.

Chapter 14

Back at work in my proper job after two weeks with my new man and thinking only about my business was a bit of a shock to the system. Meaner Nina decided it would be good to have a team-building night out. Being my regular anti-social self, I could live without these but I needed to be seen as a team player, to keep my life easy at work. She asked me to organise this for our immediate team of trainers, which is around twenty staff in total. Sue and I had coffee in the morning for a break.

'How'd the lesson go? I hear Gabby is a real taskmaster.'

'You can say that again. I felt like I'd done a round with Mike Tyson by the time I was finished. This stuff really isn't easy.'

'Nothing worth its weight in this life is easy, so stick with it. You'll be great, just give yourself the chance.'

I wasn't quite so sure I'd be great, but, as always, I appreciated her support.

'And Gary?' she asked, with raised eyebrows.

'What about Gary?' I feigned ignorance.

'You like him? I think you do and I'm sure he likes you. He's always somewhere in the vicinity when you're around.'

'Even if I did, I'm most definitely not going there. Batman and Paul are sufficient male activity in my life at the moment.'

'We'll see,' she said, then turned her attention to the forthcoming team night out.

'So, where are you thinking for the team drinks?'

We chatted about where to go as we finished our coffees and decided on a cocktail bar close to the office. We headed back up to the office.

As the night out was just for our closer team, I didn't need to write an essay in the email so I sent out a brief invite. I added a short and snappy subject heading saying: 'Let's get together'. In the email itself, I put simply: 'Meet for drinks at the Cutting Shop cocktail bar at 5.30 on Wednesday.' I addressed the email invite to our team mailing list, or at least I thought I did, and that was that; job done - another tick in the box for Fran.

With work going well on my business plan, I decided to take the chance and print a copy out so I could read through it and make some editing notes at lunchtime. Now, printing something that isn't work-related involves all kinds of risks and the last thing I need is for my personal business document to be seen on the work printer. As per any underhand activity I engage myself in, I have a cunning plan. What I do is print my own document first and immediately after it, the other work document I'm working on. When I go to the printer, my work document is stacked on top of my business plan. I pick up the whole pile and job's a good'un! Well, that was the plan...

What happened? I sent both to the printer and it damn-well jammed before anything came out. Now, as with my knowledge of anything mechanical or technical, I know seven-tenths of sod all about printers. I can just about manage to add paper to the tray if I really have to, but anything that involves opening little doors and dealing with spin-y innards is absolutely out of my skill set.

Today, however, I was dead keen to get on in there. Mark came over, flashing his cheesy-sleazy grin, and offered to help, placing one of his touchy-feely hands on my shoulder. A little too quickly, I told him I was fine and I had it covered. Thankfully he mooched on back to his desk.

I started to pull open the different compartments to find the paper jam, getting just a little frazzled in my desire to have this fixed before someone realised just what I was up to. It's amazing what skills a sudden onset of fear for your job will endow upon a person.

From her desk, Meaner Nina could hear the commotion as I pulled and prodded at the machine.

'Is everything OK?' she asked me.

'Yes, it's all good,' I said, trying to sound much calmer than I felt. 'Just a paper jam. I'll have it going again in just a couple of minutes.'

'Good, I've sent my report to print and I need it quickly,' she added as extra incentive for me to get my act into gear and fix the bloody thing.

Thankfully, just at the point I was about to give in and beat the living daylights out of the printer to make myself feel better about it getting me the sack, I found the jam and pulled out the stuck paper.

And there it was, back in action, my sheets printer and in my hand, and my job safe again.

As the day progressed, replies to my earlier email started to filter through to me.

Distracted as I was by progressing my business plan with my double document ruse, I didn't realise that my suspicions should have been on high alert after a response from someone in Manchester saying 'I'd love to meet for drinks. See you there.' Or the one from Doncaster that told me 'Drinks are most definitely out of the question as I'm happily married.'

In fact, had I checked my emails a little earlier, I might have noticed my error quicker and been able to take corrective action of recalling the original mail.

A short while later Sue came over. Seeing her coming, I flicked my screen over to my course notes document. Not that Sue didn't know what I got up to, but if anyone else approached whilst we were talking I wouldn't have to make any sudden suspicious-looking mouse clicks.

'Do you know where you sent that email invitation? Have you actually checked?'

I raised my eyes questioningly. I felt the cold creeping of dread through my bones that I often did when Sue spoke to me in that you've-screwed-up-again tone of voice.

'You sent the drinks invite to every single Allpro Power member of staff in the United Kingdom ‒ You muppet!'

My brain, quick with figures (but quick with sod all else, unfortunately) calculated that I'd invited in the region of three thousand people to come and have a drink with me (how were they to know from my extremely short note that it was a team drinks thing?). I checked my mailbox immediately, sure I really couldn't have ‒ not even I could be that substantially dumb. But there it was, the evidence was plain to see as my inbox was flooding fuller and fuller as we spoke. As they say, artificial intelligence is no match for natural stupidity and I seem to be overly blessed in the latter.

I recalled the email but the damage was essentially done; both to my reputation and to my mailbox. The IT technicians had to sort my mailbox out for me and capture and delete all of the replies to my email. The reputation, however, was my problem and mine alone.

Nina was feeling quite meaner that afternoon after my debacle with the email and a subsequent dressing down for incompetent staff management from her superior, so she had me work out the square metreage for our new office flooring, I think to make her feel better. To save time, I thought I could just count the ceiling tiles. Given that each is three quarters of a metre, I simply needed to multiply the number of full tiles by the size of each tile, then add on the measurements of any partial tiles. That way, I'd have a good representation of the size. I explained my approach to Nina. She looked completely unimpressed.

'Knock knock, anyone in there?' she said, thick with sarcasm, 'I asked for the size of the floor, not the ceiling.'

I held my face solid, even though a smile was threatening to break through. It gave me much solace to know that at least I'm not the only muppet on the planet. It gave me much less solace to know that that other muppet is someone as banal as Meaner Nina.

By the end of my day at work I have to say that I was almost looking forward to a couple of hours at the yard with Batman, where sanity might prevail.

Chapter 15

Today I was introduced to dressage markers. Surrounding the arena at fixed points these markers made absolutely no bloody sense to me whatsoever. Add to that the beginnings of a cold and I was feeling just a touch sorry for myself.

Gabby said to me, 'Halt at X.'

'What? What's this X place? Where do I find it?' OK, so I was a touch sarcastic, but I genuinely had no bloody idea what she was talking about.

'Stop and come here,' she said.

I did. She explained to me about rectangle dressage arena and dressage markers scattered thereabouts so riders know where to do what moves in the test they are riding.

'All King Edward's Horses Can Manage Big Fences,' Gabby said. 'That's the phrase you can use to remember the order of the dressage letters around the outside of the arena: A, K, E, H, C, M, B, F.' Seeing the confusion on my face, she continued: 'At school, didn't you learn that the phrase Big Elephants Can Always Use Small Exits helps you spell the word *because*?' I shook my head. It was all pretty double Dutch to me but the whole Big Elephants phrase actually made loads of sense now I'd heard it.

'In your King Edward's doobrie where is X, then? I didn't hear a word for X but you told me to stop there.'

'I told you to halt there. We say halt, not stop in dressage. X is in the middle of the arena, between E and B and between A and C. Imagine a big rectangle. X is right in the middle and the other letters are all placed at points around the edge. There are other letters but we'll not worry about those just now.'

'So why aren't they just alphabetic?' I asked.

'Don't ask silly questions,' was the response I got. 'That's where the markers go. They can't be alphabetical because there's no start and no end point. Don't make things more complicated than they need to be, Fran.'

I sneezed. In defiance. That was my take on it, anyway. Seems my false teeth had developed a whole persona of their own since I'd developed a bit of a cold. Their persistent (and frankly quite embarrassing) break for freedom each time I sneezed was a feature I could have lived without. I slobbered them back into their rightful place and turned my attention back to the dressage markers (I decided quietly that I'd Google it later and set Gabby straight, since she clearly didn't know).

Today was going to be challenging, I could tell. I still felt alphabetic would have been much easier than King Edward and all that palaver, but I held my tongue. Gabby didn't look like she was up for any more debate (or, indeed, any debate at all). I'd just have to live with it and try and remember where the hell each letter was.

'Flatwork and dressage are perhaps the most important part of your riding,' Gabby told me. I wasn't actually sure what flatwork was but I'd take Gabby's word on it that it was crucial.

'Your flatwork is the foundation of everything you do on your horse,' she said.

I didn't think it was going to be the foundation of me falling off or, indeed, of my learning to tack up but that was an opinion just for me, I thought.

We practised stopping (or halting - when I said it was a stop, she was down my throat again like a dose of Honey and Lemon cough syrup). We practised trotting then walking then trotting again.

'Transitions, Fran. Transitions - walk to trot, trot to walk, walk to halt, trot to halt. You can't do enough transitions.' I felt actually, with good authority based on my experience of today's lesson that you could, in fact, do way too many. I felt I had already.

'When you get as far as going to an event, the dressage will set you apart. That's what you've got to nail, so we'll spend as much time learning to make a good show of yourself in a dressage test as we do for the jumping.'

I must have done another two hundred transitions between walk, trot and halt before my lesson was done. I felt I might be transitioning around the arena in my sleep that night.

Back in the tea room, Sue whipped the kettle on. Sonia, Big Katie and Liv were there too. All asked how my lesson had gone. I told them it had neither gone well nor bad, it had just *gone*.

'It was bloody hard work. I had to walk, then go faster and then stop with all four feet (Batman's, of course) lined up square', although I thought, given how long he is compared to wide, it was antithetical, as it should, in fact, be rectangle. I wasn't, however, going to argue with the weight of the horsey community on this one.

Tea ready, I sipped eagerly. I liked the tea room. It was small and basic but it really was the hub of this busy yard and I was beginning to become comfortable here.

'I'm finding this quite difficult,' I told them. 'There's so much to learn. When I decided to get into this horsey game, I thought the basics of riding were stop, go and jump. Seems that's not the case.'

They all laughed at that.

'Now I've got transitions, dressage, paces, halting square, and God knows what else is still to come in the mix.'

Sonia came to my rescue.

'Stick with it. It looks like you're pretty determined and, with our help too, you'll get there.' As a benefits fraud investigator by trade, Sonia was actually larger than life and probably the loudest and possibly foulest mouth on the yard, but she seemed OK. I was grateful for her encouraging words. I was quite liking having additional friends. Maybe this whole journey wouldn't be the dog's dinner I was thinking it was turning into. I was getting to like these riding buddies and looked forward to my tea room catch-ups.

I began to think I might not be the anti-social witch I've allowed myself to think I am. I'm actually capable of being friendly! You learn something new every day. Before heading off for the evening, I remembered a little task I had planned for tomorrow so I slipped back to the stable block to pick up my tub of hoof oil. There are more things you can do with hoof oil than simply painting it on a horse's feet.

Chapter 16

When I got into the office this morning, the new flooring which I had expertly calculated the metreage for had been laid. This meant there were cables all over the place and desks needed to be put back to their original state (which in my case, looked like it was losing badly at a game of Jumanji). Tarquin had woken me super early at five in the morning for some reason, screeching to a level I simply couldn't ignore.

When I got downstairs, I saw why; he'd clearly been bursting for the loo but couldn't get out of the cat flap and, refusing to use his litter tray (there was a spec of wee in it already), had decided to crap on the kitchen table. Just what I needed to set myself up for the day. Now, at the best of times, my cat has the tendency to do explosive defecation, but given that there was half a bowl of chilli con carne on the side last night which was now just about empty, his capability for explosion had just been tripled with chilli-powered rocket fuel. Unfortunately, given the nature of his upset stomach, some had splattered onto my printed business plan. Since it was just the copy I was to give to Richard, I decided to wipe it clean carefully with a sheet of kitchen roll. He'd never know. At worst it would look like a chocolate stain.

Notes a touch smeared but clean enough in my opinion, and table disinfected, I was now wide awake so there was no point going back to bed. I went for a shower and faced what was probably my week's most terrifying fifteen seconds when I was held captive in the corner of the cubicle by freezing cold water. Paul had clearly used all the hot.

I had Batman turned out and mucked out and was at work by seven-fifteen. Early - even by my standards.

Time for my cunning Baldrick plan; I went straight to Mark's desk and wiggled his mouse to see if his screen was unlocked. It was - result! With a few swift keystrokes and mouse clicks, I'd created a new folder on his desktop, taken a screenshot, deleted the new folder and put my screenshot as his background wallpaper. I stood back and admired the result. There on his desktop, appeared a folder titled: 'My Porn'. His first reaction would, of course, be to delete it. Try as he might, he'd find that impossible because it was now just a picture on his background! It might not stop him bashing the keys on his keyboard but it would give me a great deal of satisfaction watching his reaction to my handiwork. Before settling down at my own desk, I pulled the hoof oil from my bag, opened the tin and used its brush to apply a thin coating of the clear slimy liquid across the keys on Mark's keyboard.

Next I headed under my desk to sort out my computer and monitor cables. Whilst scrabbling under there, I didn't notice the footfalls joining me in the deserted office and it was only when I heard the voices that I realised I was in a slightly compromising position.

What do you do when you find yourself beneath a desk with two colleagues canoodling, one of which is married, just above you? It was uncomfortable to say the least, I can tell you. What you most definitely don't do is notice a spider and, being completely arachnophobic, yelp, involuntarily try to lurch to a standing position only to be stopped painfully en route by the desk beneath which you are positioned. A huge bump to my head later, I crawled sheepishly out from beneath my desk, to find Meaner Nina straightening herself out guiltily.

'Fran!!'

'Just sorting my cables so I can crack on – got a busy day ahead,' I said, avoiding eye contact. I was worried I might just burst out laughing. Keyboard-bangy, sleaze-ball Mark had slunk off quickly.

'I, I was...I came in early to check all was in order with the move.' Then she turned on her heels and headed off to her desk in the corner of the office. I felt slightly on the upper-handed side of smug and decided I'd feel that way for some time to come. Sue would love this one – not that I'd be one to gossip, under normal circumstances and about people I like. This, however, didn't constitute normal circumstances and I was not a great fan of Meaner Nina nor, indeed, Mark, so in my book this was fair game. Of course, I'd tell Sue in absolute confidence, but the day had definitely taken on a much brighter outlook and it wasn't even eight o'clock yet.

I mooched off to the kitchen, made a cuppa and headed back to my desk, where Mark was looking just a touch frantic.

'You OK?' I asked.

'Erm, yes, fine...' he said hurriedly, frowning and looking down at his fingers (clearly coated with a film of hoof oil). I think if he could have thrown himself across his computer monitor, he would have. I leaned slightly over his way, just to wind him up that little bit more.

'Need some help?' I teased.

'No, I'm good, thanks.' He looked like he was starting to sweat. I so wanted to laugh. I really do need to grow up. I think it took him about half an hour to work out that the 'My Porn' folder in the middle of his desktop was part of a background image.

It actually made my day. He could now bash his keys as much as he liked.

Chapter 17

Work all done for the week, I planned a longer day at the yard today. I made myself a sandwich at home to bring with me. In the tea room, I opened the fridge. There seems to be a custom of naming your food at this yard. I named my sandwich Peter. Yesterday, I ate a sarnie called Katie and a yoghurt called Gary. There I go again. Alas, not everyone thinks I'm as funny as I think I am.

I decided today that I would spend some time grooming Batman and then I'd ride...on my own. I had to bite the bullet and just crack on. I needed to be independent of Gabby, I couldn't rely on her all the time. I started as I meant to go on for the day. I made a coffee, flicked on the TV and enjoyed a moment of peace and quiet in the tea room without the swarm of lively riders, gossiping and laughing. Not that I mind that, but this morning, in between my Batman-related activities, I wanted some thinking time for my business.

It wasn't to be, however. Just as I was about to get going with a thought process about how I was going to market my Igniss app system, Tweedle-Dum Flo walked in.

Armed with a hot cup of coffee to go with a snack she'd brought in a paper bag, she joined me. I said a cursory 'Hi' and turned my attention back to the notebook on the table in front of me, hoping that was sufficient indication that I was busy.

Flo clearly needed more obvious signals than that, because she decided to start to talk to me anyway.

'I see you're settling in well. How are you enjoying the yard and having your own horse?' she asked through a mouthful of pecan Danish pastry.

I was jotting away in my pad – writing marketing ideas down, doing a bit of self-directed brainstorming. I looked up briefly.

'Yeah, it's all good,' I said, returning to my notes.

'I do wish sometimes that I could still be in the saddle,' mused Flo. 'I used to do dressage – to a high level, you know.'

I paused writing for a sip of my coffee, acknowledged her with an 'ah!' and carried on with my notes. Flo carried on talking, undeterred by a completely uninterested recipient, telling me about her horse, the one she'd had since it was a four-year-old that she'd broken all by herself. To be honest, if I'd broken my horse, whether I'd done it by myself or with someone else, I don't think I'd be going around bragging about it to anyone else. Unperturbed, she continued, my peace unlikely to return I feared. I was tempted to butt in and say something along the lines of: *whilst I don't mean to interrupt your story, per se, I wonder if you might happen to have a completely different and possibly much shorter version*. However, I thought if I voiced my query, it might completely alienate her for the rest of my mortal, equine-enforced life, so I held my tongue and smiled sweetly as I listened to her warble on about her riding days. In the end, I tucked my notebook into my bag and turned my attention to finishing my coffee whilst Flo prattled.

Coffee consumed, it was time for me to ride. I headed off to the stable block to get Batman ready. As a result, I ended up sporting a well-deserved bruised bump on my head. How? Well, when you've got mud all over the bottom of your riding boots it turns them into slippery little critters - one of which will inadvertently slide clean off the bar it's resting on while you fasten your gaiter, and cause you to face plant on the stable gate. I didn't make that mistake again with my right foot, I can tell you.

Fortunately, as the stable block was empty of anything other than equine company at the time, my little stupid act went unnoticed by human eyes. Though it did hurt like hell when I put my hat on. The rim sat right on the exact point I bashed on the metal bar. Is that not just typical? I could have hit my head a centimetre lower or higher but no, not me.

Riding done and, I might add, without major incident - unless, of course, you consider...do you know what? Let's just not go there. It's about time I allowed myself to look just a touch more competent than I actually am. Hat, gaiters and boots off, then wellies on and there was still enough time for a quick brew and watch *Countdown* in the tea room, trying to beat the contestants, before heading for home.

As there was no-one else around when I came to put my tack away, keen not to forget to put the tack room keys back in the key box in the tea room, I sought a suitably memorable place to keep them. I've found out since that down one of my rather firm wellies (that also contains my foot and lower leg) is not that place. Having lodged themselves on the top part of my foot that has to flex to get my welly off, I found myself, yet again, stuck in a position I really should never have been in. Having tried stuffing my arm down the welly as far as I could reach (which was only a meagre halfway down my calf), my only option was to get down on my back, touch-turtle-like, with my right leg in the air to try and shake them free. To add a layer of extra insult to my current predicament, they were becoming quite painful.

So, conjure this picture in your mind's eye; me in the tea room, on the cold, concrete floor, legs and arms shaking in the air (seemed I got a better action if all my limbs were involved in the movement) and the theme to *Countdown* playing on the TV in the background. Imagine my dismay when Flo and Camilla (Tweedles Dum and Dee) came walking in.

'There's a good reason for this,' I exclaimed, with all four limbs halting immediately, mid-shake, further adding to the turtled appearance.

'And that would be?' asked Camilla (Tweedle Dee).

'Keys ‑ stuck in my welly. I could do with some help, if you would.'

Most people would have a bit of a laugh at such a ridiculous situation, but not this pair of sour faces. Everything is serious to them. Thank God I never have to spend longer than ten seconds in their presence, under normal circumstances. I think I could soon lose the ability to function as a normal human being.

The solution was for Camilla to get a riding crop ‑ one of the thinner whips ‑ and fish for the keys down my welly (or rather up as my leg was still in the air to allow

98

gravity to assist). This saw her getting right down on the floor and lying next to me.

A few extra prods with the whip and the keys were moving in the right direction.

'I think we've got them,' said Camilla, dropping the whip and reaching into my welly with her arm.

Imagine my further disappointment, when Gary walked in. I've kind of liked him since I first set eyes on him but, it seems, I'm doomed to just look like a crazed lunatic in front of him. I had twisted my head to see who had joined us. He took one look with those lovely grey eyes, said not a single word, turned and left the tea room. If there had been any chance of him noticing me ever, this was indeed it and what a bloody impression I had just made. Chances to go out with Gary? Wiped right out.

'How was your day?' asked Paul brightly, when I got home.

'Summarised in a few short words: slippery, painful, embarrassing and soul destroying – apart from that, it was super. You?'

Paul clearly didn't appreciate my attempt at sarcastic humour as he ignored my comment.

'Did you see Marcus, today?'

'And why would you even be interested?'

'Just asking,' he said, and turned on his heel and left the kitchen.

I needed the glass of Prosecco I poured.

'And you can shut the hell up,' I said to Tarquin, who was squeaking by his bowl with a little cat smile, but the Prosecco was hitting the spot and I was feeling better about my experiences for today. I fed the cat and put all of my silly little exploits right out of my mind - where they belonged.

Chapter 18

So it turns out that dressage is supposed to be elegant and controlled, not rough and distinctly agitated, as demonstrated by me and Batman. Nevertheless, this was our first proper attempt at working with markers after being introduced to them a couple of weeks ago, so that was OK, in my book, at least. Gabby had shown me an app, BE Dressage Tests, and it had a list of stuff that I had to do. Not only that, I had to memorise this stuff and do it in the right order. Well, I read the list, memorised it and then promptly unmemorised it, without even consciously trying. It just popped right back out of my mind like a little fart puffing off into the atmosphere.

While I was trotting around the outdoor arena, Gabby instructed 'Off you go. Enter at A.'

I looked at her.

'I can't remember where I'm going and when I'm doing what...Sorry!'

She didn't look best impressed.

'Fran, you are taking this seriously, aren't you?'

'Of course I am. I just forgot. It's a lot to take in, all those letters and movements.'

'OK, I'll call it out for you this time, but you can't do that at your real event. You MUST learn your test by heart. And will you sit up. Give yourself a *look-at-me* posture - you'll get better marks.'

So Gabby called the test for me so I could ride the movements and practise doing dressage. It was full of circles that had to be twenty metres in diameter, straight lines that had to be, well, straight and trot, walk and canter that had to start and finish at just the right places.

It was a bit more eighteen-metre-eggy-roundish-type-shape than twenty metre circle, a bit more slalom down the centre line and a bit more handbrake stop at G than halt, as Batman was on a mission by then but, for a first dressage test, I was actually pretty pleased.

Back in the tea room, I flicked the kettle on. I saw Richard heading my way, so grabbed a second cup. With it being still early days for this whole challenge/investment thing, I found myself just slightly uncomfortable in Richard's presence. He was suitably kitted out in his tight breeches with a little bit of belly overhanging the waistband. I just wanted to get on with things on my own and in my own way. He was paying such a huge amount out for this and, really, when I allowed myself to think beyond the seventy-five-thousand-pound investment that I was continually blinded by, I just didn't quite get it. Whilst I KNOW I'm going to join the ranks of the super rich, if I was in Richard's position I'd be thinking that there are easier ways to a) make lots of money and b) find entertainment. As quickly at the thoughts arrived, I pushed them away again, back into the recesses of my mind (although given the apparent tiny capacity of my brain, that wouldn't be very far). So, I found myself stuck in this limbo between desperately wanting his investment money at all costs and not quite understanding his motivations, which left me finding him a little awkward to be around. That then had a knock-on effect on how I spoke to him and I seemed to manage each time to actually make myself look like a blithering idiot – not a good look at any time of the day.

'Nice to have the place to yourself,' he said. 'It's not often the tea room is this quiet.'

'Fancy a tea?' I asked him.

'Yep, that would be nice. How is the riding going?'

'Challenging,' I said, simply.

'That's no surprise. And the business?'

'The business plan is in draft now and I'm pretty happy with it,' I lied. I didn't want him to think I wasn't making good progress.

'I'd love to see it. Maybe I can help refine it. Email it to me tomorrow and I'll give you some feedback.' Internally I squealed. Stupid, stupid person. Now I had no choice but to work through the night to finish it.

I made the teas and handed his to him.

He thanked me.

'I needed a nice cup of tea to keep me warm,' he added. Then a silence ensued. It became uncomfortable. To fill the silent void, my mouth opened and just said the first thing I could think of.

'Yes, it's nice when it's warm and wet.' I could hear the words coming but seemed incapable of stopping them vocalising. NO, I screamed at myself (inwardly, of course). I mean, who the hell comes out with a phrase like that? Warm and wet? Really, Fran, really? Particularly to someone with whom you have no intention of having any type of intimate relationship with. My inner cringe reflex was operating at full throttle. Outwardly, I just smiled.

'Indeed!' he said. 'Warm and wet - just the way I like it,' he said with a wry smile as I blushed. Tea drunk, Richard headed back to his house. As I finished my own tea, I busied myself looking in the arena diary and didn't look up when someone joined me in the tea room.

'You seen Liv at all?' said a very familiar voice. I looked up and nearly spat out my last mouthful of tea. It was no less than Mark the slime-ball from work!

'Oh, hi Fran. I didn't know you have a horse,' he said. 'I'm guessing you know my Liv, then?'

'Indeed I do.' Now there was an awkward situation.

I missed Sue at the yard, so I called her for a chat on the way home.

'You won't believe what I'm about to tell you,' I said.

'NO way,' she said, when I told her who Mark from work actually was. 'Look, I'm taking the morning off on Friday to pick up a Shetland pony from Bradford. It's coming as a companion for Richard's horse. We can chat more on the way.'

'Yes, work's been terminal and I'm going to do some editing on my business plan tonight so I do fancy a wee jaunt out.'

I worked long and hard through the evening, finally hitting the sack at two in the morning, having emailed the business plan to Richard. It wasn't wonderful but it was going in the right direction.

Chapter 19

On Friday morning we headed out with Sue's trailer in tow to collect the little pony. It was great to be out. The rest of the working week after my trip away on Monday was, to say the least, uninspiring. I'd managed a good deal of work on my business plan though, so that was a real plus.

'So what's your thoughts? Do I tell Liv or not?' I asked Sue.

'Well, it's a difficult one. Even though you're becoming good friends, you've only known her a short while and you don't know the background between them. In fact, didn't you say that you actually didn't see anything other than Mark and Nina looking a bit shifty.'

'And the drink invite?'

'Well, he's slimy. He could easily get out of that and maybe even leave you looking like the bad one. I'd leave it alone just for now.' I felt better for talking to Sue. I changed the subject.

'How come you're picking this pony up for Richard? Couldn't he just get it himself?'

'I owe him a favour or two and it's no big deal,' she said.

The sun was shining and it felt like it was going to be a great day. I planned to ride Batman when I got back, then home for tea and Prosecco; a perfect Saturday. When we got to Bradford, the lane where the pony was stabled was way too narrow to turn the trailer round on so Sue parked at the end by the junction. The houses in the area at this end of the lane were just amazing. We parked opposite a huge mansion with big wrought iron gates, a beautiful lawn, tennis court and rockery. That could be my type of house, I thought to myself, completely distracted from our task of picking up the pony, whilst Sue opened up the trailer ready.

'Come on,' said Sue, bringing me back from my preoccupation with the big house. 'She's waiting for us.'

I followed on and we headed down the lane to the stables. The lady was waiting for us with the pony in hand ready for us to lead up the road. I'd never seen one of these little Shetland cuties up close, ever!

'Oh my God, Sue, how ADORABLE is that little thing!' I cooed.

'Don't be fooled. They can be little horrors,' said Sue. Personally, I just couldn't see it. How could something so fluffy and sweet be anything like a little beast? Oh, I had so much to learn.

Sue had a quick conversation with the lady who owned the Shetland and then we headed back up the road to the trailer, with Sue leading the pony. Unfortunately, halfway up the lane, Sue's foot went down a pothole and her ankle twisted painfully. After yelping in pain, she thrust the pony's lead rope at me.

'Fran, you'll need to take him. I can't manage.'

I was like, *really!?* But just in my head, of course. Outwardly, I took the rope to lead the pony.

'You OK?'

'I'll be fine,' she assured me. 'I just need to let it recover. Let's just get back to the car, load the pony and I can assess the damage. I was briefly horrified that I might have to drive the trailer – never having driven one before, it felt like a huge catastrophe in the making. Little did I know that wasn't the issue I should be worried about, but, me being so ignorant of horses (and, indeed, Shetland ponies), I couldn't have visualised what was about to occur on this nice, quiet, rural and very expensive lane in Bradford.

As we approached the trailer, Sue pointed out the obvious that I hadn't registered. 'You'll need to load him for me, Fran. I don't think I can do it.'

'Me? Get him on the trailer? But, how?'

'It's easy, just walk on slightly in front of him and he'll follow you. It will be fine.'

It wasn't fine, it was anything but bloody fine. I walked on, he started to walk on and stopped. I turned round to face him, lead rope in both hands and hauled with all my might. He just stood there looking at me like I was an idiot. Just about at this point, the gates to the stunning house opened and a beautiful Mercedes emerged, then everything happened so very quickly.

All in what seemed like one swift 3D-world-integrated move, the damn cute little pony pulled back as hard as he could, ripped the rope from between my hands (and painfully, I might add) and he was then on the road and through the black wrought iron gates just before they closed.

So here's the situation that faced me at that point: Mercedes disappearing into the distance, gates to the mansion now closed, Sue crippled, leaning against the car and the not-so-cute-anymore pony running amok in the neatly trimmed garden, as I emerged from the back of the trailer in complete shock. This presented an uncomfortable puzzle: a) how to get into the mansion's gardens, given the gates had shut, and b) how to catch the pony that was razzing and bucking around what seemed like every corner of the perfect garden. I looked at Sue, she shrugged, and I realised I was on my own.

I sprang into action. I managed to climb up onto the very nice Yorkshire stone wall that was about waist high, and from there I had to haul myself up and over the spiked the iron fence. On lowering myself down on the other side, my single aim was to avoid impaling myself on the spear-shaped spikes. I thought I was in the clear until I felt the tug on my breeches (my nice, relatively new breeches) and realised I'd failed – wholesale.

My slightly excessive weight then acted in perfect harmony with gravity to pull me free from the spike, ripping the arse end out of my breeches as it did so. My arms held firm and I thought I was luckily going to be able to at least drop myself a bit more gracefully onto the wall at the other side. I was wrong about that too. The strength in my arms was no match for my whole weight-with-gravity combination and I found myself plummeting to the ground and landing splat in the mud, on my feet to begin with, but they slid from beneath me and I did an impressive face plant into a flower bed that was wet and sticky from overnight rain. I hauled myself up, arse now with integrated air conditioning and face, chest and hands sporting sticky mud. Sue was, by now, doubled over not with pain, but with laughter. Now came the task of catching the pony but the little git was running wild, lead rope twitching all over the place, like a loose electric cable on speed. He stopped by a rather smart-looking rockery for a nibble of grass, so I legged it up the drive (which was uphill, I'll have you know) towards him. My plan of catching the little beast didn't seem to fit in with his plan of causing general mayhem in a mansion-house garden as, once I was within six feet of him, he turned, bucked and tanked off up the rockery, flattening an array of impressive-looking flowers and shrubs as he went, and leaving a trail of mini hoof prints behind.

As I chased after him, I kept one eye on the house and the other on the havoc-causing pony that was now heading towards the tennis court, feet and legs caked in rockery mud. I could see it, in my mind's eye, the mess he was about to make of that pristine rubber-surfaced green court with its bright white marking lines and it wasn't going to be pretty. I broke down to the left, seeing the direction he was going, in the hope I could head him off but that would have been way too easy. The little git knew exactly what I was planning and had other ideas. He ducked off to the right and my hand just brushed his arse end as he changed direction. That was it, he made a beeline for the open gate into the tennis court, and he was in. As I'd suspected, little legs going ten to the dozen, he left a trail of black, muddy hoof prints as he careered around. My only hope was to persuade him to come to me before someone in that fancy big house realised there was a loose pony cutting up their nicely manicured and very big lawn and mud-patting their pristine tennis court. I rehearsed in my mind: 'Oh, I'm so sorry but it's actually not my pony. I was just helping out.'

I couldn't believe no one had caught us yet. They must have been deaf in that house, whoever was left behind when the Merc pulled out, because the pony was squealing and whinnying like a good'un.

I could hear Sue calling and beckoning me back. She was holding out a bucket. I ran back down to see she was handing me a bucket with some pony nuts in it. Of course

- genius! Persuade the little monster with food. I took the bucket and started to rattle it as I headed back up the drive and it didn't take him long to realise there was food on offer. Ears pricked, head high, he trotted, quick as you like, back down the drive to meet me. As soon as he was in reach, I grabbed the rope and snatched the bucket away from his eager mouth.

'Dream on, you little git,' I told him, but Sue shouted from behind me and told me to give him the feed. I pulled a face of why-the-hell-should-I.

'He came to you - in his book that's good, so give him the few nuts.'

I did, but I found myself growling at him under my breath as I did. There was a gate-release button on the inside which I tapped quickly and got out of there pronto. Just as I was leading the little git round to the back of the trailer, the Merc was heading back up the lane. That spurred me. Once inside the gates, it would take the occupant all of thirty seconds to register the mayhem and we needed to be out of there by that time.

Attempt two saw him load, no problem. Sue decided she'd be fine to drive, for which I was excessively grateful. I'd had enough drama for one day. As we set off, the gates were just closing behind the Mercedes.

Shetland pony delivered to its new home and happy with its companion, I headed home for a well-earned glass of the sparkling stuff to keep me company whilst I got going on my marketing plan. I wanted the business stuff in the bag a good way before my main competition. The last thing I needed was to win the damn competition and find the business side had let me down.

Chapter 20

The weekend finally arrived and the sun was shining on the Saturday morning. Great stuff. Today was to be my first hack, a nice relaxing ride out with my new horsey friends. Sue, Big and Little Katie, Sonia and I were heading out to Inglewood Estate for a couple of hours. I'd already sorted my stable, groomed Batman and was tacked up and ready. Indeed, I even considered myself looking forward to this jaunt out on my steed. I downed a final cup of coffee before we got on and headed off.

In the block, Sonia quickly disappeared from sight in her stable next to mine. Sue, standing opposite, saw me looking and sparked conversation to explain.

'You peeing in your stable again, Sonia?' Sue shouted over.

'You know me,' she answered. 'Can't get on with a full bladder.'

I was mildly horrified. It conjured up an image that I wasn't keen to see. These horsey types would never cease to amaze me. Why on earth she couldn't simply use the toilet like everyone else, I didn't know.

Finally tacked up and ready (with Sonia relieved) we set out across the fields at the back of the yard. I was grateful to be part of a group going out, and particularly a group containing riders who were sufficiently able to open and close gates whilst on horseback.

I felt a little, well actually a lot, insecure as we set off into the open world. I'd only ridden in an enclosed indoor arena so far, and that felt infinitely safer than being out here with no actual boundaries to keep Batman and me in one place. The world felt huge right now and I had actually no idea how Batman would fare out here. What I was certain of though was, if he didn't fare well, I would fare even worse.

As it was, he just walked happily alongside the others and I started to relax. The day was lovely and bright and I even began to enjoy the ride.

It took us about twenty minutes to hack through the quiet tracks to get to the Inglewood Estate entrance.

We weren't too far into the estate, mooching slowly through the woods, when I found myself bursting for a wee. So preoccupied was I at Sonia going to the toilet in her stable that I forgot to think of going myself.

'How long 'til we're back at the yard?' I asked, but I knew, given how long it had taken us to get this far, that even if we turned right around now, it wouldn't be quick enough.

'About two hours,' said Sonia.

I asked Sue where the nearest loo was. She laughed.

'See that tree over there?' She pointed.

'You must be joking,' I said, but quickly realised she was anything but.

So here was my issue, I was wearing very lovely looking, but very tight new breeches (my second pair without the added Shetland-induced-butt-hole) and I was wondering just how to navigate those, along with my underwear, into a position where I could crouch and wee without drenching myself, whilst holding onto Batman and obscuring myself with a tree.

Sue must have heard my brain in thought motion.

'I'll hold Batman for you.'

I climbed off and headed a bit deeper into the woods. The tree Sue pointed to was just a bit too public and, in my opinion, visible from the track. My butt, perhaps slightly plump and slightly saggy, is for selected viewing only.

I found what I thought was a more private tree, close to a brook and well away from the bridleway we were riding along and I thought would do. I looked behind me and couldn't see the girls, although I could hear their chatter, so I was comforted that I wouldn't be overlooked.

I quickly hauled down my lower half, balanced with an arm on the tree for extra support and sighed in relief - completely unaware of the dog-walker, smiling as he strolled along the bank of the little stream.

'Morning,' he said, pleasantly. I think he might have been a touch embarrassed but he hid it well. I know that because I saw his face fully and the face I saw was Gary's, from the yard. I guess that means there's not much of me that was actually hidden in my not-so-discrete loo-break location. Mid-flow, there wasn't much I could do about it but cringe inwardly and remember to a) drink less coffee before hacking and b) never assume the middle of the woods was a private-enough place to relieve oneself. Yet again, I'd made a pretty significant impression on him.

'You OK?' he asked as he walked on by, keeping his eyes straight ahead. Could this actually get any worse?

'Yep, fine,' I squeaked.

The rest of them, as you might expect, found it hilarious when I got back.

As we moved off, I wondered quite how I'd face him at the yard. But, as we trotted on, I had more immediate things to focus my mind on. My rising trot was getting better. Instead of being bounced around in the saddle as I tried to do my up-downs, I was actually getting into a bit of a rhythm that I think most of my innards were quietly grateful for.

When we reached the bottom of the park, through the gate was a huge expanse of field, running up a gentle hill. I knew just what was coming. GALLOP!

And that's what we did, right to the top. It was amazing and was probably the turning point in my relationship with riding. I loved it.

'Back down again, girls?' shouted Big Katie. Everyone agreed.

Well, how was I to know that there was a protocol of waiting until everyone was ready, girths tightened and stuff before setting off and that Little Katie wasn't showing off as she tanked past me, yelling something quite incoherent but actually was trying to stop her ex-racer thoroughbred that had taken off as I cantered past whilst she shortened her stirrups?

Never mind, no harm done. I'll know for next time.

On the ride back to the yard, they kept me firmly behind so I could cause no further chaos.

Chapter 21

I had a smile on my face all the way home after my hack. Then, my mobile rang and my heart sunk when I saw the name 'Mum' pop up. I answered anyway. She knows I always have my phone on me, except in extenuating circumstances, like in the shower, so ignoring it and pretending not to hear is really not an option.

'You in, Hun? Shall I pop round for a cuppa? Feels like ages since we caught up.'

'Yep,' was all I said, but nope, would have been closer.

I hung up and shouted to Paul: 'Mum's on her way.'

He hurried down the stairs with his jacket on. 'I'm off out and don't tell her I'm staying here.'

'Paul, that's not fair.'

'Of course it is. She'll give me a hard time and you handle her much better than I do.'

That was absolutely not true but it was an argument I wasn't going to win.

'Where are you going?'

'Just out, to see a friend,' he said.

'Bring me a bottle of Prosecco back with you, then. I think I'm going to need it.'

'Deal.' And on that note, he was quickly out the door.

Fifteen minutes later, she arrived and hearing the door go, Portia the Pug went berserk barking. Why is it that when someone rings the doorbell, dogs always assume it's for them?

Anyway, she rang the doorbell and, without waiting for me to answer, was immediately helping herself in the back door to the kitchen, where the kettle was already boiling. Her long grey hair was pulled back into her usual bun at the base of her neck and her sum-total of five feet two inches was clad in a green twinset of skirt and sweater that made her look a touch like a cucumber. That made me smile.

'So, how's the job going?'

'Good, yes, brilliant,' I said.

'And this silly business idea of yours? You've knocked that into touch?'

'Well, not exactly.'

She raised her neatly plucked eyebrows, inviting me to expand. I stirred coffee and milk into a cup.

'Sue knows this guy at her yard – you know, where she keeps her horse. Anyway, he's a big, wealthy businessman and,' I paused for strength, 'he's going to invest and help me get it off the ground.'

'Is he indeed?' Her face was its usual stern self. 'That Sue is always trying to lead you astray. She's old enough to know better.'

'Mum, I'm old enough to do my own thing, I'm not a teenager.'

'And what, exactly, is he going to want in return? Is he married?'

I rolled my eyes. 'No, he's not and it's not like that. He'll take a proper share in the business and will make money – that's what he'll get.'

'Fran, why can't you just stop getting all ahead of your station and just stick to what you're good at? You've got a good job and a nice house. Many people would kill

116

for what you've got.' I thought to myself, *I'm one of them with the mother I've got*!

'How many times have your so-called businesses failed? Four? Five?'

'Mum, lots of really successful business people have had unsuccessful businesses. It's part of the process of becoming successful. I need to learn from those past mistakes.'

'Yes, but they know what they're doing!'

'I know what I'm doing,' I almost shouted. I took a deep breath. 'Here.' I handed her a coffee.

'But you've got no experience in these things. How can you hope to do better than these well-off business people?'

'One of those well-off business people has just invested in me. He wouldn't plough money into my business if he didn't think I could do this,' I shouted, without thinking. My heart sank as Richard's words rang silently through my brain – tell NO-ONE. Bloody hell. The no-one I blurt it out to happens to have a mouth bigger than the Tyne Tunnel.

She stopped dead in her tirade, inviting me with that look of hers to tell more. The damage was done so what the hell?

'Part of the deal, well, it's not quite that simple,' I said and she eyed me sideways with a superior look I didn't like. 'Richard, erm, he's my new investor. Anyway, he has bought me a horse and I'm learning to ride.'

'Oh, where will it end?' she said, exasperated. 'In tears, I'll be sure. Why on earth did he want to buy you a horse? You've never been on one in your life! What would you know about riding at all? You've got all the coordination of an octopus on valium.'

'Well, there was the donkey on Scarborough seafront, that could count, I guess,' I muttered. 'It's a way for me to show I'm committed to the business and that I've got the staying power to show I can make it even when the going gets a bit tougher.'

'I tell you, he's got eyes on something other than just your business acumen. Men don't buy women horses for nothing.'

'Well, this one has and it's his stipulation for me getting the investment. So, I'm giving it my best shot. All said, there's other ways I'd rather spend my time than trying to ride a four-legged beast that I'm not sure I've got complete or, in fact, any control over, but it's a challenge and I'm up for it.'

'I'll believe you can do that when I see it.' She sighed.

'And Mother, you CANNOT tell anyone. You can't mention this. He's a very private man and wants no-one to know.'

'How's your brother?' she asked. 'Have you heard from him recently? In fact, isn't that his dog?' The subject was changed. She'd said her piece and was now pointing at Portia.

'We spoke briefly the other day – he called. Not much to report there,' I lied. 'I'm looking after Portia for him for a few days.' She'd never accepted that he wasn't ever going to find a good woman, settle down and give her grandchildren. The word 'gay' only existed in her vocabulary to describe a happy type of feeling.

She drank her coffee without much further comment, and hauled herself up from the kitchen table to leave.

'When am I meeting this Richard and this horse?'

My eyes widened in a brief hint of horror. That most definitely wasn't on the cards for happening.

'Well, he's very busy and the yard is very dirty. I'm not sure...'

'Nonsense, I like to know what you're up to. I'll come up on Saturday morning. Just text me the postcode and I'll meet you there at eleven.'

Glad she was leaving, I felt completely drained. I best ride before she gets there on Saturday, lest she sucks the life force from me, and Batman throws me off.

Inside, I was looking forward to the bottle of Prosecco Paul now owed me...and I wouldn't be sharing a drop with him.

Chapter 22

Facing my first jumping lesson EVER I was, I think quite understandably, dreading today. Gabby told me to be in the indoor arena at one p.m. sharp. She's not the most patient, my instructor, and I'm not best keen on winding her up. I think, as I've said before, I like to give her every reason to be gentle and thoughtful with me and today was certainly no exception.

When I arrived, she was there waiting, and made a deliberate show of checking the time on her phone, which I ignored and smiled sweetly. I have to say, smiling was the last thing I felt like doing. When I saw the line of poles on the ground and a little jump made of crossed poles, I quite honestly nearly defecated in my pants. Being in persistent contact with the ground, at all times, with the exception of flying in an aeroplane, is an absolute must in my opinion. Gabby saw my face, smile firmly wiped clean away.

'Don't worry, we'll start with poles,' she said, putting the cross poles on the floor. 'Breathe will you, woman.'

I breathed again. I didn't even know I'd been holding my breath in the first place.

I warmed up with Gabby shouting her usual stream of incessant commands: 'Sit up,' 'Kick ‑ will you,' 'Do that transition again ‑ that was rubbish.' Then there was her favourite: 'What the hell was that? Do it AGAIN!' She used this one all the time. When I get really good (ha-ha) I think Gabby will miss this particular phrase.

I was getting used to this tirade of abuse and was starting to understand it for what it was, though. At first,

I thought she was just a right witch, but she actually wanted me to learn and to learn well. Bloody funny way to show it, but there it was. Just as well she was as committed to horses as a career, because I couldn't see those particular people skills transferring into the corporate world.

Could you imagine it? Gabby in charge of an IT apprentice, for example. 'Get the hell in here and write that program again. It's a pile of rubbish.' Not sure it would go down too well.

The time came for me to trot on down the poles. There was a line of five of them. Gabby had told me to sit up round the corner, kick Batman (that wasn't actually a problem as I'd been wanting to kick his shins for some time now, this was a fairly good second option) and ride straight down the poles.

As it was, he walked when we came round the corner, Gabby told me that was because I wasn't using enough 'leg'. To my mind, being just slightly overweight, I have plenty of leg, in fact maybe even too much, but that's not what Gabby meant, I know. What she meant was nudge him more with my leg to keep him in trot. I don't know why these horsey types don't just say what they mean in plain English. I'm a great advocate of plain English. Then, I understand what's being said.

When we reached the poles, we slithered down them in a veritable snake-like fashion.

'What was straight about that?' Gabby barked.

Well, actually, there was nothing straight about it. It was about as straight as Paul's pug's tail or, indeed, as straight as Paul himself and neither of those are straight, I can tell you.

'Come again,' she yelled – another of her favourites. Given half a chance I wouldn't come ever again but, as we all know, it was out of my hands, at that point in time.

When the first cross pole jump went up, I nearly had a coronary. It looked six feet tall, for God's sake. In reality, it was about the sum total of six inches, with the poles resting on cups that were on the second hole up of the jump wing.

'He probably won't even jump it,' said Gabby with authority.

'Well, what the hell will he do with it then?' I asked, alarmed.

'Don't be ridiculous, Fran. What I mean is, he'll probably just trot over it like he did with the poles. I don't think the jump is big enough yet for him.'

NOT DAMN-WELL BIG ENOUGH FOR HIM? my tiny mind screamed. The woman was mad; it might not be big enough for him but it was ample bloody big enough for me.

'Fran, today would be good. Crack on.'

'OK, but you've left the poles in the way of the jump,' I said.

'What are you talking about?'

'The poles.' I pointed at the two horizontal poles, the ones I'd just been trotting down. 'You forgot to move them. They're in the way, I can't get to the jump for them.'

'Really? Are you actually being serious? They are placing poles,' she said, as if speaking to a five-year-old. 'They help you get to the fence on the right stride. They

122

are most definitely not in the way! Now will you stop messing about and jump the bloody fence?'

One of these days, or more precisely, in a few months, I'd be walking out of that arena door and she could kiss mine and Batman's cute behinds. That day, however, was not today, so I did as instructed and pointed Batman at the fence.

As I set off, Gabby said in a softer tone: 'Batman knows what to do with the poles, don't look at them. You just concentrate on your position. Hold onto your neck strap once you're straight, give him a kick and the horse will do the rest.'

And so he did, but his version of 'doing the rest' wasn't the version I wanted to see. Over the poles he simply ground to a gradual halt, put his head down to look at the fence and I slid down his neck. It all happened so slowly, yet I was powerless to stop it. I did a neat little roly-poly-manoeuvre at the bottom and ended sat on my butt still holding onto the reins. Batman completed the whole little scene with a gentle nudge in my back, as if to say: *What are you doing down there, idiot?* I wanted to kick his shins for him. I could have been sat at home drinking tea and eating biscuits, instead of sitting here, with a sore backside in the sand. All I could think was that I bet a cup of Earl Grey and a chocolate chip cookie wouldn't have done this to me.

'That was your fault,' said Gabby. She proceeded to tell me that if I had the capacity to learn from my mistakes, I was clearly in a position to learn lots today.

'Get back on and do it again. And this time, use your legs.'

I did, and I did – get on and use my legs. We got over. It wasn't pretty, but we made it from the take-off side to the landing side and away from the fence in one piece and together. It put a smile on my face. It felt good. And that was it, we were off and running or, rather, jumping. Still a long way to go to being anything close to competent but it was a start.

Gabby was pleased with us. There was always more to do but she was happy nonetheless.

'You did well. We need to work on your balance and togetherness with Batman, but I'm impressed. It could have been so much worse.'

I was secretly beaming from ear to ear at the compliment. There weren't too many coming from Gabby.

Back in the tea room, Gabby joined me for a brew and we chatted a bit. She had a more normal side to her that I hadn't really seen yet.

Chapter 23

If ever there was a nervous livery yard visitor, it would be my mum. At sixty-eight, she's spent her life only ever close to four-legged creatures that don't stand taller than her thighs. Yet, still she was keen to meet Batman. What could I do? I had no choice but to let her come to the yard. I just hoped to goodness that she wouldn't want to see me ride the damn thing. I was also desperate for Richard not to be around.

I thought we could see Batman, nice and safe, confined in his stable and then I'd take her off for a coffee and all would be good.

'So where is he, then?' she asked as I met her in the yard car park.

'He's in there.' I pointed to my stable block across the yard. It had been raining so the place was wet and muddy. She had come completely ill prepared, in small heels and a skirt. I mentally shook my head. But really, I should have warned her to come suitably attired. Being the experienced equestrian I was now (as if), I forgot that the uninitiated wouldn't even think to pack wellies or boots in the car.

Her face was a picture as she tiptoed her way across the yard, trying to keep her shoes clean. Knowing my mother too, they weren't cheap.

'I think you need to sweep up a little round here, dear,' she said.

'It's not my mess, this is a big shared yard and there are people who run the yard that are hired to do this stuff. It's just wet and mucky because it's rained.'

'Now that's not the attitude to take. Can you imagine if I had taken that view? We'd have lived in a pig-sty if it was left to you and your brother.'

I just smiled. It wasn't even worth the effort of putting an alternative view forward.

In the block, Batman was happily munching away on his net. He barely even looked round in acknowledgement when we came in.

'This is him,' I said, as we approached his stable door.

She scowled.

'Well, he's very big. How on earth are you managing to handle him?'

'I'm managing just fine,' I said, opening the door, going in and giving him a big pat. I actually felt quite protective of him right now, 'I've got good help and I'm learning lots every day.'

'But it's a huge waste of time. What are you ever going to do with a horse? You're not a rider. If you want a business, make it happen, don't fanny around pretending you've got something to prove.'

'But I am becoming a rider and I am enjoying it.' I think I just said this to contradict her and I wasn't quite sure enjoy was the word I'd use for it. I looked around to make sure no-one could hear and lowered my voice a little. 'I potentially have a good business partner, not just the investment. And, do you know what? This challenge is good for me. I've been stuck in my routine job, having my business ideas but never really getting anywhere. Someone said to me recently, "if you do what you've always done, you'll get what you've always got." I want to get something different now. So, I'm giving this a proper shot. Sue was right, all I do is work and dream up

126

businesses. Life was passing me by. It would be really great if you would just get behind me this once.'

'What do you mean? This once? I've supported you all your life!'

I looked at her, eyebrows raised.

'I've done my best. I may not be the perfect Mum but I've tried.'

In fact, she sounded like a spoilt child, but I said nothing. At that point, Richard walked in and my heart sank through the floor.

'How's things, Fran?' he asked cheerfully.

'Good, thank you. This is my mum, Andrea,' I replied with a huge fake smile that I was sure would convince nobody.

He walked forward and thrust his hand out to shake.

'Nice to meet you, Andrea, I'm Richard.'

'So, you're the man who's giving my daughter all that money.'

Inwardly, I cringed. Richard looked sternly at me, his eyebrows raised. That look spoke volumes to me. Your investment is history! He turned his attention to my Mother.

'Giving? Not giving, investing,' he corrected.

'And, why, might I ask would you do that for someone you don't know?'

'Well, Andrea, I'm a businessman and I like to make money. I think Fran has a good idea that will do just that. I wanted to get involved.'

'Are those the only intentions you have towards my daughter?'

'MOTHER!' She gave me one of her looks then turned her attention back to Richard.

He hesitated just a moment. 'My intentions are entirely business related,' he said with a reassuring smile. 'Although, of course, my investment depends entirely on Fran meeting my set conditions.' Again, his eyes spoke to me directly as he stressed *set conditions*.

'Let's go get some coffee, shall we,' I suggested, diffusing the tension. The only way to prove it to Mother would be, in fact, to prove it to Mother!

'Just before you go, Fran, perhaps you and I could have a private chat when you're free?'

'Sure,' I said, with a heavy heart.

I caught up with Richard a little later. As he wasn't to be seen on the yard, I headed up to the house at the back of the farm and knocked on the door. Whilst he was friendly to all on the yard, Richard maintained his privacy up at his home and it was rare for yard people to go up there. He answered and invited me into the kitchen. This was the first time I'd been to his house. It was warm from the Aga and very homely which, for some reason, surprised me. His face was stern.

'I know what you're going to say,' I steamed in.

'You do? I'm impressed then, because I haven't decided quite yet what I'm going to say. Tea?'

'Yes, please.' He took out a mug and poured me a cuppa from the pot he'd made. I kind of wished he'd just get this over with.

'You told your Mum about our deal.'

'I didn't mean to. She goaded me into it.'

'So you're easily influenced in the heat of the moment? That's not a good business characteristic to have.'

'No, not at all, it's just...' I tried to find the right words, but Richard was quicker.

'How did she goad you into it if she had no idea about it in the first place?' he asked.

'You don't know my Mother. She finds a chink and picks away at it. She's got no faith in me to do anything other than sit in what she thinks is a normal routine life. I just snapped, I wanted to show her I can do something else and...' I paused a moment, '...that *someone* has confidence in me.'

His stern look softened.

'OK, Fran, I can understand that.' He took a sip of his tea. 'When I said you couldn't tell anyone, I meant most people. I didn't expect that you wouldn't tell your family. It's reasonable they should know.' I felt relief seep through me. 'I didn't, however, expect to get the third degree from your Mother so you need to make sure she's kept in check in future. If she spills the beans to anyone on this yard, the deal really is off.'

I'd been given a second chance that I hadn't really lost in the first place...or wouldn't have lost if Mother hadn't opened her big mouth!

Chapter 24

The next six weeks passed in a blur of work, jumping lessons (sometimes three a week), flatwork and hacking. The aim, in Gabby's words, were 'confidence and competence'.

'We need to get you to the level we can start to get you out to little competitions. And, we need to get you to the stage you can jump independently, without me being there to hold your hand.'

Transitions were the order of the day for these six weeks. Walk-trot, trot-walk, trot-halt, trot-canter, canter-trot; you name it, I did it - and I did over and over and over again. If I did a transition once, I did it a thousand times, or at least, it felt like a thousand times.

Gabby's favourite phrases during this time in my learning-to-ride experience were:

'Crap! That was crap!'

'Do it again.'

'What the hell was that?'

'Nope, no good.'

All of these phrases were interchangeable and could be put together in any order. In fact, there came a point where I would say:

'That was crap, wasn't it? Shall I do it again?' And, she'd just nod.

There then further came a time where I wouldn't even ask, I would just go, on my own volition, and do it again. I guess, that was the sign that things were really starting to sink in. If I was realising, without being told what was good and what was not and fixing it for myself, I must be really learning.

I learned how to canter in a balance – so it helped that Batman could already do that and I just had to learn how to sit on that canter without wobbling about all over the place and, indeed, falling off. I learned how to do a proper working trot and how to do my up-downs without a double-bump when my slightly ample backside hit the saddle on each sit stride.

I also noticed Gary lurking around at points when I was riding. I could even convince myself that he was watching because maybe he was a bit interested in me as a person, rather than just watching me learning to ride.

Gabby gave me lunge lessons and persecuted me suitably to make my balance and seat in the saddle better. I went round and round and round in circles with Batman attached to Gabby with a long lunge line so he couldn't go anywhere unexpected. I had to make aeroplane wings with my arms, circle my arms whilst trotting, lose my stirrups whilst cantering, and all of this a) without scaring the bejesus out of Batman and b) staying in the saddle and avoiding any unnecessary injury to myself.

In truth, I was starting to feel both more confident and competent. I wasn't stupid, the competent part could only come with experience. The level of competence I was actually feeling was a watered down version of what it needed to be but that could also only be achieved with the passage of time, lots of riding and lots of instruction. In the case of all three of those components I was severely handicapped, so I had to work with what I had: lots of instruction. Whilst I felt like I was doing lots of riding, so was everyone else, and that had to span a number of years to count for anything in their book. I decided I would read a different book! Mine was called *Fran Comes To Town Riding (Competently) On A Pony Called Batman* - and everyone else can just get lost. At least I was giving it a go.

Lots of these people at the yard didn't like my way of achievement. Not my new group of friends, but others. It's a big yard. I found it difficult to understand their mentality, to be honest. I heard Bridgett talking with some of the women in the top stable yard as I passed by. They were yard people I didn't really know but they clearly took an interest in what I was doing.

'She thinks she can actually do a proper event with no real riding experience,' said one. Immediately it was clear they were talking about me. I was the only one around the place that fitted that bill.

'She'll simply screw the horse up and it will serve her right.'

'Batman will just stop jumping. He won't put up with her swinging off his mouth on the end of the reins.'

'Is she so arrogant to think she can ride better than the rest of us?'

With support like that in the background, what type of environment is that to learn to ride in?

It just made me stronger, more determined. I know I have a different outcome, my own goal, but working with people who have my back along the way might be a nice touch. I called Sue.

'People at the yard,' I told her on the phone, 'they're talking about me and it's not so nice.'

'Don't worry, Fran. This is often normal in the horsey world with some people. Don't take it to heart. Let's have a coffee and a chat before work.'

She made me feel better and I was able to enjoy the curry and Prosecco that I'd decided might be a good end to the day.

Chapter 25

Curry last night saw my stomach suffering a combination of fire and pain. That then translated into slack bowels that felt almost, and I stress, almost, beyond control. I managed to do Batman with only three desperate sprints to the toilet. I pitied anyone that might follow me in there as the smell was less than rose-like aromatic. I resolved never to eat hot Thai green curry ever again. Particularly when it was washed down with two bottles of Prosecco.

Anyway, I got to work and having parked my car, I felt the familiar pang of desperation overtake me. My planned coffee and catch up with Sue was absolutely out of the question and I'd just have to stand her up. I decided absently to text her when the immediate crisis was over. I had little time to get myself through the security barrier, up in the lift (I usually take the stairs, but today was to be an exception) and head straight to the ladies. Under normal circumstances, I'd be timing my poo-break to coincide with every other female on the floor being busy elsewhere. Our toilets at work are less than anonymous. With simple partitions that don't even stretch the full floor-to-ceiling length, how is a girl supposed to go about her daily business without the fear of expelling a whole orchestra of interesting sounds? Anyway, today that was no longer a consideration. I could have let rip with the sound of the loudest fog horn in history and I wouldn't have cared - at least, not right at that moment. I might have cared if the toilet block was full and I had to face the other occupants later.

When the lift landed on my floor, I ran, stumbled and in the end minced my way into the toilets. Second-hand Thai green curry was threatening insistently to re-enter the world via my large intestine. The battle was on. Who would win? Me or the Thai-green-curry-infested-colon? I'll tell you exactly who won and it wasn't me. As I pushed open the door into the ladies, I was now doing a kind of crouched-crab-style-shuffling movement, completely unable to stand up straight. My pelvic floor muscles were in serious revolt-mode right about now and I was scared I was about to lose the fight.

I did a pincer-style movement with my arms high, to keep my balance, and my backside low to stop it from shedding its load, into the first cubicle I could reach. I thought I was actually going to make it. All I had to do was unzip my trousers and sit my arse on the seat and I was home and dry, so to speak. It just wasn't to be, though. As I was sliding the lock shut on the cubicle with my backside in sticky-out-daren't-stand-up-or-indeed-move-at-all-for-fear-of-accidentally-crapping-myself-mode...I accidentally crapped myself. No joke, I, a big grown-up girl, couldn't hold it in and actually REALLY in real life crapped my bloody pants - AT WORK! Oh My God! Was I at home, I could just clean myself up and pretend like it didn't really happen. Perhaps I could even persuade myself that it really hadn't happened. Even at the yard, it smells so bloody awful there all the time that,

134

again, I could perhaps have just about escaped the complete mortification of such a misdemeanour. But no, not me. I couldn't do this somewhere anonymous. I had to do it in the most bloody open and public toilets going – in the working world.

And so, it slipped out. I felt it happen. It was, to put it mildly, abso-damn-well-lutely gross. Well, actually, just a little warm and comforting, but in reality truly gross. So, in this situation, what do you do? Simple plan – trousers off, soiled underwear off, wrap up and dispose of underwear and go commando for the rest of the day. Simples! Actually, not simples. Not on Planet Fran! NOOOOOO, it's just never going to be that easy, is it? The toilets had no internal bins. I wrapped the offending article, and I can tell you it was very bloody offending from an aroma point of view, in toilet tissue. I waited until the voices died down and I heard the door squeak, which I hoped meant they had left the toilets. I could hear no other sounds so I assumed they were gone. I whipped out and was heading round the corner to the sinks and the lidded-bin when the door opened. Without thinking, I quickly dropped my crudely wrapped package into the smaller, open waste paper bin. What I didn't realise was that the bin hadn't been emptied for two days due to ill-health in the Facilities team and that I hadn't wrapped my parcel as well as I'd thought. And that's where things took a turn for the worse, if that was at all possible.

Back in the office, Sue was there, taking her coat off.

'Where were you? Eight-thirty, coffee in The Bean?'

'Ah,' I said, quietly. 'I had an urgent need to get straight in. Bit of a jippy tummy. Sorry about that.'

'It's fine,' she said and then our attention was caught when one our comedienne colleagues waltzed into the busy office, over to our bank of desks and hollered out:

'OH MY GOD, DISGUSTING OR WHAT!'

Everyone, and I mean, everyone looked round. I almost daren't ask the question. I could feel a little bead of sweat trying to escape and make me look guilty. I mean, really, there's no way it could be...

'I dropped my bloody glasses in the waste bin in the loo, fished my hand in to get them.'

My heart was sinking so fast, it was close to the ground floor by now and bearing in mind my office is on the seventh, that's a pretty long way down.

'SOMEONE dropped a pair of crappy knickers in there! Who the hell in a professional office would do such a vile thing?'

I morphed my face from the look of abject guilt it was trying to assume to one of complete disgust.

'No way!!' I exclaimed, trying to sound as convincing as possible.

'Just gross. My hand went right into it. It's for bloody paper towels for God's sake! Just who in their right mind would do that? I had to wash my glasses off, it was all in the creases of the arms!'

Sue was wide-eyed, looking right at me, silently saying *you didn't?*

I screwed my face up in a kind-of *well, I might have done, sort of* way and she rolled her eyes, chuckling quietly to herself.

People in the office were now looking around at each other, clearly trying to work out in their own mind who the culprit was.

'So, someone in here's going commando, then,' said Mark with a snigger. 'Could it be you, Fran?'

JESUS! Grow up. Some poor sucker, i.e. me, has had the crappiest (literally) of days and just wants to brush this under the carpet and move on in life, is what I thought.

'I bet they belong to Nina,' is what I actually said.

Thank God it wasn't politically correct to ask to see if anyone was sans-underwear in the office, as I would have been seriously rumbled.

Sue and I managed our coffee and catch up at lunchtime.

'You know, you don't need to listen to the gossips around the yard. They will always find something or someone to be overly concerned with.'

'That's sometimes easier said than done when it's me they're concerned with.'

'Well, focus on this instead; I heard on the yard grapevine that Gabby has an interesting activity planned for you, something to help you cement your partnership with Batman,' she said, with a wry smile.

'And that is?'

'I'll let Gabby tell you all about it.'

Prosecco was in great need when I got home, as was a shower and a change of clothes into something far more comfortable.

Chapter 26

'Hunting? What do you mean I'm going hunting?'

'It makes you brave,' Gabby told me, sipping at her cup of coffee in our tea room.

'Brave? BRAVE? I'm brave enough, thank you very much. Anyway, I don't agree with hunting.'

'And what, exactly, do you know about it? Not much, I would hazard a guess at. It's hunting within the law, which isn't the real thing. You'll just be chasing a scent.'

'Ah,' I said, as if that really meant anything to me, which it didn't. 'Let me get this straight, it will involve galloping all over open country, jumping things on the way and drinking sloe gin from a hip flask, whilst following a pack of dogs?'

'They're called hounds, but yep, that's about the long and the short of it.'

'And people enjoy doing this?'

'They do, most definitely. In fact, they pay a pretty penny for the privilege. Batman is a super hunter apparently, so you will be fine. You will hold onto your neck strap, lean forward over the jumps and he will do the rest. We'll only take you over the smaller fences and we'll go round the others.'

'Oh, well I'm quite reassured by that!'

'Don't be sarcastic. Look on this as a new and wonderfully exhilarating experience.'

I didn't. I looked on it as a new and, frankly, bloody scary and potentially-Fran-damaging experience.

Thursday morning was our day and the hunt was at a place called Peacock Farm. Batman had his mane plaited and looked very smart, all tacked up and ready to go. Marcus had done that for me. As instructed by Gabby, I was pretty smart too; in my borrowed tweed hunting jacket. Gabby drove us in the yard's little three-horse lorry. She told me there were likely to be a few others from the yard there, too. I was so nervous when we got there that I was desperate for the loo. No-one told me that hunting involves being out in the middle of nowhere with no conveniences like toilets or eateries or coffee shops. The horsebox had no on-board toilet, so once we had the horses off and tied to the side of the lorry, Gabby told me just to go in the back partition.

'Everyone goes in the back of their lorry at some point in their horsey life,' she told me. I was quite horrified. Portaloos were bad enough but I was desperate and needs must, as they say.

Two minutes later, I yelled out to Gabby:

'Is there any toilet roll?'

'Toilet roll?' I could hear the astonishment in her voice. 'Can't you just shake?'

'Good idea,' I shouted back, realising I had completely misunderstood the whole everyone-goes-in-the-back concept. Oh crap, I thought. There was no way I was going to shake this off. Have you heard that joke 'What do loo roll and the Starship Enterprise have in common?' 'They both wipe out Klingons!'?

Just as well I'm smart and resourceful, is all I can say. The straw bedding at the back of the partition doubled as acceptable, if particularly prickly, toilet paper. I resolved to make sure I mucked out the back of the lorry so there was no chance that Gabby would realise my mistake! Desperation resolved, I hauled myself back together and was ready to get on Batman. As I emerged from the back of the lorry, I was mildly horrified to see Gary chatting with Gabby. He smiled over to me with those wide, knowing, almost-laughing eyes. He'd most definitely heard my toilet roll request, I was sure of it, and my heart sank.

It was a cold crisp morning but at least it was dry. It had rained a bit during the last week so I was grateful for better weather today.

All of the hunting people met, on their horses of course, in a courtyard on the farm. It took us just five minutes from where we parked on the side of the road to get to what Gabby referred to as 'The Meet'. We stood around there for some time waiting to go (to be fair, I really could wait to go as I was literally pooping my pants with fear - the evidence was now buried loosely beneath a small pile of straw in the back of the lorry).

'When you first talk to someone here, start by saying *good morning*. That's proper hunting manners and proper behaviour matters, so don't show me up with that, please.'

'Sure thing.'

Gabby seemed to know many of the people there and was slowly mooching around the courtyard on her horse talking with them. I stayed put. It seemed too much effort to navigate through the whole throng of horses. On the plus side though, some nice people were wandering around on foot, offering us riders sausage rolls and cups of what I think were brandy and whiskey (not mixed, though). I had a good three cups of the brandy-type stuff, saying *good morning* to each and everyone of the people who were handing them out, and felt a very nice warm glow inside. I found my nerves were dissipating a touch so I had another.

Everyone looked so smart. It was actually a nice sight to see. The courtyard was quite full. I estimated there must have been around thirty horses there. I saw Gabby making her way back to me and my heart fluttered as I guessed it must be nearly time to get going. I think the worst of my nerves were coming from the fact that I really didn't know what to expect at all from this experience. I vowed silently to myself that I would, above all else, stay on! If I could do that, I'd be happy.

'When we set off, make sure you stay behind the hunt master – the guy over there,' Gabby pointed, 'in the pink coat. Don't stand on any of the hounds and be generally polite.' I thought she had managed overnight to turn colour-blind. He was clearly wearing a red coat. I cleverly thought to myself that this must be related to the horse-colour ridiculousness.

'Pink coat? It looks perfectly red to me.'

'Fran, when will you learn that in the horse world, all is not as it seems. Pink is an old-school term based on a tailor called Pink who made hunting coats. Some also call them scarlet but fewer refer to them as red.'

'Clear as mud,' I said. I decided internally to myself, that I would stick with red.

'Looks like we have a good field today,' said Gabby, changing the subject.

'What only one field to ride in? And how can you tell from here?'

Gabby looked at me with her stupid-Fran expression, one I'm getting pretty used to seeing, telling me I've said or done something ridiculous.

'The field refers to the mounted riders, you muppet.'

After a brief speech of thanks from the guy in charge, in the red coat (it really was most definitely red and not pink in my eyes), we were off. We started in trot, round some roads and then we were on grass and that was it, like a herd of something very fast, we were galloping at what felt to me like top speed. I was scared and excited all at the same time. The wind whistled past me and I felt free. The fear gave way to me relaxing a little and starting to enjoy myself. That is, until the jumping began. It was only a little one but it looked like the Great Wall of China from where I was approaching. Gabby was cantering close to me.

'Remember what I said, sit up, hold your Jesus Christ strap and Batman will do the rest – he'll just follow on. I'll go in front of you,' she called to me, with a big grin on her face. And so we were heading to the stone wall that led into the next field.

'Why did you just call it called a Jesus Chr...' Batman took off what felt like a mile from the jump. 'JESUS BLOODY CHRIST!!!' I yelled, clinging on tightly to the strap with both hands. We landed, in one piece. Bloody hell, what a rush that was. My heart was pounding so hard it felt like it would beat itself right out of my chest to freedom. But there was no let-up. We were off and running again. After what felt like a while, we eventually stopped for a breather. The hunt master and his cronies were mooching around with the hounds whilst the rest of us stood having our break. Instantly hip flasks were out, being passed amongst the crowd. Gabby produced her own and passed it to me.

'Gin?'

'Too bloody right,' I said, taking the flask eagerly. 'So, we get breaks then?'

'We stop when the hunt master and the whips are working out where to go next.'

'Whips?'

'Whipper-in. They help the master organise the hounds.'

I took a good swig from the hip flask and shuddered slightly as the warming, sharp, sweet gin hit my stomach. Before I had time to digest my drink, we were setting off again. Batman was keen and I nearly dropped the flask but managed to flip the lid, thankfully permanently attached, back on and slip it into my pocket.

The next jump came at the end of the next field. It was a hedge. As Gabby was indicating for me to follow, I assumed it was a 'small' one that I could do. She was a bit ahead of me now and a few others were going to the jump before me. That was fine. I knew what to do. As instructed, I just pointed Batman, kicked and held onto my much-needed Jesus-Christ neck strap. Seems, however, on the landing side, we needed to turn a sharp left to avoid riding straight into a tree that was rooted in the biggest muddiest puddle going. Batman realised this fact very quickly, it seemed he'd weighed up the whole mud-tree-sharp-turn scenario even before he'd reached the jump because I swear he'd made the turn mid-air. I, on the other hand, didn't even see the obstructing tree until we landed. So, long story short, Batman turned and

I didn't, landing me in the rather large muddy puddle. Fortunately, I narrowly missed bouncing off the tree.

Nowhere in sight, Gabby was probably way up ahead. As I was now covered in mud and feeling quite sorry for myself, I would have quite happily walked back to the lorry and left Batman to fend for himself (perhaps after kicking him in the shin to make up for him dumping me in a mud-bath), but that was not to be and some kind guy had already hopped off his horse and was offering to leg me back on. Seems this kind guy didn't realise his own strength because right as he launched me off the ground, before I could get my leg over the saddle to sit back on board, I was plummeting to the ground on the other side of Batman, having been flung right over the other side. On the plus side, if there can be such a thing when the ground is approaching rapidly and it's your face that is suitably placed to break your fall, I was still positioned in the soft mud-bath I had originally fallen in, so my landing would be cushioned somewhat. My arms instinctively went out ahead of me and resulted in me kind of diving into the mud. I'm sure it wasn't a pretty sight but made for good amusement.

'Oh, I'm so very sorry,' said Mr Kind-Guy as I face-planted for the second time within three minutes in a pile of wet mud.

At that point, Gary sailed the jump and pulled up.

'You OK, Fran?' he asked.

I prised my face out of the mud and pushed myself up enough to look up at him.

'Just super,' I said, through a dirt-encrusted face.

'There are easier ways to have a mud-pack if you want a beauty treatment,' he said, smiling.

I was about to give him a few choice words about where to go and ensuring it involved some kind of reproduction but, at that point, Mr Kind-Guy piped up.

'Let me help you...' he offered, and hauled at my arm to pull me on to my feet. 'Let's get you back on.'

'Thanks but I'll climb on from the fence, if that's OK?' If I was to have to get back on, this seemed a much safer option. I did, however, trust him to hold Batman for me. I was quite sure Mr Kind-Guy couldn't manage to screw that up and I didn't fancy face-planting a third time. Gary had headed off.

Back on board, I headed off to catch up with Gabby and the others. Gabby was clearly oblivious to the fact that I'd fallen off. As I was approaching the rest of the group, Gabby was heading back my way to find me. She took one look at the state of me, covered in mud, and decided we could think about finishing for the day.

'Come on, Fran, we've been out about two hours so let's make tracks home. I think you and Batman have done enough for one day.' I was so relieved. 'We just need to follow correct etiquette and take our leave of the Hunt Master and we'll head back to the lorry.'

As we walked past the master in his smart red or pink or scarlet coat, Gabby held up her hand and called: 'Goodnight,' to him, which I just didn't get as it was still the middle of the day.

I followed suit and took my own leave of the master.

'Bye, see you again, I had a great time,' I called, adding an enthusiastic wave into the bargain.

'You muppet,' said Gabby, growling at me which took me by surprise. I looked at her with my best what-the-hell-did-I-do expression. 'It's "goodnight"! Goodnight is the proper etiquette when leaving the hunt. Did you not hear what I said?'

'Well, how was I to know? You only told me about *good morning*' Christ, there are rules for everything in the equestrian world. Safe to say, hunting wasn't one of my greatest successes in life. When the business was up and running and this challenge was done, there would be no more confusing hunting etiquette for me because there would be no more hunting for me.

Chapter 27

It was a crisp Tuesday morning and I'd arrived at the yard quite early to get Batman done. It had taken me a few days to get over my hunting experience so I hadn't ridden much over the weekend. In fact, I hadn't done much bar eat chocolate, take-away and drink a couple glasses of the fizzy stuff. I wasn't working today and was looking forward to some dedicated business time. I rode him, then turned him out in the field. I'd learned, very quickly, that it was a good idea for him to have daily time in the field so he had burned off any excess energy he was feeling, running around amusing himself, rather than trying to do it when I was on his back. I wandered into the tea room, having finished my immediate jobs. Richard followed me in as I was making myself a well-deserved brew.

'You seem to be making good progress,' he said lightly. 'I'm really pleased.' He paused. 'I want you to succeed. In fact, I think you are maybe ready to be getting out and about.'

I smiled but said nothing. My Richard-dar was on full alert and, in its view, something was about to escape him that I was surely not to like.

'I was thinking, you could borrow my lorry to get around for now. You need to be getting out there and trying your hand at some small competitions.'

'That's great,' I said, quickly, not liking the direction of this conversation one little bit. 'But I don't know anyone that can drive one of those.'

'Given your age, I'm assuming you can drive a small lorry on your current license.'

'I wouldn't know,' I said. It's bad enough that I have to learn to ride (and stay on whilst I'm doing it) without having to cope with driving a bloody great lorry.

'Take it from me, I know about driving licenses. You can. You'll be a great trucker - just like me.'

Trucker wasn't a word I wanted to use for him right at that moment, but it was close. Anyway, I wondered, how would Richard actually know what sort of age I am? I guess my wealth-seeking has taken a bit of a toll. Perhaps if I was a touch more girly and made a real effort with my appearance, I'd look better. In fact, my only attempt at looking younger is when an '80s song comes on and I try to look completely confused and slightly disgusted.

'I've taken the liberty of booking you on a crash HGV course,' he said with his biggest cheesy smile.

'You start in three weeks' time, after which your own lorry will be ready for you and you won't have to share mine. Don't get excited, though, it's an older lorry borrowed from a good friend of mine who's having some time off, out of the country. It's in the garage getting its MOT, at the moment.' Don't get excited. There was an understatement if ever I'd heard one. I could completely contain my excitement. In fact, I struggled to hide the disappointment on my face. He noticed.

'There are loads on this yard that would give their right arm for what you're getting here.'

'You could give these things to someone more deserving and just give me the investment,' I suggested. As they say, nothing ventured, nothing gained.

'But that would be no fun at all - for me at least - and I'd be depriving you of another life experience.'

And that, as they say, was that. The decision was made. I would do the driving course and I would drive his friend's lorry.

I spent the rest of the week at work completely distracted by my forthcoming lorry adventure. Yet again, I wondered what the hell I'd gotten myself into.

Chapter 28

After weeks of preparation, Gabby had decided it was time for me and Batman to do our first competition. We were to do a dressage test – a simple one; Prelim One, and it was about the easiest test going that had canter in it. There were tests that only did walk and trot but Gabby said, given my challenge timescale, I didn't have time to mess about with more baby stuff. I just needed to crack on.

She sat me down with her to do my entry, was going to drive the lorry, help me get ready and do all the stuff I'm told you need to do at a competition. My entries require an emergency contact. Seems reasonable, taking into account my actual riding ability. We decided, as Marcus would accompany me to most events, we'd use his name and number.

'It'll be good for you and Batman to go out and do this,' Gabby told me.

Mentally, I begged to differ on that front because I suspect what Batman and I do is not going to be considered *doing it*. I'm game, though. Bring it on!

We had a run through the test yesterday and I think I managed all the right movements at about the right(ish) time. It helped that Gabby was shouting out each move for me and she told me that as she was allowed to do this for me at this particular competition, she would but just to get me going. In future, I would most definitely have to memorise the whole test.

Gabby had instructed me that she would meet me at the yard at ten a.m. prompt and that both Batman and I should be clean, presentable and ready to load onto the lorry.

When I turned up to the yard to get ready, I was introduced to the 'in joke' about Batman being grey. He was actually covered, and I mean covered, in green crap and there was no way I could take him anywhere looking like that. All the nice brown-coloured horses can have a quick brush off taking all of maybe five minutes. There was no way this green stuff was coming off without a full body bath and that was going to take some considerable time. There went my quiet sit-down for a coffee before the off. I've actually never seen him so dirty. It's like he took one look at me as I said goodnight to him yesterday and thought: *If she thinks she's taking me out looking clean tomorrow, well she's got another think coming!* Then sprayed green poo like a blanket all over his stable and then rolled and rolled and rolled in it, mashing it into every light patch on his stupid, hairy body.

When I looked in his stable, there were only two piles of poo visible, the rest were hidden amongst his bedding. How the hell had he gotten so dirty from just that? He must have taken the time to roll each individual part of his body. Now that's dedication to your cause, isn't it? I almost had to admire him for being so bloody minded. Now, I know every horsey person would tell me that horses just don't think like that, but I'm telling you, Batman saw me coming and decided to make a complete idiot of me. And he was doing a bloody good job.

Well, I got my own back. Fortunately, with Gabby's *be ready promptly* phrase ringing in my ears, I'd gotten up to the yard early to make sure I had all my stuff together. Head collar on, I dragged him off to the washroom and gave him a nice cold bath. He wasn't smiling after that, but he was clean.

Our trip today wasn't too far. We were to drive in Richard's lorry but it wouldn't start. Given that my entire effective knowledge of vehicle repair is derived from the song 'The Wheels on the Bus Go Round and Round', I thought it best that I didn't touch anything mechanical so we reverted to the yard's little lorry.

The centre I was competing at (if you could call it competing) was about half an hour drive away. Gabby helped me and Batman get ready, stuck my competitor number on his bridle and helped me warm up in the collecting arena that sat behind a fence from the main arena where I'd do my test.

'When it's your turn,' Gabby told me, 'ride around the outside of the arena until the judge rings the bell, which means you can start. I'll stand by the side of the arena and I'll call the test for you so you don't forget any of the movements.'

So, I rode round and round and round the arena but no bell. The person in the car at the end of the dressage test arena beeped the horn a few times but I didn't know what that meant. The only use of a horn in a car, as far as I'm concerned, is to tell other drivers either get the hell out of my way or you're an idiot.

Gabby went running over to the judge in the car, said something I couldn't hear, and then came running over to tell me to start my test.

'You said a bell.'

She told me to use my brain, in the absence of a bell it was horn. Oh, well, I should've known that then, shouldn't I.

152

So back to this calling the test concept – I would call it bloody awful, based on mine and Batman's performance today. But, on the plus side, we stayed in the arena when we were supposed to, left the arena when we were supposed to and did some moves in between. When I asked him to trot, he did and when I asked him to canter, he did...eventually.

Gabby told me it was OK and that it had gone as well as could be expected for a first ever test. My score was sixty per cent. Gabby told me the judge was generous and that my collective marks (apparently, this is how I ride and how the horse goes) would need to improve for when I did my main eventing competition. In my view, generous would've been getting out of the car and explaining about the horn instead of making me look a right idiot.

Still, my first competition was over. There were no rosettes for me and Batman, but I still had a kind of warm feeling of achievement. I even gave Batman a Polo once he was loaded on the lorry again.

The first place I wanted to go to was the burger van. I found, although I couldn't eat before I rode my test, I was now the most ravenous I'd ever felt. In fact, I felt like I could eat the entire van in one go – including all the food inside it.

'Next outing, we'll go and do a clear round show jumping. Just something really small,' Gabby told me.

'A bit optimistic to think I'll jump a round clear for my first time out, don't you think?'

'No, you muppet. Clear round is what the competition is called. It's an introductory level to show jumping for beginners.'

It all sounded very complex to me and, for today, I was keen just to get back to the yard, get Batman settled and get a wee glass of the fizzy stuff I like so much. This competing lark was proving to be stressful. More terminology, scoring, bells and horns to understand. I couldn't imagine the day when all of this would make absolute sense and would be second nature to me. Perhaps, in fact, that day would never come.

Chapter 29

My weekend of riding and competition over, today's training course was at our site in the centre of Sheffield, teaching project staff how to use Microsoft Excel to do fancy calculations. As Sheffield is not a place I'm really familiar with, and based on previous experience of my navigational deficiencies, I set off in plenty of time to make sure I had a getting-lost and can't-find-anywhere-to-park contingency plan.

The car park that was close was busy. I had to circle a couple of times before I could get a space. Like buses, a few came free at the same time so I hiked it quickly to the single ticket machine. The last thing I needed, with a meeting starting in ten minutes, was to get stuck behind the silver brigade on pension day and their failing eyesight trying to work out what coins were what in their wallets. The pensioner in front of me was peering closely at the ticket machine slotting coins in at a painfully slow pace and at the rate he was going, the pound would have dropped another five per cent on the FTSE by the time he was finished. I rolled my eyes and sighed with impatience. As he fumbled his remaining coins back into his wallet, I hovered close to her, showing that I wasn't keen on waiting much longer. I did, however, owe a debt of gratitude to the kind old lady who tapped me on my shoulder as I fed my coins into the ticket machine, at the front of a nice long queue, to tell me that my skirt was tucked into my underwear. That must have come from my brief loo stop on the way, which must have made a nice spectacle for all the other visitors at the busy services. The smiles on the faces of the queue behind just added that touch of insult.

My mind wasn't on the training course though, it was on my new app system that needed more work. That's where I wanted to be and what I wanted to be doing. If Richard would give up this stupid game and just invest, I could have it to market in three months and he could be on his way to being rich. Well, more rich, I guess. For a guy like him, where's the fun in that, though? I spent my lunch break working up some more of my marketing plan. I was, I have to say, finding it difficult. The technical stuff I could do, no problem, but the more fluffy stuff, didn't come easy. I wasn't going to worry, though. I'd make it come together.

When my day working in Sheffield was done, I was running about half an hour late and that meant that the traffic was likely to be horridly busy. I could see out of the window that it was raining heavily as I was packing up ready to leave the training site to head back to my car. Always without one, Paul had bought me a compact umbrella as a stocking filler for Christmas last year. I put it in my car boot for emergencies. And there it remains, neither use nor ornament in this heavy rain. I wrapped up well in my coat and scarf. As an afterthought, I took my glasses off their usual pew on top of my head and tucked them safely in my coat pocket. When I say the rain was heavy, I mean horizontal, sheet rain of the sort that makes you feel like you just stepped out of a shower. So, it's not rocket science to guess that I got wet. So wet was I, I stripped off my coat and scarf and threw them along with my laptop and handbag into the boot of my car before quickly jumping in the driver's seat, thankful to be out of the rain.

I got going quickly, as I could see queues already building. Once in the flow of traffic, I felt I could relax a little. All being well, I'd be at the yard to sort Batman by about six-thirty and I might catch Sue for a quick brew too. As I drew to a standstill at the first traffic lights, I thought I'd just use my Sat Nav to check the best route back to avoid the worst of the traffic. That was where I realised my oversight. My phone, with my maps app, was sitting happily on the passenger seat, next to me. My glasses, however, were tucked into my soaking wet coat in the boot. Given that at close range I can see sweet sod all in any sort of useful detail without my glasses, I was, to put it bluntly, buggered!

Not to worry, I told myself, how many times have I used the keyboard on my iPhone? (That was rhetorical - I knew exactly how many times, well not exactly, what I mean is, I knew I'd used it lots) I decided I could put the postcode in anyway as I could make out the keys. After doing so, I pressed the large green Go button. Big mistake - BIG mistake. DN13 6RG became DN14 6EG. The difference might only be two alpha-numeric characters, but the actual difference sits around the twelve-mile mark. I might have realised my mistake, if I had any remote semblance of a sense of direction but, alas, that's a department (along with many others) that I am liberally under-blessed in.

The Sat Nav took me up the Sheffield Parkway, a dual carriageway leading to the M1 motorway that was more like a car park at this time of rush hour. Sat, again in a long queue of traffic like the non-yacht-owning loser I am (but only at the moment!), I used the stationary time to text Paul and ask him to put out the recycle bins, to save me a job whenever I finally got home that evening.

An hour later, I was on the verge of losing the will to live and seemed no closer to home. The scenery, whilst now glum and rainy, looked entirely unfamiliar (this would be the result of a 4 and an E in place of the correct 3 and R, respectively). Turns out, I found myself the other side of Doncaster to where I intended to be. That turned out to be an extra hour of driving I needed like a hole in the head. To be honest, I use a Sat Nav because it's fairly idiot proof. However, it seems that if you make it idiot proof, you're pretty well guaranteed to find a better kind of idiot! That better kind of idiot, in many cases, would turn out to be me!

So grateful to finally be home, I sank at the kitchen table completely knackered. Paul busied himself retrieving fish and chips, still in the paper, from the oven. My eyes were drawn to two wine glasses on the draining board.

'I'm assuming it wasn't Mike that was here earlier,' I said, nodding my head toward the two glasses.

His eyes widened and I'd swear his look said he'd meant to get those dried and put away before I got home.

'No, it was a friend.'

'And that friend was who?'

'Just a friend from work.' He was being evasive and I was not buying it.

'Just tell me it wasn't Marcus.'

'And what would be wrong if it was? He just popped round to see if you were home. We had a quick drink and a chat, that was it.'

'I don't need to tell you what is wrong with that and you know it.'

'I'm a grown professional man. I don't need a lecture.'

'You're a grown professional man who can't help but flirt where you shouldn't. Marcus is out of bounds!' He didn't reply. I wasn't convinced he'd take any notice of me. 'Did you hear what I said?'

'Yes, did you hear me ignoring you?'

I shook my head. These coming months were going to seem even longer if I had to try to keep my kid brother away from the handsome groom.

Paul picked up his phone and changed the subject.

'I'm intrigued at what it was you asked me to put out,' he said.

I frowned. 'What do you mean?'

'Your text! It says: *Please will you put the recycler bisexual out?* What the hell is the recycler bisexual? I didn't even know you owned such a thing!'

'Ah, my glasses. I didn't have my glasses on. Isn't it obvious? Recycle bin.'

God only knows what the hell I typed for the autocorrect to come up with that interpretation.

I do, however, know that in future, I should most definitely not leave my glasses anywhere that is out of reach if I plan to either find my way somewhere or plan to communicate with anyone other than myself or, perhaps, Tarquin – because he won't care in the slightest, no matter what comes out.

Chapter 30

After a couple of days off riding, through me being taken up with work, and Batman being confined to his stable due to a severe spate of heavy rain, I thought it best to turn him out in the field for a while before riding him. A roll, as soon as he got out through the gate, saw his legs catch in the electric fencing and send him houlie-ing around the field like a demented horse that had been electrocuted. I was thankful for my decision to turn him out. I thought a nice quiet walk around the block at lunchtime would be in order to get ready for lessons starting again tomorrow. Now that we've really started to get to know each other, Batman is normally a super horse to hack – he'll walk past anything unusual, provided it's in a new location that he's not familiar with. If it's anything within his own environment, it's a whole different ball-game. For example, round the block from the yard, the local farmer grows peas in the fields. One day, the farmer cut down one of those fields and Batman was then terrified to walk anywhere near it because the peas were missing.

Sonia was at the yard.

'Day off?' I asked.

'Yep, thought I'd have some R&R with my boy today. Fancy a hack?'

I did, indeed. Company was always welcomed. Whilst my confidence was growing, I was not a fool. Batman, good boy though he was, was still a bloody great animal with a mind of his own.

Today we set off on our quiet little hack to find a chainsaw on the go over the road, temporary road-works (complete with multiple road-side signs, barriers and a lorry with trailer partly blocking the lane) and finally a group of unexpected shooters with dogs and guns were creeping around in the woods. This saw Batman then jog, twitch and canter halfway round the hack. Given his behaviour, I think there might just have been some pixies hiding in the undergrowth too.

'He's full of himself today,' Sonia commented with a smile.

'You don't say!'

'He'll calm down.'

I hoped so. We tootled up the lane together and he did, indeed, calm down somewhat, with me and Sonia passing the time of day.

'He's a nice sort of a horse, your Batman, to be learning on. Bit feisty at times, though?'

'I don't have much to compare him to, starting riding as recently as I have, but he's a good lad.'

'Strange thing to take up so late in life, you know, when it's not something you've been interested in at all.'

'Hey, I'm not that old!'

'Ha-ha – you know what I mean. To just decide to ride and then like, get your own horse straight away. That is a bit unusual. I've been around horses a long time and I've not seen that happen really.'

'Well, I guess I had a bit of an epiphany. I needed something all-encompassing and this was it.'

She looked at me like I was on day release from the local psychiatric unit and then was quiet as we rode on.

'Richard's a bit of a catch for someone, don't you think?' I wasn't quite sure where this was going but I was quite sure by now that Sonia wasn't just making idle conversation.

'Is he?'

'Well, he's very wealthy and he's single. Horsey, too. The ideal catch for someone who's into horses. Someone might even become interested in horses in the hope... you know?'

'Not sure I do know, Sonia,' I said, trying to keep the sharpness out of my voice. 'Are you suggesting...'

'I'm not suggesting anything,' she cut in quickly. 'I'm just making conversation. He's a catch, is all I'm saying.'

'You interested, then?' That took her aback a little. I saw the briefest of flinches and I might actually have touched a bit of a raw nerve. As they say, *"The truth shall set you free..."* unless, of course, you're in court. Then you should probably shut the hell up.

'Of course not. He's not my type and I'm happily attached...And you're not interested?'

'Definitely not. Happily single. Enough on my plate with my new hobby, don't you think?'

'So, there's nothing between you and Richard?'

Nowt like being direct, I thought.

'That's about the long and the short of it.' Not sure she was satisfied with that, I quickly changed the subject. 'Did I notice earlier that you've had your hair done?'

'Yes! You like it?' She seemed pleased I'd noticed. I wanted to add: *I just love what you've done with it. How do you get it to come out of your nostrils like that?* But I thought, on reflection, that it might not go down too well, so I held my tongue and kept it to a simple: 'Yes, I

163

do.' We rode on and talked useless rubbish for the rest of the ride.

I spent a good deal of the hack wrangling with Batman who was taking exception to just about everything he encountered. Big leaf? Spook. Lamppost? Spook. Puddle? Spook, and so the list went on.

Just when I managed to persuade him that all was right with the world and he wasn't actually in mortal danger, we returned to the lane to find the workforce had doubled and were just starting on dismantling the road-works. Needless to say, he was clearly in fine fettle after his couple of days off. I think continued work would perhaps be preferable in future.

Leaving the stables, I felt in serious need of a chocolate fix on my way to my afternoon meeting. I managed to mash a whole family-sized bar of Galaxy into my mouth within the space of around three minutes and IT TASTED LOVELY. What I didn't realise was that some of my precious chocolate had dropped onto my driver's seat. What was also unbeknown to me was that said chocolate was now working its way between the butt cheeks of my very light-coloured trousers. Add to that the warmth of my heated driver's seat and I'm sure it conjures up an appropriate image in your mind.

So, when you walk into a room full of your colleagues, managers and other seriously important business people, what do you say to a senior manager who asks you:

'What's that on your rear end? I'm assuming you've maybe sat in something and it's not actually what it really looks like?'

Oh my good God, I wanted the whole of the meeting room to just open up and swallow me right where I stood. Feeling extremely self-conscious now, I had to not only excuse myself from the meeting and leave, displaying my rear end to the entire room of my colleagues who were all now looking with interest and sniggering, but I had to walk through the open plan office to reach the ladies and it seemed that everyone was looking. Having done a bendy-turny-roundy-type of movement so I could try to see my butt in the mirror, I realised I had no choice but to take off my trousers and wash them out. Hand foam out of a wall dispenser, however, doesn't double as the best of chocolate-removing detergents so I just really managed to smear the brown substance rather than actually remove the stain.

The Dyson blade hand driers also don't double as the best of trouser-butt driers either and it was a painfully slow process trying to make them wearable again. The outcome looked even worse, like I'd crapped myself, as I was left with just a dried brown stain. At least with the chocolate in situ, it looked like chocolate! Of all the days to wear a short jacket ‑ damn you, mild weather. There was no option but for me to take the rest of the day off and go home to change. The consolation was that Prosecco time would arrive early this evening and tomorrow was a yard day.

Chapter 31

My jumping felt like it was going OK. Only jumping small, my confidence was building and I was secretly starting to even enjoy it, although I was reluctant to admit this to anyone. Seeing my improvement, Gabby decided it was time for us to tackle our first proper solid jumps. I'm not so sure I liked the sound of that but I knew it was a necessary evil to allow me to compete in a proper one-day event. Gabby had booked some time at a place locally called Harper Farm that, she told me, had a good selection of fences for me to go at. We arrived just after eleven in the morning and I busied myself with putting on Batman's tack whilst Gabby went to find the owner and pay for the use of the facilities. Suitably armoured up in my body protector, hat and air jacket, I found movement to be a touch restricted. It occurred to me that I might be more safe if I could actually breathe and move my limbs but Gabby disagreed.

'I've seen your jumping,' she said. 'You need all the protection you can get.'

Once on board, we set off down the hill to the cross-country schooling field that sat in the valley. The array of fences I could see immediately struck fear into my heart. They were all shapes and sizes and not one of them looked, at least from my vantage point, like they were small enough for me to jump. I knew immediately that this lesson was going to be more of a battle of wills between me and Gabby; me trying not to jump and Gabby trying to make me. That questioning voice in my head, or is it the rational voice, was asking me to reconsider my sanity right about now, but it was countered by the determined and ever-so-slightly greedy voice that really, really wanted the cash investment that was dangling ever-so-effectively as a metaphorical carrot. So, instead of running (or rather galloping) for the hills, as they say, I headed down onto the field and began to warm up under Gabby's expert eye. Trot this way, canter that way, move the canter forward a bit, bring the canter back. I was getting with the lingo and, in fact, didn't even realise it was happening. I was just understanding what was being asked of me.

When it was time to start jumping, Gabby told me to start with a little log. To be fair, it didn't look that little to me but I think my perspective, when it comes to anything riding-related, is a touch skewed by my absolute of fear of falling off. I had unintentionally departed from the saddle (whilst it's been attached to Batman) a sum total of six times already and, whilst I'm continually reminded by everyone equestrian that you have to fall off at least seven times to be a good rider, I'd be quite happy to remain the novice I am at six times. To me, when I'm on board the horse, gravity seems to double its strength as it has this uncanny knack of pulling me right off the horse even when it seems I should just remain in the saddle. The slightest overbalance and there it is; good old gravity reminding me that the ground is really quite hard.

Today, seeing as we were now jumping round a set of fences in a field, the ground really was hard and I had no intentions of testing its firmness with any part of my body except the soles of my feet - and that would only be when I actually chose to get off. That was the plan, anyway. As with most of my plans, they never quite come to fruition.

The log went well. Batman came in what felt like a good canter and popped over it nicely. My spirits raised immediately – it was a good start to my first cross-country schooling session. That was about extent of the riding for which the adjective *good* could be used that day. Batman got a bit keen and that made me a bit less keen. The keener he got, the faster he got. The faster he got, the more I froze into doing nothing, including telling him to slow down.

'Will you pull that horse up?'

'I'm trying,' I yelled. 'He's not listening to me.'

'Well, make him listen! If you just sit there like a wet fart he's just going to take the mick. Tell him who's in control.' She was now going into lecture-Fran mode. I didn't think I was sitting there anything like a wet fart at all, but I don't tend to argue with Gabby. Even if I'm pretty sure I'm right, she always has a way of showing me that I'm actually completely wrong.

'Look, let's make it nice and simple. Trot to the log and when you've jumped that, trot him over to the water and just let him paddle in. Nice and steady.'

I did just that and he paddled into the water like an old pro, his little hooves splashing around as we circled and walked back out.

'Now do it all in trot. Jump the log, trot into the water, trot through the water and out up the little ramp at the other side.'

The log, again, went well. Nothing else did. As I approached the water, Batman must have seen piranha or some other such flesh-eating creatures because he slammed the brakes on right at the edge, pitching me right forward until I found myself looking right at his left

168

ear. Unperturbed, however, and determination in full swing, I hitched myself back into the saddle and gave him a full legs-off-his-side kick. Under normal circumstances, Batman will do his utmost to ignore most of the signals I give him with my legs. Today, however, he decided to be different and completely overreact, which saw him launching, all four feet off the ground in one go, over the fictitious horse-eating fish into the water. Had that been the end of the manoeuvre I might have been all right but then on landing, he effectively stubbed his toe in the water, causing him to trip. In tripping, the whole front of the horse seemed to disappear from in front of me and I pitched head first into the water. It was a rather neat move that saw me somersault and ensure that every single inch of my being had been submersed and was, as a result, drenched. Now, I'm not a great lover of water, in fact, I'm quite terrified of it and, in particular, drowning. Well, I can tell you, I thought I was drowning. The fact that it was only twelve inches deep was irrelevant – I was, in my mind, in mortal danger. Not only was I under water, I couldn't breathe. It took me just a moment to realise that was as a result of the air jacket inflating, squeezing the very life breath from me. My breathing, as you might imagine, returned to normal when the air jacket deflated.

As I sat there in the water, now recovered from my immediate panic, all I could see was Batman eyeing me up suspiciously from the safety of the bank. I myself was eyeing up the hill back to the lorry thinking what a long walk it was going to be. I mean, who could get back on a horse and ride it in this state?

'Come on, let's get you back on. You need to do that one again,' said Gabby, taking hold of Batman and heading towards me.

I hauled myself up out of the water and hung my arms wide as the water started to drain from my hat, clothes and body protector.

'What? WHAT? Again?'

'Er, yes, again. What, you think you can just leave it at that? Fall off and not get back on?'

'But I'm soaked!'

'And? Maybe it'll teach you to glue your backside to the saddle and keep your shoulders back in future. He just pecked; tripped on landing. If you hadn't been leaning so far forward, you would have been fine. Consider it a learning experience.'

As I was so very wet, she decided I could use a jump as a mounting block rather than giving me a leg up. Once on I did, indeed, have to go and jump it again. And, in the true spirit of learning, I kept my shoulders up and stuck my backside in the saddle. This was how I completed the rest of the lesson: wet and cold. I guess now she could really say I was sitting there like a wet fart. The added incentive, however, was that I wanted it to end quick-smart. That meant, where possible, doing everything right first time. Doing it wrong meant doing it again, and again, and again, until it was right.

'You can't sit in the lorry like that,' Gabby said. 'You'll soak the seats. I assume you have a change?'

'Well, now that you mention it, no-one suggested that to me.' She didn't look impressed.

'Fran, am I right in thinking that you are academically capable?' I nodded. 'Am I further right in thinking that you have fallen off, in the space of eight weeks riding, no less than six times?' I nodded. 'Would that not indicate that if you engaged that brain of yours it might suggest there's a possibility you and Batman might realistically part company and that out in the field, that might require a change of clothing?'

I felt her tirade of questioning here was more rhetorical than practical so I declined to answer and instead, gave her my best weak smile.

As even my underwear was wet, I had to strip off pretty much everything. I found a pair of Richard's breeches in the back along with a tee-shirt. That was the sum total of the clothing available to me. I pulled the breeches on and they immediately fell back down to my ankles. I searched the drawers and found some of the orange string used to tie up bales of hay and straw. I used that as a makeshift belt. (Sue later told me that bale twine is THE most useful substance in the equestrian world, being the horsey equivalent of duct tape – It most certainly was very useful in helping me cover my arse). I peeled off my top half and put on the tee-shirt. It was only then that I realised it was emblazoned with a large capital W and a picture of a ship's anchor. Yes, it took me a second to work it out but I had no choice other than to wear it. It was that or go in the buff. It's a bit how I was feeling actually, so it felt apt.

When I climbed in the cab, Gabby just burst out laughing.

'Suits you,' she said.

And so it did.

On the way back to the yard, it was good to get an opportunity to chat to Gabby. I'd been too tense on the way there to even think of having a rational conversation.

'I'm having a birthday party soon. Some of the girls at the yard are coming. You can come too. It will be fun. It's themed so I hope you like dressing up.'

'That sounds great, I'd love to come.' I beamed inside. I felt like I was becoming one of the crowd.

'It's back at home over Cheshire way.'

'You're a long way from home. What made you move over here?'

'I came to go to uni and never left. Now I work and live here.' She looked across at me. 'I admire you taking this on, learning to ride. It's good to follow your dreams. I'd love to move out to the US but it's such a big move, I don't know if it would or even could happen,' she confided.

'My elderly uncle moved to America. It was a huge move for him, especially at his age,' I told her.

'What state was he in?' she asked.

'Well, although he was old, he was in pretty good shape, to be honest – at least until he died, then he wasn't in a good state at all.' Gabby looked at me, I saw her eyebrows raise and then I realised, lowered my voice and added: 'Texas – he was in the state of Texas.

Chapter 32

All dried off and ready for the week ahead, Monday came and I started my intensive HGV driving lessons. I turned up at six-thirty am as instructed, ready for my seven o'clock start. Standing in a cold, dark HGV yard with a group of other potential large-lorry-driving individuals, all of whom were men, I found myself slightly horrified as the driving instructors, young and capable looking, came out and peeled off the new students, leaving me on my own (bit like being the last to be picked for the rounders team at school). Finally, Tommy arrived – little, old and looking like he needed a good, long sit-down. Just my luck to get the ancient guy who would probably need to turn his hearing aid up when I spoke and would probably get confused with where we were going. I nearly died when I got in the eighteen-tonne Scania and saw what looked like an airline control centre in front of me.

I knew then that this was to be a very long week.

Unlike my car, the lorry had a total of nine gears, with a handy little switch mounted on the front of the gearstick to move from the higher to the lower gearing thingamajig. At least I didn't need to know the technical terms to pass my test.

The way it works is that gear one is also (at a flick of the handy little switch I mentioned) gear five and gear two is also (same flick, same switch) gear six, and so it goes on. With that in mind, rearrange these words and you're close to what I was thinking at that point in time: *hell can what the I that do with!*

This was actually my first real challenge. Now, given I don't know my left from my right, my up from my down and inside out from my...well you get the drift; how the hell was I supposed to work out which way the stupid little switch was supposed to be, WHILST negotiating a junction WHILST driving a big lorry that I wasn't used to?

Turning out of the end of the driveway was a trauma. These big beasts take a bit of manoeuvring and even minor understeering around a corner can lead to added decoration down the truck's side, in the form of scrapes and dents, if there happens to be any type of obstacle, like a parked car or lamppost, in the way. Fortunately, good old Tommy was onto that one very quickly and saved me, screeching 'Stop!!', from taking out the whole side of the lorry within my first two minutes of being on the road.

I did just that, I stopped...dead. Those lorry brakes are pretty damn sharp. I think Tommy and I felt a touch like Billy Splat, although our seat belts helped prevent the splat part on the windscreen. Who the hell puts a great lamppost right on the first corner out of an HGV driving school anyway? There's just no cure for that kind of stupid!

Tommy instructed me to take my corners wide. He stressed the word wide, so I'd make no mistake in future.

We got under way but that just signalled the start of my difficulties.

Hills were a challenge, both up and down. Roundabouts were obstacles that just got in the way and mini-roundabouts might as well have been non-existent; going round them was simply not an option, so I just kind of drove straight over them. I got the feeling that passing this test wasn't going to be quite as easy as I had hoped.

'Tyres and tarmac,' said Tommy, as I nearly mashed into the back of a transit van at some traffic lights.

'What?'

'When you come to a stop, you should be able to see tyres and tarmac!' he told me.

All I could see was the tail-end door of the van. Definitely no tyres and most definitely no tarmac - not even an inch. This, I'd have to get better at.

'I'll try and remember that.' I was sure if I could, life might be safer for everyone on the road.

When we got back to the lorry yard to drop my beast off, I felt quite frazzled yet somewhat pleased with myself. I'd managed not to hit anything, except the brakes a little too sharply on numerous occasions. Oh, and an inconvenient overhanging tree branch that scraped right up the side of the lorry, but that really wasn't my fault.

Back in my own car, it felt small and the brakes didn't respond in quite the same way, but I think that was a good thing.

Boy was I ready for a glass of Prosecco that night.

I was subjected to four hours driving each day. Turned out though, that Tommy was actually not such an old geezer after all. In fact, he really knew his stuff. I think I actually lucked-in for once.

And (should you actually start a sentence with 'And'? Actually, do I care?), I really tried to do as I was told. I found, as the first lesson progressed, this had become a bit of a challenge. I started out not caring if I passed or failed. I mean, Richard put me in this position, made me learn to drive a lorry, even paid for it. What did I care? Maybe it was pride or my competitive nature, but I wanted to pass and to pass first time.

Tommy would issue his gentle instructions and I would try really hard to follow them. Simple you might think, but then you must remember my whole left, right, up, down, inside-out, right-way-out handicap. In that kind of world, nothing is simple.

'At the next junction, Fran, would you like to turn left?' I'd hear Tommy say, on more than one occasion. I'd indicate, position in the road, do all the good stuff, make the turn, and make it well in my opinion. And, on more than one occasion, I'd also hear Tommy say:

'At the next junction, Fran, I'd like you to take the OTHER left turn, please.'

I had some interesting challenges in my driving week, in preparation for my HGV test, such as avoiding free-wheeling a potential load of thirty-two tonnes down residential streets towards small roundabouts and stopping at red traffic lights (that concept seemed to be particularly difficult for my tiny brain to grasp). But, other than taking out a set of road-works signs with my new, large motorised fiend and scraping the side down some awkwardly obstructive bushes, I thought I got off to a rather good start.

On Wednesday, I did lots of practise at the reverse exercise. I got a bit cocky, like I do, after I had done it three times and nearly took out the side of a container with a touch of over-steer but on the whole I managed well. Tommy was quite pleased with me today, particularly when I narrowly avoided rear-ending a police car at a roundabout.

And then it was here, the dreaded Thursday. The day of my test. Tommy took me for a cup of tea at a proper truckers' greasy caff on the way. When we were done, we threw our polystyrene cups in the bin and Tommy took to the driver's seat to take me to the test centre. I felt condemned. When my test started, right from the get-go, what could go wrong, did go wrong...along with a few things that absolutely couldn't go wrong! My brake warning light came on twice during the test. The problem is that at the same time as warning you about air pressure, it simultaneously stops you from moving forward, which is, in fact, a basic requirement in a driving test. Also, and I can't blame it on age, confusion struck mid-way round a roundabout, which saw my indicators going left and right like luminous yo-yos whilst I tried to fathom out where the hell I was supposed to be going.

On track again having got myself together, of all things my examiner decided to MAKE CONVERSATION. So, at this point, I've screwed up on leaving the test centre, I've screwed up big time on the roundabout and I'm progressing down a narrow country road and he wants to know why I like riding.

Because I'm a mad, psycho bitch that is having to learn to ride to extract a good deal of funding from a mad, psycho rich man who thinks it would be funny to make me learn to ride, drive an HGV and win some stupid competition – was what I wanted to say.

'They're such lovely creatures, how could you not like riding them?' was what I actually said, hiding the sarcasm that was trying to escape.

I had managed to go all week with only mounting the kerb once (which is an instant fail in your test). What happened today? I'm sure somebody was out last night and re-concreted the left edge of the entrance to the mini-roundabout at the top of Skipton. I clipped it badly with the nearside rear wheel. I thought quickly on my feet (so to speak, as I was, you'll be glad to hear, still sat down).

'Could that have been a little pot hole?' I heard myself say.

A little further round the test, driving down one of the quieter roads, I faced an interesting problem that I really could have done without on my test. Heading down North Road there, sat right in the middle of the road, was a little black cat. Are black cats in your path supposed to be good luck or bad luck? I had a feeling that whichever it was for the general population, it would amount to bad luck for me in my current situation.

I brought my lorry to an impressively smooth stop. What to do? In my hesitation, I found myself muttering quietly 'move, cat, please move, cat, please move, cat,' whilst my completely distracted mind was working overtime on how to get rid of the cat. The damn cat was going to see me fail. That is, if all of the other screw ups weren't bad enough to fail me, so in fact, the cat might not be the one to get me failed, but I really didn't want to take the chance. I needed the damn thing to bloody well move.

'He can't hear you,' said my examiner, kindly. As if a light bulb went on in my head, I looked across at him and then shouted: 'MOOOVE OUT OF THE BLOODY WAY, CAT!'

The cat persisted to sit there in direct defiance of me.

'I actually meant, beep your horn,' said the examiner. And, quite predictably, that was the tactic that did the trick. I was stumped as to why I didn't think of that.

For the remainder of my test, unlike the rest of this week, I managed not to nearly rear-end, hit or inappropriately flatten any other road users, so that was a positive result. Imagine my surprise then, on returning to the test centre, suitably sweated up and planning my re-take for next week, that I was told I had passed (he told me to be careful of clipping the kerb in future.)

Tommy was suitably delighted as, indeed, was I. I was keen to drive back to the lorry park, but Tommy told me that was out of the question whilst in my euphoric state, so he took the wheel and I sat with a very stupid but very well-earned grin on my face all the way back. It surprised me just how pleased I was with myself.

I got back to the yard a little after lunchtime. Having texted Sue to let her know the good news, I arrived in the tea room to find a card and a Yorkie bar. The card was signed by most of the people in our block. Both the card and the chocolate made me smile. That was it; Batman and I were now mobile. There would be no stopping us now.

Chapter 33

Still beaming from passing my test and a couple of days' worth of good riding, I had a very busy Sunday morning. I hacked Batman and then I baked. You might as well have called me Nigella; I did lots of mixing. Although, I guess Nigella wouldn't mix up teaspoons with tablespoons, mix up plain flour with self-raising, decorate the kitchen with mix by lifting the mixer lid whilst it's still on or, indeed, mix up the ingredients from two entirely separate recipes through not realising she'd turned the page to read on and not turned it back. But hey, I gave it a bash and what came out of the oven looked like a cake. Even Paul was impressed when he came in.

'You had a good day? Been anywhere nice?' I asked casually.

'Just met a friend for lunch, nothing special,' he replied.

'Friend? What friend?' I asked, turning just a touch suspicious.

'No-one you know, just a guy from work.'

'No word from Mike yet? It's really about time you sorted this out with him.'

'No, I've not heard from him. He'll be in touch when he's good and ready.'

It was clear there was also no point in me pushing it with Paul, so I let it alone. I wasn't convinced, though, that he hadn't been up to mischief and I suspected, if he had, I knew who it would have been with.

It was nice to have a somewhat relaxing Sunday without lessons, competitions or business, at all. I felt human again and liked the feeling. I slobbed on the sofa, ate my cake, drank tea, watched *Independence Day*, again, and generally relaxed. Paul went out and left me, Tarquin and Portia the Pug to it. When the movie finished, I made myself another brew, grabbed a pack of Hobnobs from the pantry and settled down to watch another movie, refusing to feel guilty about the cake and biscuit binge.

It was only as I was rounding off my cup of tea that I realised I'd lost the pug. In fact, the last time I'd seen her was when I was making my tea. I found her buried in a five-kilogram bag of cat biscuits in the pantry (I don't like to risk running out.) There was no head, just a curly-tailed pug backside with wiggling legs sticking out of the oversized bag. She was a very happy pug at that point in time – at least, until I extricated her from the food bag.

My easy day really recharged my physiological batteries and by early evening I found myself raring to go, both on the riding and business front. I loved feeling that motivated.

Chapter 34

So, it was party time. Gabby was turning twenty-five. Oh, to be that age again. Actually, to be honest, I'm not sure I would want to be given the opportunity; I might like the youth but along side the added life experience I have now, or maybe even someone else's life experience instead of my own – someone with a modicum of common sense would be ideal. Anyway, back in the moment: The party was taking place in an old castle on the hillside next to Gabby's parents' house. It was a big affair that had apparently taken months of planning to kit out the old castle with tables and chairs, erect the marquee and create a wandering path up the hill to the venue. The theme was 'medieval' which is great because I love dressing up. Dressing up in someone else's clothes saves me having to try and coordinate colours, another life skill which I'm lacking in wads. I don't see clashes, which poses a bit of a problem. With that in mind, I tend to stick to safe colours, ones that are tried and tested and that I know go together. Adventure in this area can see me dressed like a dog's dinner.

I hired an outfit. Sue and I went together. She got a nifty long green velvet number and I went for a floating floor-length wench's dress with a long pointy hat, trailing a long scarf-like decoration.

Suitably installed into our hotel and ready for an evening of serious horsey partying, we headed off in a taxi to make sure we arrived fresh as daisies. When we got there, the scene was just amazing; there were fairy lights along the path to the castle, fire pits blazing, music filling the air and people milling around. When we reached the castle at the top of the path, Gabby was there to meet us. She looked stunning, all kitted out in a Renaissance maiden's outfit.

'Hi there,' she beamed. 'Grab yourselves a drink.'

It was good to see Gabby in a social sense. I realised that, for all my lessons and horsey time with her, I actually knew very little about her.

The room quickly filled up and there was a buzz of conversation vibrating just below the music. Liv and Sonia had arrived just ahead of us and were already with glasses in their hand.

'Bloody amazing,' said Liv, guzzling her glass of champagne and looking just a touch sombre. 'Bloody amazing,' she repeated, almost to herself.

'Second glass already,' Sonia leaned close and confided.

'You OK?' I asked Liv.

'Oh, me? Yes, I'm good. Well, I guess as good as you can be when your husband walked out two days ago.' Well, that was a bomb-shell-and-a-half.

'Oh my God, why didn't you say before?' asked Sue.

'I didn't want to believe it. I thought he'd be straight back.' Her eyes watered. I didn't know what to say, so I didn't say anything.

'Right,' said Sue with authority. 'Tonight is for celebrations. Think of his worst trait and we'll celebrate the fact that you don't have to put up with it anymore!'

'Well, he leaves piles of crap out of his pockets all around the house.' We raised a glass and drank. 'He actually chews with his mouth open and makes the most gross noises when he eats and it drives me up the wall,'

Liv was getting in the swing of it now. 'He eats honey out of the jar with a teaspoon. And, to top it all off, what really drives me mad is that he breathes!' We all laughed and so did Liv.

'Let's get partying, ladies,' said Sonia. We drank and danced, and after fifteen minutes of vigorous alcohol-inflicted boogie-moves, we stopped for a break.

Gabby joined us, sporting a gin and tonic.

'How are you enjoying the party?'

'Aw, it's just great,' said Sonia and we all agreed.

As we chatted with the birthday girl, someone across the room caught my eye.

'Hell's bells, is that Gary over there?' The girls all looked round. Yes, there in the flesh, looking all King-Arthury, was Gary from the yard talking with Richard, who was suitably attired as a peaky-hatted jester.

'I teach Gary, too,' said Gabby. 'He's a pretty good rider. I do think he has a soft touch for someone at the yard, though.'

'Oh, who?' asked Sonia.

Gabby just smiled and looked directly at me.

'Fran!?' gasped Sonia.

'And why not? What's wrong with someone liking me?'

'Well, nothing, I just thought...oh, I don't know what I thought. I've had a few glasses of vino...'

'Why don't you go and talk to him?' Gabby asked.

'Oh, I don't know about that. He's talking with Richard, and well, I'm not interested in a man.'

'I'm not asking you to marry him, just talk to him. Do it for me, for my birthday - do it to please your instructor.'

'Go on,' added Sue.

Fuelled by much horsey-friend-encouragement and much wine, I mooched my way over, hat scarf flowing behind me, to where Richard and Gary were chatting and drinking.

'Hi there,' I said, just a touch too enthusiastically.

'Fran!' said Richard. Gary smiled at me, his hazel eyes bore into mine, making me melt a little. This wasn't helping my absolutely-no-men-complications resolve.

'I see you lot are having a good time.' At that point, Sue motioned for Richard to go join her on the dance floor and he quickly obliged. 'Time to bust a few moves, I think.'

There was a moment of silence when Richard left. I found myself looking at my feet. Gary broke the ice; 'Great party,' he said.

'Yes, isn't it? Lots of free alcohol, always a good sign,' I said, raising my glass. Internally I scolded myself; was there nothing better I could think of to say?

'So, Fran,' his saying my name gave me a little shiver, 'I know you're into horses, having watched you learning to ride but what else do you like?' There was a mischievous glint in his eyes.

'I'm into teaching people how to use computer software and I'm into making shed loads of money and buying a super yacht. You?'

'I'm a fundraiser for a mental health charity.'

'Ah,' I said. 'And of course, with such super wealth, when it arrives, I would obviously be donating muchos amounts to charity.' He looked less than convinced.

'Philanthropy, now that's a trait I like.' I looked at him quizzically through the fog of wine, wondering if he

185

was teasing me. 'Philanthropy,' he repeated. 'You like to help others?'

'I know what it means,' I said, a touch defensively.

'Of course you do.'

Sue and Richard came sauntering over, chatting and giggling, dancing all done for now.

'Come on Fran, the buffet's open now. Let's eat; I'm starved.' She grabbed my arm and led me away.

'Catch you later maybe,' said Gary. I just smiled and nodded. I mean, how the hell could I, millionaire-in-the-making and mercenary-bitch-extraordinaire, be involved with a charity fund-raiser?

The food was fabulous and the alcohol continued to flow freely. I felt truly honoured to be there. As such, I celebrated with muchos more of the free stuff - as did my cohorts. In other words, we all got completely mortal.

So, after an amazing night and knowing I was on the completely plastered side of sober, I went to find Sue to see about finding our way back to the hotel. It was only a short walk so there was no point in worrying about a taxi, since being daisy-fresh was now irrelevant.

On my way up the hill from the toilets to find Sue, I bumped into Liv. She looked a bit worse for wear and was complaining about falling out with Big Katie, with whom she was sharing a room. The excessive amount of drink was pitching her into tearful territory and I was keen to avoid that at all costs. Dealing with a spurned, upset person when completely sober was bad enough, but when I'd consumed a skinful of my own along with someone else's skinful too, it was just too much to handle. I urged her to come with me to find Sue and that if she really didn't wanting to share with Big Katie tonight, she could come and bunk down in mine and Sue's room. I was quite sure Sue wouldn't mind.

Inside the marquee, we headed to find Gabby, who was swirling extravagantly on the dance floor, to say our goodbyes and a massive thank you for the super party. The next task was finding Sue, whom we hadn't seen for at least an hour.

She was sat, comatose, by a table in the corner, little snoring noises emanating from her still form. I lifted her chin gently (as gently as I could whilst trying to hold my inebriated self still), just to confirm she was actually going nowhere. And, she wasn't; going anywhere, anytime soon, that is. She wasn't the only one, either. I covered her over with a coat I found discarded nearby and headed off with Liv for the hotel.

We made it down the hill to the long driveway, which was a feat in itself given the steepness, darkness, inappropriate dressedness and drunkenness involved. Although, I have to say, it did include some impressive arms-waving-in-the-air and some holy-crap-where-the-hell-did-that-come-from movements, trying to stay upright. Getting out of the drive, however, was another matter. At the bottom was a cattle grid that was inconveniently placed between Liv and I and the road beyond. It seemed a simple matter to traverse the metal poles - I mean, why wouldn't it?

It wasn't. I tentatively placed my first foot and then my second on the bars, promptly lost my balance with the result seeing my left foot falling down between the bars, closely followed by my right foot. It had been raining so I now found myself shin deep in muddy water.

As I overbalanced, I instinctively reached out with my left arm to stop my fall, resulting in my left arm coming to rest, not on a nice dry bar, but between them, full to the brim with cold, muddy water. This was followed closely by my right arm. It conjures up quite the picture doesn't it? A woman, kitted in full medieval dress (complete with pointy, floaty hat), on all fours through a cattle grid, now unable to get any purchase to get back up.

I looked to Liv (although it was difficult since it entailed stretching my neck backwards from my rather awkward position) to help me out. Unfortunately, she was by now completely incapacitated; doubled over and uncontrollably laughing. I'm quite sure it wasn't actually that funny – it was the drink that was fuelling her mirth. So, there I was, stuck with my hands and feet down a rain-filled cattle grid, in full medieval get-up, and getting up was something I wasn't going to be doing any time soon. Through my wine-induced fog, I wondered at the sheer brilliance of myself – my ability, like no other person I know, to get into the most ungettable-into positions and situations. It has to be some kind of unique skill...though maybe not one that is sought-after.

'There's sumwum coming, I carn't make owt who it is but 'opefully he'll be sober enof t'be of some use,' slurred Liv. 'I'm waving so he'll stop,' she said, giving me a running commentary from behind my stuck position.

'Liv, if he's walking down t'drive, he's obviously gonna stop – he's gotta walk over the bloody cattle grid to geroff the drive. As it is, I'm in the cattle grid so I fink it's grid locked and I fink your stupid waving is a bit not needed,' I garbled.

She ignored me. He must have been by now within hearing distance.

'We need some help. Poor Fran hashadabit of a mishap wit cattle grid.' I hoped the person she'd *flagged down* would be no-one I knew. When I heard his voice, I knew immediately that I'd hoped in vain.

'Fran McBride, you do get yourself into some pretty unusual positions.' My heart sank, yet again.

Between Liv pulling on my right arm, Gary pulling on my left arm and me trying to get some purchase with my feet, we finally managed to get me both out of the cattle grid and on the right side of the road, so we had a hope of making it to the hotel. Had I been left on the other side, I might just have completely given up, laid myself down and slept for the night right there on the track.

'How exactly were you two getting back to your hotel?'

'Er, walking,' said Liv.

'Don't be ridiculous, it's pitch black, late and that's a very busy road down there with no path. I'll call a taxi.'

With the taxi on its way to meet us, we headed for the road at the bottom of the long, long drive. I stumbled at one point and Gary, quick as a flash, reached out and steadied me. Even in my drunken state, his touch sent a fizzle of niceness through me. Well, I think that was it. We made it back to the hotel, though probably only because Gary was there to keep us on the straight and narrow.

Having seen us safely to the hotel, Gary headed off into the night. I was too inebriated to even wonder where he was staying.

Breakfast the next morning was a sombre affair, entirely hangover controlled. My head was thumping, as was Liv's, and we sat in almost silence throwing as many carbs down our necks as physically possible, washed down with strong, sugary tea. The party had been great, although I wasn't quite sure how I'd face Gary when I saw him next. For now, it was now time to head back and get cracking on making my millionaire dream a reality. We decided we'd pick hopefully-no-longer-comatose Sue up on the way. It was an extremely long drive home with the three of us well in the grip of a decent hangover. The thought of work again on Monday seemed almost unbearable. Unsure just how I was going to make it (both home and into work on Monday), I decided to switch to autopilot and hope it would see me home.

Chapter 35

The Sunday after the party, I wasn't sure if I was dying, hung-over or just hungry for a stack of carbs. Monday came too quickly, and I felt like work as I felt like another case load of champagne. I did, however, at least find myself at work alive and functioning like something vaguely resembling a human being.

I headed on up to the tenth floor to check the room setup ready for Nina's senior management team meeting, but there was somewhere else I wanted to be; I was finding myself thinking more and more about Batman and riding than I was about working; it was a most unexpected turn of events. I found that I wanted to be at the yard, tacking up and heading out for a ride – just me and him. No busy office, no inane gossip, no bossy bosses; just the countryside and peace to think.

I don't see why the hell Nina can't get off her fat backside and check these things for herself, but it was too much effort to complain, so I didn't. I'd normally use the stairs; I like to get the exercise, even if it is just a floor or two, but today I was feeling just a touch under the weather so decided the lift would be a better option. There was a pile of folders that had been left on the meeting table so I thought I'd best take those back with me to the office. Arms piled high with the folders, I caught the lift back down to seven. The lift was empty and, as is often the case when I'm in a lift on my own, I pull funny faces in the mirrored doors. I call it 'Lift Roulette' and when the doors start to open, I see how long I dare keep the face in place not knowing, of course, if there's going to be someone on the other side. I usually chicken out right at the last minute.

Today was no exception and, under the weather or not, I found my face morphing into some contorted version of a squashed tomato. For added effect, I pushed my bottom false teeth plate out of position and rested it on my bottom lip. The resulting face was quite amusing and cheered me up no end. The lift pulled onto floor seven and the doors started to open. As is usual, I chickened out, which is just as well because Nina was stood there with the Director of IT and the Director of HR. Unfortunately, however, as I had been so creative as to involve my false teeth in the game, that was an extra dimension to handle and they weren't for playing ball nicely today. As I curled my lips inwards in the hope of pushing the plate back into place, completely the opposite happened: The teeth were propelled out of my mouth. Hands full of folders, I had no hope of stopping their unfortunate trajectory, as they landed (quite impressively, actually) in the right hand of the Director of IT who had, in an involuntary and instinctive movement, reached out to catch them. So, there they sat, Fixodent strands, spittle and all, in Tom Grainger's hand. As you might imagine, I was mortified. Nina's face said more than any words could possibly say and my interpretation was along the lines of; 'you are SO fired'.

Tom Grainger said nothing and just held out his hand to me as if the plate of plastic teeth it contained was the very plague.

'I'm fo forry,' I said ('S's' become quite difficult without my teeth in).

I juggled my armful of folders and picked up the plate from the IT Director's hand. I couldn't help but catch the almost imperceptible shake of his head in disgust.

It took a sort of double-over-stretch-my-neck-to-meet-my-hand kind of movement to get the teeth back in their rightful place: inside my mouth. Back in one piece, I scuttled off quickly to the office, leaving the senior management team to continue in the lift up to their meeting, most likely ever so slightly traumatised by what must have seemed a very surreal experience.

Sue almost wet herself laughing when I told her all about it.

'I reckon I'm in proper trouble with Nina when she gets back,' I said.

'No way, she can't have a go at you for losing your false teeth! I'd forget about it. It'll give them something to talk about. I bet that'll be far more interesting than their usual rubbish small talk anyway.'

Perhaps she was right. It's not every day you catch a set of false teeth when waiting for a lift. When I'm in *Hello* magazine with a photo on my super yacht, I could turn out be Tom Grainger's claim to fame.

Chapter 36

Thankfully, the weekend had arrived again and it was time for me and Batman to head out together. So, how difficult could it be to get a horse to walk on to the back of a horse lorry? Well, I can tell you; it can be incredibly bloody difficult, particularly when that horse is called Batman and that horsebox belongs (not actually, but for the purposes of my challenge) to me. All set and ready for the off, Batman and I were heading to some so-called 'Stressless Dressage'. This is where you turn up as you are; no need to bath and plait up your horse and no need to wear competition gear. The idea is to take the stress out of the competition and let you concentrate on riding by reducing all the unnecessary preparation - a great idea, in my view. I dragged him in from the field, gave him a brush, stuck on his competition rug and head collar and took him out to the waiting lorry. I'd decided that, without the added stress, it would be a good test and a good bonding opportunity for Batman and I to get out just the two of us.

'Stressless' my arse is all I can say. Irrespective of the competition itself, at this rate, we were unlikely to even get off the yard, never mind arrive and compete.

He simply stood at the bottom of the ramp and said 'no', metaphorically speaking that is, as he was actually silent and his legs, or rather the lack of movement in his legs, did the talking. I tugged on the rope but he wouldn't budge. He just looked at me with that blank expression he seems to have developed every time I ask him to do something he doesn't want to do. He's so damned unreasonable; I tried cajoling him, sweet-talking him and growling at him but nothing worked. He simply remained, feet firmly planted, refusing to move. Why can't he just understand that if he does what I ask him to do, life will be just so much easier (well, for me at least)? It was sod's law too, that there was no-one around to help. He'd been on this lorry I-don't-know-how-many times. He knew, I'm sure of it, he knew I was on my own and could do sweet sod all about it.

OK, think about this logically, I told myself. What's his motivation to go on the lorry? Actually, when I thought about it, there wasn't much motivation. He was standing quite happily at the bottom of the ramp and clearly had no desire to go any further.

Incentive - that's what I needed. Motivated primarily by his stomach and food, I decided a bucket with feed in it was the way to go. I tied him to the side of the lorry, he was fine to move in that direction, and headed off for my bucket. Armed with pony nuts, I rattled the bucket so he knew I had food, untied him again and approached the ramp. Still no desire to go on. I climbed on the ramp myself and held out the bucket, close enough that he could smell the lure of the feed but far enough away that he wasn't getting a mouthful until he complied. It's amazing how stretchy a horse's neck is when they want to reach something. I was near the top of the ramp, swinging off the end of the lead rope and Batman's nose, stretched to its limit, was almost touching the bucket, but still his legs refused to move.

My frustration was building. I put the bucket down and, in temper, put two hands on the rope and hauled as hard as I could. That was the point that I'd effectively lost the battle. It's not rocket science to work out that half a tonne of horse on four legs is going to be stronger (and better balanced) than ten stone of Fran on just two legs. In response to my outburst, he simply lifted his head sharply and pulled me down the ramp. I slipped on the rubber and landed full on my backside, painfully. I was snarling and muttering under my breath at this point. His shins looked prime for being kicked but I decided wisely against that as I wasn't sure he wouldn't kick me back. In a Fran-versus-Batman kicking contest, I was surely going to come off worst. Hauling myself back up onto my feet, keeping hold of the lead rope, we were at an impasse.

From nowhere, Richard appeared.

'Looks like you need some help,' he remarked, casually.

'You don't say,' I said, still hauling fruitlessly on the lead rope. 'Have you been watching me struggle?' Investment or not, I was feeling pretty miffed at the moment so was less concerned about speaking my mind.

'Well, I couldn't help but notice that Batman was being a little obstinate but I thought I'd let you try and resolve it yourself first. Look, give me the rope and stand back.' He took hold of Batman, walked him round in a circle, aimed him directly at the ramp and, walking quietly next to his shoulder, simply proceeded up the ramp. He tied Batman, then brought him straight back off again.

'Your turn now. Do it just the same as I did.'

I took Batman and, indeed, he went straight on as I walked quietly by his shoulder. I closed the partition and I'm quite sure the horse was laughing at me – internally, of course, because we all know horses can't actually laugh.

But, he was on and we were good to go.

'Thanks,' I said. 'You know, you don't have to test me at every single point along this whole equestrian journey. You could just come and help straight up.'

'And what would that achieve, Fran? In this instance, you would get yourself out there to a competition and not be able to get home. You won't always have people with you.'

My resolve to get my crap together and make this whole partnership work was unshaken though. Had I just taken a moment to consider the whole 'partnership' portion of this relationship, I might have saved myself much time, effort and mental trauma. Instead of trying to enforce my will on him (mostly unsuccessfully, I might add), I could perhaps have worked on developing an understanding between us and building a little mutual respect, but I knew so little about horses that such an approach hadn't even crossed my mind as a possibility. Once I got there, the Stressless Dressage did not go particularly well but it did go. So that was good. I was another step closer to my critical competition and I felt like I was still vaguely on track.

Chapter 37

I was looking forward to a day out with Sue at the weekend, without being on the riding side of things myself. The girls from the yard were riding in a team chase. I didn't know what that was until Sue explained. And, now I know, it sounds like complete and utter madness. Four horses all galloping along together, jumping solid fences, and the team with the least faults, that is closest to some unknown optimum time with three horses is the winner!

To get there I borrowed Paul's nice new Audi A4 as my car wouldn't start. He was going to be away overnight. 'Boys' night out', he said.

The team chase competition was at a big estate south of Leeds, called Parkbank Hall. Rumour had it that Big Katie had been 'having relations' with the squire of the hall, having met him out hunting and had, at one point, been seen butt-ass naked climbing out of a first floor bedroom window when his wife arrived home early. I didn't know how true that was but it made for a good story.

I could have gone in the lorry with Sue but decided that if I went in the car I could make a quick getaway. I was looking forward to a bottle of Prosecco and a movie that evening since Paul was away and I had the house to myself.

The last thing I wanted was to be knee-deep in mud and horse crap for no desperate reason.

As I pulled into the Parkbank Estate, my alarm bells should have been ringing loud and clear. I parked up, changed into my wellies and went to find Sue and the team.

Our Meadowgrove Farm Livery Yard team was Big Katie, Sue, Little Katie and Sonia.

They were all tacking up and buzzing with nervous excitement. I helped a bit by holding a couple of the horses. In fact, I felt a little bit a part of the in-crowd and I quite liked it.

At the start line, Sonia actually looked like she might throw up. Her face was sheet white. It made me wonder why people actually put themselves in that position. I mean, if you don't want to do it, just don't! Didn't seem like rocket science to me.

Sue's horse, Robbie, a big ginger (not chestnut!) thing, was bouncing about all over the place like Zebedee on speed. Although it looked like my worst nightmare, Sue seemed to like it and sat with a confident smile. It would likely have seen me flat on the floor, to be honest.

The starter counted down from ten and then they were off. I was now a touch excited for them! As I saw them head off out into the distance and over the first jump, my heart was actually pounding.

There was no shouty-loud-speaker thing to tell me how they were going so I just had to wait. They were out there for about five minutes and then I saw them come back into sight. It was Sue and Little Katie coming first, followed by Big Katie and Sonia behind.

'Poor Sonia had a dreadful round. Two stops on track,' Sue told me as we led Priscilla back to the lorry park. 'When Sonia gets back to the lorry, say something positive to her.'

As Sonia arrived back, I looked at her and smiled supportively. 'At least, it can never be that bad again!'

Sue just rolled her eyes. Maybe that wasn't the kind of positive she meant.

Horses all sorted and the team heading for the beer tent, I said my goodbyes and made my way back to the car. I loved driving Paul's car; it was so big and comfortable – and HEAVY. I turned it on and eased my foot off the clutch but the car went nowhere. I tried again, but it was stuck fast. The more I tried, the further in I was digging the wheels.

Bloody hell!

Why didn't I just leave it on the road? Well, I didn't, so now I had to deal with it. To be fair, lorries were stuck, too. There was a tractor pulling them out. I went to find the tractor driver and he followed me slowly back to Paul's car. He took a look at the car and then at his rather large chain.

'Well, love,' he said in his broad Yorkshire drawl. 'I could pull you out with this,' he held up his heavy chain like a trophy, 'but I suspect I'd pull the front bumper off your car.'

My eyes were wild. Bloody hell!

'Well, what do you suggest? You can't pull the front off the car!' I think, by this point, I was sounding just a touch hysterical and if I wasn't, I should have been, as it's exactly how I was feeling.

It was a Land Rover that eventually came to the rescue and the car was pulled out whilst leaving my, or rather Paul's, front bumper intact. The car, however, was sporting a new mud-styled coating that I knew my brother wouldn't appreciate on his pride-and-joy, so first stop on the way home was the car wash.

I decided I could do with much less exciting days out in future and looked forward to the evening to myself. Well, not counting Portia and Tarquin. A Chinese, a bottle of Prosecco and not a horse in sight. Just perfect!

Chapter 38

Putting the prawn crackers, complete with enclosing plastic bag, in the oven for safe keeping from Portia was maybe not the best idea. How was I to know Paul was going to cook sausages for lunch the next day when he got home? That'll teach him not to check the oven for plastic bags before switching it on!

I planned to quiz Paul about where he'd been the night before, but before I could get the chance he was already on the offensive, putting me on the back foot.

'So, how was your day yesterday?' Paul asked, clearing up the melted plastic from the oven. His eyes were shifty and I was suspicious.

'Good, thank you!' I said.

'No problems or issues, at all?'

'What do you mean?'

'If you want me to narrow it down, I mean with my car? My NEW car?'

'And...' I hesitated. 'What would make you ask that?'

'You washed it! Last time you washed your own car, there was a full moon and an eclipse all at the same time.'

Well, that was indeed a good point. I considered myself well and truly caught out and assumed I'd never again be allowed behind the wheel of his car. I had no choice but to come clean (pardon the pun) but I left out the bit about being dragged out of the mud. Now was not the time to ask outright exactly who he was away with last night. One thing I did know; it wasn't his other half, Mike.

Fillet steak for tea; perhaps that would go some way in making up for my little indiscretion with Paul's car. I took two out of the freezer and left them on the side to thaw whilst I went to the yard.

Today, I was doing some flatwork (get me with my terminology) with Gabby in the outdoor arena. I was even slightly looking forward to it.

Tacked up and ready, Gabby texted me to say she was running five minutes late so I thought I'd just get on and walk around the arena until she arrived. The air was cool and crisp. My phone pinged again, so I dug it out of my pocket to read the text, reins looped loosely over my right arm.

It was Liv sending me inane text chat and it made me smile.

I was feeling a like a bit of a pro. But, a loud bang in the stable block close by soon changed that.

I was told, early doors, when Batman arrived that he was 'bomb-proof'. *That's brilliant*, I'd thought, *if I'm likely to find myself in terrorist country*. I later found out it means he's pretty unflappable in most situations.

Seems no-one actually told Batman this, as whilst he might be completely bomb-proof, he sure as hell isn't loud-bang-behind-him-proof!

In fact, he went from nought to gallop (well, perhaps fast canter) in approximately one-point-two seconds, doing the wall of death around the arena. In rocketing off like that, unfortunately my slouched position whilst messing with my phone saw me pitching backward, nearly falling out the back door, legs (with feet still inside the stirrups) akimbo in the air, arms flailing causing my phone to sail through the air like a little iPhone-shaped missile, embedding itself in the arena. I pulled myself upright (thank God for a fairly firm core), hauled in my reins, and after a good two circuits being totally out of control (me not the horse – he was very much in bloody control), finally ground Batman to a halt.

Gabby would often tell me that I leave my brain at the arena gate when I get on Batman for my lessons. She was probably right. When Gabby flounced into the arena, she took one look at me and asked: 'Did I miss something? You look a touch frazzled.'

'No,' I squeaked with a painted-on smile. 'But, could you maybe pass me my phone, please?' I pointed to the phone in its landing place in the middle of the arena, upended in the sand.

'How did it get there?' she asked. 'On the other hand, let's forget that and just get going.' She picked up my phone and handed it to me. I wedged it firmly into my pocket and growled under my breath at Batman. One of these days this horse might just cut me some slack and give me a chance. How the hell am I ever going to win this damned competition with a horse that continually tries to catch me out?

Today, we worked on going forward and straight. It's more difficult than you might think, I can tell you. Forward was fine and if that was all we needed to worry about, we'd have been top of our one-person-one-horse lesson. Straight was another matter. And to be fair to me, it was Batman that was wobbly, although Gabby told me if I used my legs correctly and rode better he would be much straighter. Sometimes I feel like I'm back in school: 'Fran could try harder.'

Positively knackered when the lesson was over, I was grateful to be home. It felt like it had been a long day. Fillet steak and nice cold glass of Prosecco would be just the ticket!

I opened the door to a pug that I could swear was smiling. I thought it was a nice welcoming touch, that was until I saw the single fillet steak on the worktop where there once was two.

Since Portia was here to stay for a while, I decided that things really were going to have to change in my household. One two-kilogram packet of mince, one loaf of bread, one block of butter, several leftover meats and veg, along with one very expensive fillet steak later, I finally realised she would eat literally anything that wasn't nailed down, frozen or hidden in a cupboard. With a kitchen made out of units with shelves, it was nigh on impossible to stop her from climbing up.

I managed to stretch the remaining fillet steak to double its original size by bashing it with the rolling pin. I cut it in half and hey presto; steak for two again. I was careful to put the two halves of the steak in the fridge to keep safe until I was ready to cook them. Abandoning them for even minute or two whilst I stoked the wood burner would be tantamount to carelessness and an open invite to the naughty pug.

Chapter 39

A morning of mild irritation around my neck confirmed, yet again, my top was the wrong way round! I think I'm going to invent an anyway-round-upside-down-right-way-up kind of garment so I can feel competent in my ability to get dressed every day. I'm also beginning to think I might benefit from a full-time carer as I sure as hell struggle to care correctly for myself.

I'd booked the afternoon off for an extra jumping lesson with Gabby. When I got to the yard, I quickly tacked up and was in the outdoor arena in ample time ready for my lesson. I was there before Gabby which was good. I used the time to walk and trot Batman around the arena. I didn't have any idea what Gabby had in store for me but I knew, whatever it was, it would be stretching me. Every time I turned up to a lesson, I'd look at jumps that were set up and think *yeah, I like the look of those*. But, it didn't matter how big or small (in my opinion) they were, she'd change them and put me completely out of my comfort zone. And so, that came to be what I expected. Today was no different. I knew I was jumping rather than doing flatwork, but that was about it. Gabby seemed to have this knack of putting together exercises for learning to jump that no-one else in their right mind could possibly think of. I guess I should be grateful. This is top-class training. She's a competitor on the way to the top of her sport and I'm lucky (?) enough to have her train me twice a week.

'Skinnies and turns. That's what we're doing today.'

I wished desperately that I was a skinny and, to be fair, I think Batman wished that too (the diet was still not going so well).

Gabby built a very narrow-faced fence in the bottom end of the arena and then another towards the top. If I was to follow the line from the first to the second, it would look a bit like the shape of a banana. Looking at the first fence, the wings looked pretty damn close together. 'Breathe in,' I said quietly to Batman.

'So, Fran, you're going to ride your first skinny jump.'

'Bit like a skinny latte, but not liquid and not coffee?'

'Be serious, will you. You need to keep him straight all the way to the jump. Think of him like a tube of toothpaste and you're using both legs to squeeze him forward.'

To be honest, I thought it was a dreadful analogy. I'm a bit of a literal person, and I've never yet seen a tube of toothpaste the size of Batman and, if I did, the last thing I'd want to do would be to sit on top of it. Squeezing my legs didn't equate to toothpaste to me, but I thought I'd not bother contradicting her.

'So you come round the corner to the fence and you're looking at it – keep your eye on it all the way...' Gabby was now not only walking the line to the fence, she was actually doing this loping kind of lopsided lollop that I think she thought represented a human version of canter. It looked plain stupid to me but this was yet another opinion I kept to myself.

'Keep your leg on and don't assume he's going to take off until he's actually taken off. Don't come too fast, he needs time to look at the jump, think about the jump, then go.'

This was becoming a lot to take in for my tiny brain, and I was beginning to fear it was close to bursting. I did as she said and we approached the fence. All was going well, perhaps a little too well. Our pace was good, not too fast, I was focussed on the jump, my legs were squeezing, as instructed. We even got off the ground heading in the right direction, that is, between the wings, but Batman must have seen some fairies hidden in the jump itself because he felt like he went into orbit, and with him went me. I was catapulted out of the saddle and managed, on my re-entry into the arena's atmosphere, to strike the fence with my boot, snapping one of the (what-really-must-be-way-too) flimsy rails on the surrounding post and rail fencing. Air jacket inflated, I bounced quite nicely and was grateful for such good padding.

'Ooops,' I said.

Gabby just frowned.

'Get back on and do it again,' she said. I assumed she could see I was uninjured.

Back on board, the fairies seemed to have done one and disappeared. Second time round, Batman jumped it less extravagantly and we stayed together. Another couple of times and I was feeling quite confident again.

Confidence I find, when working with horses or, in particular, a horse called Batman, is a very finely balanced commodity. You can have it in abundance one minute and severely depleted the next. Our next task, according to Gabby was to link the two jumps on a nice curving (banana-shaped) line. Fence two turned out to be the problem as Batman got a bit too keen and found he was really quite enjoying himself; a by-product of such

equine enjoyment is often, I'm led to believe, a buck -
and Batman was keen to be part of that club.

When I exited the saddle again, propelled by
Batman's exuberant ways, I managed to hit the
surrounding post and rail fencing with both my arse and
my head at the same time. Impressively, I managed to
break the fence in both places too.

'Will you please stop breaking the arena fence?'
screeched Gabby.

'Well, for God's sake, I'm not doing it just to wind
you up,' I screeched back. She was right though, the
fence was now broken in three places. I wondered
absently if Richard might deduct such fence repairs from
my investment.

The lesson was a difficult one but we did it. I
managed both fences together without falling off and in
such a way that it put a smile on Gabby's face, so I must
have done good. I may yet make an eventer. Rephrase
that – I best make an eventer. I've expended too much
time, pain and effort to get this far and not secure my
investment.

Chapter 40

First stop this morning in the office was the ladies – to turn my jumper the right way out. My underwear, however, could stay inside out as I had no plans for anyone to see it – that's unless Batman later decides to deposit me in a manner that requires some type of medical intervention. This, I certainly wouldn't put past him. I've found he likes to challenge me, particularly at the points in my life when I have the least time available to deal with it. Quick half an hour ride? Batman sees that one coming from a furlong away and uses the time to plan his dissent. It's like he's a finely tuned radio that picks up my brain waves. He just knows when I'm short on time and there seems to be nothing I can do about it. Unfortunately, it only works one way and I have not the faintest damn idea what he's thinking or planning at any single point. Usually the first I become aware is of his plot is when I'm sitting on my arse on the floor, when I'm actually supposed to be in the saddle, hopeful for an early finish.

Hopeful I might have been for an early finish in this training session, fortunate enough to achieve, I was not. One delegate was an older guy who looked prime for retirement and could only be described as a philistine when it came to his computer skills. Not only was he plain bloody useless, he was quite clearly resistant to being shown what to do and must have been forced onto the course by his management. Just what I needed – NOT! It only takes one person to ruin it for everyone. He was clearly going to be that person today.

Once I've introduced myself to the course delegates and regaled them with my extensive educational qualifications, hopefully escalating myself in the I-know-so-much-more-than-you-do stakes, so they don't question my authority during the day (this really works well for when I screw up and tell them something wrong too), I often start a course by telling my new tutees that, whilst within the bounds of my training room, there is no such thing as a daft question. I should have hesitated to put that one out there today because if there was a daft question to be asked, he asked it. It took me half an hour to get into the first topic of the day. He wanted to know if he could keep the notes – yes, I told him. He wanted to know if there would be coffee and lunch provided – no, I told him. He wanted to know if my qualifications were genuine! YES, I told him. He wanted to know if I could make the screen a bit bigger, as he couldn't see it properly. Did he think it would even matter? I mean, I was teaching him basic skills and, at this rate, I'd be teaching them all absolutely sod all as I'd spend all day answering his inane and useless questions. As the day progressed, it was clear he couldn't use the mouse, he couldn't use the keyboard and he was lacking even the most basic of skills, all of which in his humble view appeared to be my fault.

At lunchtime, when I would make the most of half an hour to myself to catch up on some of my own business work, he refused to leave the training room and insisted on talking at me about rubbish I was so not interested in hearing about. This is the type of computer course delegate that nightmares are made of. I made a mental note to be off sick if I ever saw his name on the delegate list of one of my courses in future.

I was finding myself a touch pre-occupied with Paul and the fact that he might like Marcus in a way that he didn't need to be liked. I'd messaged Sue during the day to pick her brains.

'You seen much of Marcus these last couple of weeks?' I asked her.

'Yep, he's been around, why do you ask?'

'I think Paul has a bit of a crush.'

'NO WAY!'

'Yes way, but it can't happen – he's committed to Mike.'

'Fran, you're not his mother. He's a grown man. He can make his own choices.'

'I know that, but if he gets involved and things go wrong...'

'Look, stop worrying. What will be, will be. Try to chill out.'

She was right, although I'm not sure I felt muchos reassured.

I was so grateful to finally sink into my chair at home, completely knackered, that I sat there for a good ten minutes before even getting up to take off my coat. Paul was out and had left a note to say I could eat without him. I searched the pantry for something nice (I'd be lucky), as did Portia – the pantry always being her first stop when the door is open, as she knows that's where the treasure called 'Food' is stored.

Three times this evening, I have had to extricate Paul's pug from the large cat food bag in the pantry. It seems she has now learned how to kamikaze jump, with all four legs at once, and land right in the middle of the biscuits, face first. I'd find it quite amusing (well, if I wasn't quite so tired and could be bothered chasing around a hyperactive pug) but I worry that, since she has an amazing ability to sneak in there behind me when I'm not looking, that I'll shut her in there and one day find her the size of a balloon.

Two glasses of Prosecco later, I was ready for a good night's sleep and another business day ahead.

Chapter 41

I'd been invited round to Liv's, along with others from the yard, for a 'horsey' night. I'd been told that these horsey nights were actually really good fun and often involved muchos alcohol, which suited me down to the ground. I made a small promise to myself that, no matter how many bottles of Prosecco were on offer, I was going to behave and stick to just one. Difficult, I know, but I'm a woman of determination and resolve.

In preparation for going out, I decided cash, phone, one bank card and my house key would be sufficient to take. Any additional baggage, such as a purse or handbag, was liable to be put down somewhere along the line and lost. I had learned this lesson the hard way over a number of years. I put my card and cash inside my phone case. I looked at my key – where best to put it? My pocket came first to mind, but I quickly thought better of that. My jeans pocket was no way secure enough to keep my key safe. With a flash of inspiration, I hooked the metal key ring onto the belt loop at the front of my jeans. That baby was going nowhere. Not without my jeans, anyway!

The invite list, apparently, was quite small, some of whom I knew and some I didn't really. Big and Little Katies, Big Katie's little sister, Cecily, Little Katie's big sister, Meg, Sue, Sonia and me, of course. I was becoming one of the crowd! That, in fact, seemed a good reason for celebrating, so I thought my one bottle might just extend a little bit. I had no work tomorrow and my lesson with Gabby wasn't until ten in the morning.

Cecily was a bit obsessed with her appearance before we went out. After a couple of glasses, I wasn't quite sure why she was complaining about her appearance; from what I'd seen so far, her personality was much worse. I think she might just have slipped into the gene pool when the lifeguard wasn't looking. Shame to say really, because I liked Big Katie. But hey-ho, she was driving us there and that was good.

Liv's house was a small but lovely terraced cottage in a village just outside Leeds. It had a country feel to it and I felt comfortable and at home straight away. There was a picture on the wall of Liv and her other half, or rather ex-other half as it was at the moment.

'He's still gone?' Big Katie asked, Liv.

'Yep. He says that's it. He's not coming back. He's blaming it on all the time I spend with the horse and at the yard but that's just an excuse. I don't spend *that* much time there. To be honest, I'm pretty sure he's been seeing someone else and, to me, that's unforgiveable so I doubt I'd have him back anyway. My four-legged Harry has always been more reliable than my two-legged Mark.'

'The best revenge you can have on a woman that steals your man is to let her keep him. Whoever it was that said "*money can't buy you happiness*", never paid for a divorce!' We all laughed.

'The it's time to move on. We can help you with that,' said Big Katie, pouring Liv a drink.

Liv had put a few nibbles out, and a crisp crumb had got itself stuck beneath my bottom plate so I popped to the loo to rinse it before we headed out. At that point, Mother Nature (or whoever the hell presides over the crap-that-happens-to-Fran area) decided it might be amusing if my whole set of bottom teeth (barring the two remaining real ones) snapped clean in half. I tried my best with the right half (which included my front teeth) Fixodented in, but talking saw them randomly adopting a rhythm of their own that a) I had no control over and b) gave me an inadvertent slur, making it sound like I'd emptied the whole wine rack! I think my next stop will be the emergency dentist in the morning.

Thankfully, armed with a tube of superglue, Sue came to the rescue. After a false start, super-gluing her finger to my front incisor, she managed to glue the stricken plate and I was then sporting a nearly full, if slightly wonky and lumpy set of teeth! We were, however, extremely inebriated by the time we set off which played havoc with our coordination in getting into and, indeed, staying in Cecily's car.

We decided to hit Otley. Apparently Thursday nights there were the night to be out. The Edge Bar was our destination, a downstairs, bit-of-a-dive type club but good for a boogie and a few bevvies. Otley, though, is known to be a bit rough at times.

My alcohol levels were directly proportionate to the extravagance of my dance moves that night – arms flailing wildly to the music, feet and legs just a touch unsteady. Whoever coined the phrase '*it takes two to tango*' obviously hasn't seen me drunk. Unfortunately, I danced (more like fell) into a neighbouring woman who was also busting some moves. Without a breath, she turned round and pushed me. Before I could register it, I was on the floor. I'm not one to give up easily and no way will I be pushed around, so I hauled myself back onto my feet, walked (staggered, in plain language) over to her. It took me a moment to get there, so she was back to her dance moves by that time. I tapped her on the shoulder. I mean, such unsociable behaviour is unacceptable in our modern world, after all. I was entitled to let her know that.

In my head, what I meant to say was: *You shouldn't have done that because I only knocked you by accident.*

No way, though, was my brain working that coherently at that point in the night. What actually came out was: 'Wanna fight?'

It was like my mouth had taken on a will of its own.

To make matters so much worse and to my absolute surprise, she said 'Yes!'

Fortunately, Sonia and Liv were watching carefully as this was unfolding and steamed in, stopping any altercation from happening. They were proving to be good friends; they were looking out for me and I liked that.

The rest of the evening went in much of a blur. The later it got, the more I had drunk and the less I was aware, until I decided enough was enough and headed home. The girls all decided the same. We headed towards the taxi office near the bus station and outside was a driver sitting with his engine running. I tried the door. It was locked. I knocked urgently, he opened it and I climbed in, urging the girls to pile in the back.

'Two stops in Pool then onto Arthington and Bramhope, please,' I slurred.

He looked at me, just a touch shocked.

'I'm just waiting for my wife to pick up fish and chips,' he said. So not a taxi then!

'Pile out girls,' I said and we climbed out.

Sonia shared a proper taxi with me as she lived quite close. That was handy because she was sober enough to find one and tell the taxi driver where I lived.

I woke up with a jolt the next morning when I heard Paul calling my name from the doorway of the lounge. It seemed that I'd managed to fall asleep on the sofa. I moved to get up and assess the world with a hangover-weary head.

Under severe movement restriction, my legs, whilst desperately trying to find purchase, only managed to trip me right up, face-planting me on the carpet. Paul just stood, hands on hips, looking down disapprovingly.

'Too much last night?'

'What on earth gives you that idea?' I croaked, now sporting a 'ladette' tone from too much alcohol, shouting and singing.

'Apart from your pyjama top being on your legs, look at the front door. Problem with your key?'

A memory was vaguely forming in my alcohol-fuddled mind. I was standing at the front door and I tried to get the key ring off my belt loop, which was wishful thinking of the greatest magnitude. My fingers refused to cooperate in any coordinated way and my eyes struggled to focus on anything in particular, never mind just the key ring. Looking down was also having a slightly nauseating effect, so I gave that up as a bad job, looking up and regrouping myself. I then reached down for my key, aiming for the lock, and realised that my five foot two inches wasn't high enough for it to reach the lock while it was attached to my belt loop, even standing on tiptoes.

That's about the point my dim memory gave out. I could remember nothing else in my Prosecco-induced stupor.

Lying there, flat out on the floor, I raised my heavy head and looked out of the room door, along the hallway to the back door and there was the answer: the key in the lock, with my jeans hanging from it.

'You actually must have stripped your jeans off in the street last night to get in. Is there a point in your life that you will actually grow up and behave like an adult?'

To be honest, I wasn't sure there was. I thought I was behaving like an adult – my kind of adult, anyway.

I smiled sweetly at my brother (I think it looked more like a grimace) and let my head fall gently back to its resting place on the carpet. I decided I'd think about moving a little later in the day. My lesson was no way happening today.

Chapter 42

So, working and caring for a horse is proving time consuming and bloody knackering at points. Today, I was due at one of our offices in Durham to deliver a day of training to the staff, although work is now just starting to be an intrusion on the other activities I want to be getting up to. I do, though, mostly like the training delivery part of my work. I get to interact with lots of different types of people. Granted the idiots amongst them drive me up the wall, but it's character building in helping me to learn to keep my cool.

Five am came way too quickly and I struggled to get up. I hit snooze once too often and then found myself like a headless chicken trying to get ready. That manic ten minutes just HAD to include a quick caffeine fix though, so I threw a coffee in my flask cup and had it on-the-move.

Instead of the planned three hours, I now only had two hours and twenty-five minutes to get Batman done, myself changed, drive up to the client and get set up and ready to deliver a day's training. It was pissing down too. Just the added dimension I needed for my already screwed-up day.

I dragged my wellies from the box by the back door, grabbed my suit bag and headed out. I threw my suit bag and laptop in the boot and jumped quickly into the car, trying to avoid getting completely soaked.

I did Batman in record time at the yard, then thought about nipping into the toilet to make myself presentable for work. It takes careful precision to change from yard clothes into a business suit in a draughty, dirty out-house that doubles as a toilet, whilst keeping your suit immaculately clean and free from any hint of a horsey whiff, so I thought better of it and decided to change when I got there.

The drive was slower than I'd have liked, with rain heavy on the A19 northbound. As it cleared, a little later, I took the opportunity presented by the straight road to apply my makeup as I drove, to save a little time. Having been late many times, it's a task I'm quite well practised at and can do much of it without a mirror. Life, however, would have been easier if my black eyeliner had been sharp. Using a pencil sharpener whilst driving at eighty miles per hour up the dual carriageway isn't, I'm sure you'll be glad to hear, one of my incumbent skills. As we know though, creativity and improvisation are indeed well within my expertise. So, glued-in false teeth at the ready, I gnawed the edge of the wood away from the liner, to leave a nice black pencil edge that was now fully functional. Again, liner is something I can do a) one handed and b) without a mirror, so all was good.

I'd hoped that with a quick change and my face already made up in the car, I could trek straight onto the client without delay, but my on-the-move-coffee this morning was now moving once more and seemingly determined to renter the outside world. I was bursting.

I managed to hold tight for the services eight miles up the road and, on pulling in, had to just about abandon the car and walk quickly, if a little squiggly due to the burstingness, for the ladies.

The services had a nice little café area that was filled with truckers and business people alike, enjoying a morning break on their travels. As I opened the door, faces turned. And those faces smiled. If I'd not been in such a rush, I'd have felt much brighter at that. Well they do say that the further north you go, the friendlier people are!

Suitably relieved in the ladies, I washed my hands and, about to leave, looked up briefly at the mirror. The black mess I saw around my mouth and teeth explained the smiles of the café patrons better than the whole north-more-friendly idea!

Not to worry, I wiped it off (it took some doing – have you ever considered just how indelible eyeliner is? I bet you haven't. I sure as hell hadn't). I scuttled back out to my car, my head held low, mouth glaring red from all the rubbing in the hope no-one would notice me, to retrieve my suit to change. Time was not my friend at that point. As it stood, I was going to struggle to make it on time, was likely to leave eight Allpro Power staff waiting for me to grace them with my presence and I'd be starting on a serious back-foot. Not ideal. Could today get any worse? Well, now that was the question and, in my experience, if you ask that question out loud (or, indeed, in your mind) the answer invariably is a big, fat YES! Today, however, I hoped the outcome would be different.

I grabbed my suit bag and headed back into the ladies. I changed quickly, throwing my mucky yard clothes in a pile. When I went to pick up my shoes, I was just ever so slightly confused. They weren't there! They should have been in the bottom of my suit bag. In a panic, I scrunched the empty suit bag into a ball to make absolutely sure that it was indeed empty, and do you know what? It was.

My heart just sank. Having just sorted my blackened face out, I now had to walk through the same café full of business people and truckers in business suit and yard wellies. If ever there was a day that I looked special needs, today was it. I could do nothing other than hold my head high and walk out there like it was a deliberate fashion look.

To be honest, that was the sole focus of my attention at that moment in time – getting from the ladies to the car without looking a complete idiot. It was only once I was back on the road and had taken a huge sigh of relief that my anxiety rose again. I had no shoes!

I parked in the office car park five minutes before the time I was due to start the training session. No time to even think of buying a pair of shoes, never mind actually buy them.

Why the hell didn't I put trousers on? Was my last thought before I opened the reception door and waltzed in to introduce myself. The look on the receptionist's face just said it all.

'I'm here to see Mrs Gray. I'm due to deliver a training session here today.'

'I'll call and let her know you're here. Please take a seat.'

The seat I took was in the busy reception area: a slightly overweight woman, dressed in a really posh skirt suit with a pair of crappy green wellies on, oh, and a laptop bag. I screamed care-in-the-community.

When Mrs Gray finally collected me (in reality it was about two minutes but it felt like two years), we headed to the training room down the corridor. She looked me up and down, almost instinctively. I motioned to my designer but very dirty wellies.

'There's a story here...' I began.

'I'm quite sure there is,' she said with a feigned smile. 'You're in here, today. I'll send the ladies in, in five minutes, if that's OK?' It wasn't really a question.

Lunchtime saw me strolling down the small town high street to the sandwich shop, drawing lots of amused looks.

On the plus side, my feet were well-equipped for when I arrived back at the yard that evening.

Chapter 43

There's actually a name for a dog that eats cat poo and it's called Copraphasia (in fact, it means just eating your own or another's poo – and to be honest, in anything other than dogs and cats, it really doesn't bear thinking about!). So what could be more disgusting than a cat that does explosive diarrhoea, on a regular basis, and a pug that likes to eat it? Well, I'll tell you what can be worse, it's a pug that won't wait until the pungent diarrhoea has landed in the litter tray before she's in there. Tarquin is a cat that doesn't actually like to stand in a litter tray, so he balances on his back tiptoes with his front tiptoes on the box rim. It's actually quite a feat that he can both balance and do his business in that position. When it was just he and I, all was good. So, it was a bit smelly but in the light of recent developments, if smelly was all I had to deal with, I'd take that any day. Little pug-face Portia, however, has now taken to strategically positioning her head beneath Tarquin's backside so she is best placed to receive the smelly awfulness straight from the pump, so to speak. Unfortunately, her positioning is anything but perfect and has seen her now on two occasions come mooching into the lounge with little brown spots on her head. Further examination wasn't really necessary to work out what it was; the smell alone was a dead giveaway. It's funny though, she seems to do this whenever Paul is not around to sort it out. Who has to deal with it? Muggins here. I do like to think that there are other families out there that face similar challenges to mine.

Paul was going to be late home from work so, once I'd cleaned up his dog yet again, I decided on a simple tea of boiled eggs. I just couldn't face much else but I needed to eat something as I planned a wee glass of Prosecco to watch *The Apprentice*. What else could be my favourite programme, after all? I headed into the lounge and fired up my laptop. I wanted to do some brainstorming around a logo design. I had some ideas based around the front-end app but I wanted to have a play with these before taking them forward to a designer. I think that's a bit of the control fanatic in me.

I was deep in thought when I heard an almighty bang. In one fell swoop, I had managed to redecorate the kitchen in a nice shade of hard-boiled egg, with added shell. If I'd tried to get into every nook and cranny I don't think I could have managed it quite as well as I did by simply ignoring the boiling pan. And to boot, I'd ruined my small saucepan too. The time I had saved by not cooking myself the meal I deserved, I had just squandered, and more, in the time it was about to take me to clean this damn mess up.

Half an hour it took. Half a bloody hour. First the dog's head and now the kitchen. I wondered what would be next. Whatever it was, I was sure it had better not involve either poo or boiled eggs. Settling back down to my design, I became completely engrossed. I was just loving this. I could choose the direction I was going in. I could work on what bits of my business I wanted to. I was making the decisions. Whilst I wasn't yet earning out of my business, I knew I was moving towards it. I could have used some of the investment to keep myself, take the plunge and leave my crappy job, but that just didn't feel right. The investment was for the business, I had to be genuinely earning out of that business before I could leave my job. It was coming, though. It felt right and, mad though Richard appeared, I also felt he was a shrewd businessman. I mean, who gets to be that rich without some serious business capability? I for one, was grateful to have that kind of ability in my camp and supporting me. My 'Igniss' app system was on its way to market. I knew it would take time, I mean, I only had the starting part of the investment. The real work to deliver it to the world would come after I secured the rest of the investment but if I could do a lot of the preparatory work now, the stuff that didn't cost too much, I'd be in a strong position to push ahead quickly once I win this infernal competition.

My thoughts drifted to Batman as I played around with colours in my sample designs. I was finding my thoughts straying to Batman more and more as the days and weeks passed. And I'd started to realise that with those thoughts, mostly came smiles. I was finding that not only did I like him, but I was enjoying him being a part of my life and me his. And, do you know what? It had crept up on me unawares. I just didn't see it happening. Is it a good thing? That, I don't know. He's taken my time, he's decked me and I've been hurt, he's looked at me like I'm an idiot sometimes, but then at other times we've achieved stuff together that I didn't think we could – didn't think I could. I've spent time with him in the stable and, for all his bravado, sometimes he's had a look that feels just special – like it's just me and him in the world. Heavens, if I could find a guy that looked at me that way, I'd be laughing – well, that is if I wanted a guy. The only guy I vaguely like looks at me like I'm the village idiot almost every time he comes across me. In reality, in my opinion, men were more hassle than they could be worth, and that was before I had a horse to contend with. With Batman, I seriously didn't have the time, at all. I'd spent my time busying myself with getting on in life, striving for the next step, the next development. My current situation though, made me realised I was starting to really appreciate the here and now, my time developing my business. Yes, the end result of course would be important; the success and the riches, but the journey to get there – well, I was finding some serious enjoyment in that. I was also, and I hated to admit it, finding some serious enjoyment and sense of achievement in my, albeit little, successes with Batman. And those that stood on the sidelines and criticised? Well, they're clearly not doing enough in their own lives to be happy with their own equestrian pursuits. I think it really galled them to see a novice like me really progressing.

In fact, Gabby took me to an event to watch. I was fascinated. It was amazing to see how smart people looked in their tweed jackets and light-coloured breeches. They looked so elegant to me. I watched as they warmed up and Gabby explained what was happening. Some had trainers, some had friends to help and some were working on their own. Any was OK. The thought of working on my own immediately terrified me. I absolutely knew that I wanted Gabby or someone experienced with me at all times! The whole environment was filled with atmosphere. The dressage was set behind the trade stands and the cross-country course was spread over acres and acres of land, but the show jumping was in an enclosed arena (as you would expect) within the bounds of all of the trade stands. I mean, it was really bloody scary. All those people just invited to watch you jump all those BIG fences! It dawned on me that this was my destiny. I had to do this. In front of a crowd (OK, so it might not have been a pop-star-gig-type crowd, but a set of attentive faces it most definitely was). We got a coffee and watched some show jumping. We were stood close to the collecting ring where the competitors were warming up before going into the arena. I heard a woman standing close to us commenting on a competitor who was in the arena.

'She'll be jumped off. Just look at her. The horse is too big for her, look at her position...'

I looked over. She was unconcerned.

'Gabby, did you hear that?'

'Hear what?'

'That woman next to us! She was so critical of the rider in the arena!'

Gabby looked at me like I was an alien.

'Critical? Fran, that's normal. Stand at any event by the show jumping and this is the type of comment you'll hear. Not everyone is like that but some are, so you need to get used to it.'

Get used to it? Bloody hell – the girl in the arena looked to be doing a bloody good job, at least compared with what I could do. I was in awe. It started to sink in just what I was going to be faced with when I got to the point of competing seriously. Given my inability to coordinate myself in everyday life, I don't think I was going to be much of a reference point for future riders at my level. I was here to succeed, quite simply, to succeed.

I had thought that competing on your horse in an event was about how the two of you do together. I had also thought that those around you would be supportive and keen to see you succeed but I think I'm wrong in that. People seem to be keener to see you fall flat on your face. My God, I've never known anything like it. In my world, you support effort and success, you try to boost people up, not pull them down. What is this horse world, where you pull down those around you? How could I succeed in a sport where everyone around me wanted me to fail? I so needed to succeed, my investment rested on it.

I think I shall invent a new club. It will be called the I'm-A-Newbie-To-Riding-(And-Maybe-Also-Eventing)-And-I'm-Doing-Damn-Better-Than-You Club. I'll be the first member and others will be seriously vetted for their attitude towards their fellow riders before they're allowed anywhere near my clubhouse. There will also be a sister-club called the I'm-Actually-Out-There-Doing-It-Whilst-You're-Damn-Well-Not Club. If you don't belong to either of these clubs, then shut THE HELL up, as you don't have the right to say diddly-squat about how I'm riding.

Chapter 44

I was feeling cocky now jumping. Not only was I staying on, but also I was actually feeling like I was close to being in balance with Batman, which was really saying something given my coordination challenges.

I decided I'd pop into the indoor arena, have a little jump on my own and then join the others when they got back from their hack for a cuppa and a chat before going home.

Tacked up, Batman and I headed for the indoor arena. It was empty which was a bonus. Not always the best at keeping out of other people's way, life was much easier on my own. I'd had the pass-left-to-left rule instilled in me but to be honest, that's only useful when you know which is your left! And, as you'll remember, that's just one of the areas in which I'm significantly challenged.

Gabby was pleased with my jumping progress so far. So what harm could a little pop over a little cross on my own do? Well, those are famous last words if ever they were said.

Given my complete incapacity to lift my left leg up further than my thigh, I tootled up the indoor arena to get my little cross ready so that once I was on I didn't have to get off again, at least until I'd finished. Then, off Batman and I headed.

I warmed up quickly – get me, using the terminology. What I did was walk, trot and canter on each rein. I asked Batman if he was ready and, mentally, I assumed he'd said *yes*, so off we went. I picked up canter, put my eyes firmly on the jump as Gabby had instructed me to do every single time. Round the corner we came, I counted down our strides to the fence and three, two, one, we jumped.

I was absolutely thrilled, patting and good-boying Batman like a proper little pony kid. It was never going to last, though, really, was it?

Filled with the enthusiasm and buzz of success, I approached from the other direction. Again, eyes on the jump, round the corner but this time we screwed up. I don't even really know why. The other way we were about at the right place to jump but this time we weren't, resulting in me jumping the fence without Batman. He clearly thought better of the whole too-close-to-the-jump situation. I do wish he'd keep me informed of these executive decisions when he makes them. I'm not a bloody mind reader.

As it was, I managed to twist my ankle, rotate not-quite-so elegantly, like a lumpy sack of potatoes onto my back, at which point I noticed in a fleeting moment that the poles were headed in my direction, well on their way to meet my face. One pole deadened my arm as it fell and the other hit me smack in the mouth making me, of all things, bite my tongue! I immediately tasted the metallic iron of blood.

Now, I consider myself to have a sufficiently high pain threshold. You won't find me bellyaching about a headache or complaining at a minor injury, but by God did that hurt.

I'm sure if that horse could smile, that's just what he was doing right about then as he gazed down at me, reins slumped by his ears.

I've already had it drilled into me that, if you fall off and you're not carted off in an ambulance, you get back on. I decided better of it though. Once on the deck on my own was enough and I could feel my tongue swelling.

There was nothing to do but drag my wounded self and Batman back to the stable block, where I untacked him. He seemed completely unconcerned at the pain he'd caused me. Of course, it was his fault. He was the one that didn't jump the fence. Again, I felt the urge to kick his shin but restrained myself. I really had to be more grown up than him. I was the adult and I should behave as such.

'You're an idiot, horse,' I said to him, but it actually came out a bit more like: 'Oowr agn iyot, owrs,' due to the swelling on my poorly, bitten tongue.

Horse settled, I headed, or rather limped, my way over to the tea room. A quick brew was most definitely needed after my traumatic experience. The room was a flurry of laughter and chatter. All I needed with a sore ankle, a tongue the size of a large haddock and a dead arm dangling.

All the faces looked over as I hobbled in.

'Oh my God, what happened to you?' a voice asked, I wasn't quite sure who.

'Batman stopped at a jump and I fell off,' my brain told my mouth to say. My mouth, however, actually said something a little more like: 'Bvarmah sdubt ad a jzup ahd ah feh orwph.'

The faces looked at each other then back at me.

'She's had a stroke, I think she's actually had a stroke,' said Big Katie.

233

'Look, her whole left side's gone; arm hanging, leg limping and just listen to that speech. I've never heard anything like it.' They spoke as if I wasn't standing there. Big Katie looked at me, eyebrows raised in concern.

'Fran, can you smile?' she asked slowly and deliberately, as if talking to an imbecile (to be honest, that might have been a fair assessment). 'I know you probably don't feel like it but...'

'Ahm fiy' (translated into non-swollen-tongue language, that was, 'I'm fine'). 'Juss bih mah turng.'

'Sue, let's get her to the hospital and quick, before she deteriorates any further. I can't make out a word she's saying. The damage might be irreversible,' said Big Katie.

Things were now getting just a little out of hand and I was starting to get a touch cross at everyone's complete inability to understand a God-damn plain English word I was trying to say.

I grabbed for the arena diary and pen.

'Muh-fuhn iyots,' I muttered to myself.

'Did you just call us mother-fudging idiots?' Sue asked. 'We're only trying to help.' Now she understands me!

I ignored Sue, scribbling quickly on a blank bit of today's diary page then held it up for them all to see.

Fell off and bit my tongue. I'm FINE – no stroke.

'Why didn't you just say so?' asked Big Katie. 'Instead of letting us think you were seriously in trouble.'

That didn't even warrant an answer – even if I could get the words out without them sounding like a drunken special needs case.

I just wanted to get home. I'd lost the desire for my cuppa and chat. The cuppa was just going to hurt like hell to drink and the chat was proving far more painful than any injury from my fall.

A nice, hot bath and some relaxation was what I needed and that was now top of my what-to-do-with-my-evening list.

Prosecco would definitely be in order tonight. I'd stop on my way home but would remember not to try to speak. Just smile sweetly and pay. I mused that a straw might be in order. The way I was feeling, straight out of the bottle would be the optimum consumption method tonight. At least any resultant slurring would be suitably masked by my tongue-related speaking incapacity.

My dead arm was now becoming more alive again, so that was good. I lived in hope that the Prosecco would dull the pain in my mouth and my ankle and that I'd wake up in the morning suitably refreshed and with a tongue that was its original size. Particularly, as I was delivering a training course the next day.

For the moment though, I decided just to put an Out of Order sticker on my forehead and call it a day. On the plus side, at least Gary was spared this particular scene of human incompetence.

Chapter 45

It took me a good week to recover properly from my last fall off Batman. Surely by now, I was considered a good rider with a total of eight involuntary dismounts under my belt. Perhaps now I could just remain in the saddle.

Pairs (not the eating kind)! That was today's riding activity. Sue had persuaded me mid-week, having already schooled cross country, that it would be a super introduction to cross-country competition for me if we did a pairs class at the East Fardon hunter trial, over twenty or so solid obstacles. All we had to do was finish clear, closest to a previously set optimum time and we would win.

Sounded a bit dodgy to me, but then most of these horsey activities sounded dodgy in some way or other, to me. They all seemed to carry some significant risk of falling, being stood on, bitten, head-butted, kicked, barged and I thought that adding another horse and rider into the equation in a competition like this brought the extra risk of crashing. To be fair, I wasn't keen on any of these outcomes but I said yes anyway. There was no getting away from the fact I just had to get out there and get this thing done to secure my funding.

We loaded up in Sue's lorry with Batman and Priscilla and off we set. Sue was her usual excitable self, babbling about all sorts of rubbish. I was just quiet, subdued by nerves for what I was about to do. Schooling seemed so easy compared to this. Practising meant I had Gabby on the ground, helping me, instructing me, telling me what to do, how to ride the fences. But now, I'd be out there on the course, Batman and I, making our own decisions. I wished Gabby were here now to shout at me. I never thought I'd say those words.

Sue would be there, but Batman and I would be following her and Priscilla. They had to navigate their own way round the course with me in tow.

Practically the whole yard was coming to watch too. 'Support' was the word they used. *We'll come and support you in your first hunter trial.* I wasn't convinced. Of course, the Katies and Liv would support, but I wasn't so sure some of the others were just coming to see if I fell flat on my face. I decided early doors that I most definitely wasn't going to do that and that was a decision I intended to stick to.

Sue and I were doing the first class; the smallest, measuring a whole seventy centimetres. It might not sound big but to me they were like Everest when I saw them. As we pulled into the lorry park, I could see the first of the flagged fences. The flags made it seem so real and my stomach lurched.

We got parked up and it was nice to have all the help of our yard cronies to tack up. Liv held Batman for me whilst I headed into the lorry to get ready. I'd been warned by Gabby to wear long sleeves.

'Never go cross country without sleeves on – even if it's hot,' she'd instructed me seriously.

I decided it was good advice given my current balance capacity over a fence. I remember scrubbed elbows hurting as a kid. Added to my long-sleeved top, I then donned my body protector. On top, went my air jacket. To be honest, the amount of kit I was wearing alone would cushion any fall. Last to go on was my number. I was thirteen. Thank God I'm not superstitious.

We warmed up well. Batman and I were ready for this. It was time, so we headed to the start. Sue had a killer look on her face. As a long-standing friend, I knew that was her game face. She was out to win. I, however, was most definitely not. My principal aim was to leave the start, stay on and come through the finish on board my horse. That, in my view, would be a win! But today turned out to be less 'across the country' and more 'embedded in the country' as Batman persuaded me to christen my air jacket in my first cross-country competition! Gravity called and I answered.

We were counted down from ten and then that was it, we were off. My heart was pounding. Sue took the lead as we'd agreed and Batman and I followed. The first fence was a little log and we jumped it well. We jumped the second fence well, too. This was feeling easy. I relaxed a little. As we galloped onto fence three, which was a rail in a hedge line, I noticed a group from our yard standing close to the track we were approaching on. They were shouting, 'Go Fran!'

It was Bridgett with some of the girls I saw in passing from the other stable block, and...was that Gary? It was indeed. He was here to watch me ride, too. I was touched. I put my reins in one hand and waved to them, shouting so they could hear me: 'Hi there!'

In reality, my attention would have been better placed directly on the rapidly approaching jump and, had it been in that more appropriate direction, I might have been kicking Batman to jump it instead of flapping my waving hand at the bunch from the yard and socialising on-the-move. In that case, I might not have somersaulted over the fence whilst Batman remained on the take-off side, having not, in fact, taken off at all.

The bang that accompanied my short unaided flight was followed by that familiar almighty crushing sensation just before my unceremonious impact on the ground. That was the air jacket going off. You might think that such a loud crack would scare the bejesus out of any normal horse, but Batman was unconcerned. In fact, Batman stood looking over the fence. I'd swear there was a grin on his long face, but I'm sure that's not physically possible.

Bridgett and her cronies were now in raptures of laughter. I could swear they distracted me deliberately. I absently made a little mental note to wreak some revenge in the near future, and it would be focussed specifically on Bridgett. In simple terms, I'd decided all by myself that I didn't like her at all. Gary just stood, a blank expression on his face. There I go again, making an impression. Of course, not that I'm interested at all, and perhaps I'm just trying to make myself feel a little better, but maybe these impressions are at least getting a touch healthier each time?

Sue pulled up and came back to sort me out, which was much needed as at that point I was lying on my back like a cast turtle; legs and arms flailing, with an air jacket that had all but immobilised me. The judge, who was manning the fence, launched herself from her camp chair, practically throwing her polystyrene cup of tea through the air and came rushing.

'I can't move,' I said, wiggling my legs, adding to the stuck turtle look. 'Help me get up.'

'Oh my God,' said the fence judge, mistaking my 'can't-move' for 'really can't move'.

'No! Don't move,' she screeched. Then into her radio: 'We need an ambulance – she needs immobilising.'

'Screw that,' I said, and rolled myself over onto all fours. By now the jacket was starting to deflate and I could breathe again. 'Look, I'm all good,' I told the overeager fence judge.

Back on my feet, I dusted myself down and climbed back over the fence to the take-off side. I used the fence to re-mount Batman and set off back to approach the fence again.

With the approach still lined with Bridgett and her buddies (and Gary in the background), I was determined to get over the fence, this time with Batman. I did. It wasn't a pretty sight. We got very close to the fence. Batman did a jump that Gabby calls a cat leap which saw my backside flying well out of the saddle but I landed on the other side still on top of my horse so that was good.

Said distance of my backside from the saddle would be likely to invoke one of Gabby's favourite sayings: 'Shall we paste some jam on your saddle and invite your backside to tea?' – In other words – get your ARSE in the saddle!

Onward we went. My initial optimism over the first two fences had quickly faded into please-God-let-me-get-to-the-end-in-one-piece-ism.

I learned a few new things today. One is that there is a jump called a coffin. Its name is quite descriptive, basically a long dark, ditch between two fences. Liv told me later, as they were watching us motor round the course again, one moment I was there, following Sue and the next, they were all like, 'Where's Fran?'

Then, Liv shouted: 'There she is. She's in the coffin!'

And so I was. I hadn't even seen it coming. Batman, on the other hand clearly had seen it coming, the ditch that is, and he didn't like what he saw one little bit. So much so, he slammed the brakes on (brakes I'd have been grateful to have had just a few fences ago). The result was, yet again, I flew over his head, landing perfectly laid out in the coffin ditch. In fact, I couldn't have done it better if I'd tried.

Batman stood there, reins round his neck, looking down at me. After a moment's respite in my new-found resting place, I hauled my ass out of there, which wasn't so easy given the coffin ditch wasn't actually that wide and my body weight had managed to wedge me and my rather bulky body protector within its confines. Always the optimist though, I quickly realised it could have been much worse. As my air jacket had already popped its canister, that was one less coffin-padding layer I had to worry about.

Back on my feet, I got back on Batman. Sue had waited for me.

'You OK?' she called.

'Yep, just coming,' I shouted back, far more cheerfully than I felt.

Two uneventful fences later, I rode through my first cross-country finish line. And even though I'd hit the deck twice, it felt like an achievement. When you think about it, two falls in one day would be considered impressive in spheres! From the amused look on my peers' faces when I got back to the lorry, I didn't think that this was that sphere. I decided I might become superstitious.

The second thing I learned was that a substance called Vet Wrap is incredibly useful. My second fall, saw me earn myself a nice little cut on my arm. So much for the long sleeves; my top was ruined. My adrenalin was so high though, that I didn't even notice until I was back at the lorry. Liv took Batman, Sonia took Priscilla and the Katie's set to work getting them untacked, washed off and rugged. Sue dragged out her first aid kit – her horse first aid kit – cleaned my cut off with a rather syrupy-looking red liquid, slapped on a dollop of cotton wool and wrapped it up with a bright pink strangely unsticky, yet actually very sticky, crepe bandage.

Sonia fussed around me, making sure I was OK.

'You'll be good as new now. Vet Wrap is almost as useful as bale twine!' she told me.

I've yet to find any use for bale twine, other than to hold bales of hay together and Richard's breeches up covering my arse, but hey, I guess the way my life is headed at this point in time, that will be coming my way soon too.

My next stop was the burger van: a fried egg butty, as was becoming usual for me, and a tea without the tea bag. I saw some pretty good-looking almond slices and asked for one of those too. When it came, I proceeded to pick off all of the almonds and Big Katie watched me with interest.

'So, you have eggs without the soft yolk, you have the tea without the tea and now you have the almond slice without the almond. Is there anything you have in its original form?'

I'd not thought of it that way before. I guess I really am quite fussy. I might be persuaded to have Gary in his original form, that is a) if I was at all interested in having a man and b) I could stop looking a complete muppet in front of him!

On the basis of my performance today, I think I am going to redefine success – it's now 'going from failure to failure without losing enthusiasm.'

Chapter 46

My two falls in the pairs competition resulted in a nice bit of whiplash to finish off the longest day ever. Thanks Batman, I'm sure I can do without turning my head to the left for a few days. I was surprisingly shattered when I got home. It was seven in the evening and I was aching too. The air jacket did its job for the first fall and protected me well, but that was it, canister blown. When I fell off the second time, I was left to bounce on my own and, at my age, bouncing wasn't the best idea for my poor bones.

I decided on a bath, glass of medicinal Prosecco and then an early night. Tomorrow, Batman would have the day off. Gabby informed me, reliably, that the horse deserved a day off after a competition. I wasn't complaining. A day off for him meant a day off for me, well, from the riding at least. I'd still have to muck out, do nets, blah, blah, in the morning, but Sue had agreed to bring Batman in from the field and put him to bed so I could crack on with work.

My bath was heaven. Super hot and bursting with bubbles, it was like nectar to my aching muscles. Batman had a lot to answer for and here he was getting a bloody day off for his troubles! It seemed completely wrong but, like I say, I was keen for a day off.

Out of the bath, I dried and dressed in my warm 'jamas, comfortable again. I went to drain the bath and decided just to leave it. With no chain on the plug, I'd have to reach in - it could wait until tomorrow. Prosecco called and wanted some chocolate to keep it company. Perfect evening.

I don't really understand why people have to 'get ready' for bed. I'm always ready for bed.

I used the remainder of my evening to build the social media side of my marketing plan. I was flying now. My adrenalin was running once again, but for a very different reason than this morning. Building my business gave me such a high. The thought of being rich, not just rich but REALLY rich was even more of a buzz. I could certainly do without the added bodily trauma along the way but it would be worth it. I just needed to keep my eye on the fifty-thousand-pound prize that was still to come my way.

Paul came in to see if I wanted a brew. He found me with glass in one hand, laptop on my little table and chocolate all eaten. He correctly pointed out to me, as he watched me picking a brown splat off my laptop table and sucking it off the end of my finger, that not every brown spot was necessarily chocolate! I think I'll bear that in mind in future, especially given Tarquin's propensity for creativity with his toilet locations. I think I shall also make a second challenge for myself that at the same time as securing the remainder of my investment, I'm going to educate my wayward, special needs cat that there are only two places in the whole world that he is allowed to poo: in his litter box and out-bloody-side. I think this might be an even more difficult challenge than the one set by Richard.

'Can I ask, all these evenings you've been out, have you been seeing Marcus?'

'It's just been a couple of drinks as friends. Nothing more, I promise.' He looked sheepish.

'Is it any wonder that Mike has his suspicions?'

'As it's his choice for me to be here and not at home with him, I'm not sure you can take the high ground over this. Marcus is good fun. I like his company but nothing has happened. I promise.'

I believed him. My worry was how long that would last for.

When I finally hit the sack, I was wiped out. My muscles were aching, even post-bath, head was just a little fuzzed from a glass (and it was only one) of Prosecco and my brain was bursting with thoughts of moving my business forward and also what to do about my brother's preoccupation with my investor's groom. Sleep was, thankfully, quick in coming.

The almighty screech I heard in the night woke me clean up and scared the bejesus out of me. I jumped straight out of bed and headed out into the hallway to see what the cause was. I had visions of Portia having trapped herself somewhere or the cat clawing at her puggy-buggy eyes. It dawned on me, as I saw Tarquin streak across the landing looking a touch more like a sewer rat than a nice fluffy Scottish Fold cat. It seemed he'd found out the hard way that his occasional sleeping place, in other words the bath, was otherwise occupied with my leftover bath water.

Panic over, well, for me at least, not for Tarquin, I headed back for the rest of my beauty sleep. Tomorrow was another day.

Chapter 47

Tarquin scowled at me this morning but at least he'd dried out. I gave him an extra half of a handful of his favourite biscuits for breakfast as a peace offering. Portia wanted to join in too.

Today, I had a bit of a shock. One minute, you think you're all hunky-dory with the world, or rather the world is hunky-dory with you, and the next, you find out there are people gunning for your blood. In reality, it wouldn't be so bad if they were up front about it. It seems I'm learning the quick way that the horsey world can in fact be quite a bitchy one, with people out for themselves and who just want to see others fail. Now, is that a sad state of affairs or what?

So there was me, with the upset stomach from hell. It was killing me and saw me spending more than my fair share of the morning in the privy at the yard. With explosions threatening through each wave of cramp, I was doing my best not to share the associated sound effects with the rest of the yard – more for my benefit than theirs, to be precise. The fact was I was doing a good job of being quiet and, if I could get off there for long enough, I planned to just go straight home. For now, however, I was stuck where I was. That was when I heard people come into the tearoom and a conversation pick up.

The voices were quite clear. It was Sonia and Bridgett, of all people, given that Sonia had professed on many occasions her definite dislike of the latter.

'How she can be so arrogant as to think she's got half a chance, I don't know,' said Sonia. 'Never ridden, knows sod all and thinks she can compete and ride better than the rest of us!'

It sounded, from my vantage position, more like a rant than an actual question.

'Have you seen her jump? It's dreadful. No balance at all.' Bridgett had now taken her place and strapped her seatbelt on the bandwagon.

'Taking advantage of Richard's good nature. I mean, what was he thinking anyway, taking her onto the yard? She's clearly just after his money,' added Sonia, with what sounded like real venom, immediately characteristic of plain and simple jealousy.

That was the first correct thing she'd said. I was very definitely after his money. But the rest of it? I couldn't believe what I was hearing. With that sort of cut-throat attitude, I think she'll go far in life and the sooner she starts going somewhere, the better.

I'm not sure who must've pissed in her Weetabix this morning but my earlier plan for revenge was now widening from just Bridgett to include Sonia. I guess, if we're honest, we all have that special someone we'd pay a personal visit to if given a tank to drive for a day.

At that point, an almighty cramp struck and what happened next was a noisy version of cramp minus the 'm'.

The voices stopped immediately on hearing the noise from the toilet, hushed voices followed and then footsteps quickly left the tearoom.

Perhaps they thought they'd not been heard. They certainly didn't know it was me in there. I decided it was best that way; I felt I had the upper hand and I intended to keep it.

I chose though, not to be downhearted by what I'd heard. The Romans didn't create a great Empire by letting others get them down; they did it by killing all those who opposed them. Bit extreme in my case? Answers to planetfran@gmail.com, please. I'll take them under consideration.

I waited a few minutes before hauling myself out of the toilet and back out onto the yard. When I saw Sonia emerge from the stable block out on the yard, she smiled and waved at me. I wanted to give her a nasty look but she already had one: two-faced summed her up nicely and neither of them were pretty. But, not to be put down by petty jealousy, my brain was already working on a creative comeback. I wouldn't rush this though. I'd let it marinade a little before formulating my plan.

In all honesty, I didn't care about Bridgett. Like I said, she was openly scathing about me and my riding attempts. I can live with that type of up-front conflict. What I can't live with is someone pretending to like me, pretending to help me and be my friend, when all the while they're stabbing me in the back and actually wanting me to fail. It was a mentality I just couldn't relate to at all.

To be fair, I don't know what makes Sonia so stupid, but whatever it is, it really works.

Chapter 48

As it was Monday, the yard was really quiet, with most people at work or otherwise engaged with normal weekday living. I liked it this quiet. And it was today that the opportunity for my revenge on Sonia just accidentally dropped right into my lap. My mind had been working hard on some pretty elaborate ideas but this one was to prove so purely brilliant, I couldn't help but chuckle to myself at the simple genius. Don't get me wrong, when I say revenge I just really wanted to get my own back on her for being such a two-faced, hard-nosed, thoughtless bitch, nothing really nasty or anything like that. That's definitely not my style. I like to wreak a type of revenge that's a bit higher class, if you know what I mean – something with a bit more intelligence behind it.

There were workmen around, up ladders, attaching things to walls in each of the blocks. I guessed this was the installation of the new CCTV system that had been threatened over the last few weeks. In honesty, I was grateful for the added security, particularly being a novice equestrian, often finding myself in the stable block on my own. I wasn't so sure some of the others would want the intrusion.

Richard came into the tearoom with Bridgett as I was eating my lunch. He was here in his capacity as owner of all things yard based, rather than as a rider or my investor.

'The cameras are all installed. As it's quiet, we'll be running some tests throughout the day but they won't go live until next week. I'll put a notice out to everyone when they go live but, if you see anyone in the meantime this afternoon, would you make them aware that we're testing the cameras today. Best behaviours all round!'

I smiled. I'd certainly be on my best behaviour. I wasn't quite so sure about others though.

It was about two pm when Sonia arrived in the block. I was humming away to myself, with my earphones in as I brushed Batman's thick tail. She shouted 'Hi' to me. That's when it struck me. My plan then took form in my mind within about thirty seconds and a grin widened on my face. I made sure I reduced it back to a welcoming smile before I turned to face her.

'Hi there.' I sounded cheerful. 'What are you doing here? No work today?'

'Been to the dentist – just a check-up, and I have somewhere to be at four, so I thought I'd skive off for the rest of the day and come up and ride quickly.'

'Good idea,' I said. 'Fancy a hack?'

'Sounds good. We'll go the quick loop if that's OK so I can get off for my appointment?'

That was just fine by me.

As predicted, Sonia tacked up, had her usual wee in her stable, and off we headed.

The hack was lovely. Batman was very well behaved. I like him very much when he's not being an arse. Sonia and I chatted like the oldest of friends.

She told me how proud she was of what I was doing, learning to ride like this in such a short space of time. She told me how I should be so pleased with myself being able to jump like I can. What liar she was.

I told her I was very grateful to have such a good group of friends to support me, including her. Now I was the liar.

Back at the yard, Sonia was untacked and heading off in her car before I'd even finished sorting Batman. I headed off to the tearoom and sure enough, about ten minutes later as I sat sipping a piping mug of tea, in came Richard, piece of paper flapping in his hand.

'Is Sonia around?' he asked me.

'Just left,' I said. 'Why, is there a problem?'

'Did you tell her about the camera test we're doing?'

I put on my best oh-hell-I-forgot face.

'Oh, bloody hell, I forgot! Really sorry. Why?'

Richard wafted the paper in my face. He was clearly cross. There, in all her glory, was Sonia, squatted, breeches and pants round her ankles and ample (and might I add, not too photogenic) arse on view for the camera.

'I wouldn't mind this behaviour if we didn't provide adequate toilet facilities, but we do. She's a grown woman for Christ's sake!'

He slammed the picture down on the table and left.

I took the picture and stuck it up on the wall. I couldn't wait to hear about Sonia's reaction to it. It would be perfect if I could be there, but that wasn't essential. With that, I went to finish Batman off for the day and left the yard feeling very, very happy with myself.

Now that I'd gotten my own back, I could forgive Sonia, after all, what better way would there be to pee her off?

Chapter 49

Today was to be my last lesson with Gabby before my first British Eventing competition. Although I didn't need to win this one, it was still a real deal and was my opportunity to get a feel for what the main competition was going to be like. I was getting close to make or break, as they say. To be fair, I had nearly broken, literally, many times in the last few months. It had been hard going, but I was here and still in with a shout.

As I was a bit early, I headed to the tearoom, which was full of chattering and laughter. I was delighted to see Sonia's picture still posted on the wall providing much amusement, and further delighted to see her walk in. She didn't notice it at first but, when she did, she erupted. It was all I could do not to laugh.

'WHAT THE HELL?' She tore down the unflattering photo.

'Ah Sonia, I'm so sorry, I forgot to tell you about the camera tests they were doing,' I said in my best apologetic voice. She looked at me, eyes wide.

'You stupid cow!' she said with venom.

'Hey, that's a bit harsh,' said Big Katie. 'Fran wasn't the one that got your arse out for the camera. You did that all by yourself!'

'You did that deliberately!' she hissed at me.

'And, Sonia, why on God's green earth would I want to do that to a friend?'

'You just wanted to make me look stupid. I know you did that deliberately. You come in here, think you can ride and compete after five minutes, think you can get on Richard's good side. Swanning around in your swish gear thinking you're better than the rest of us.' The tearoom bustle had died completely and everyone was silent, aghast. I suspected this was a side to Sonia that they hadn't seen, judging from the looks on their faces.

'I think you tar me with your own brush, perhaps. Not everyone thinks like you do.'

She looked around at the expressions watching her and seemed to realise just what she'd said. She turned and left, saying nothing else.

'Bloody hell!' said Liv. 'She's got issues! I think we might be giving her a bit of a wider berth in future. Fran, you know none of us think like that. You've done so well and we're right behind you.'

I smiled. It was good to hear, but I hadn't doubted it.

'Thanks, guys.'

My lesson went well. No dramas, no fall-outs with Batman, no falling off. I felt ready.

Chapter 50

The time had come for me to venture out for my first British Eventing competition. Though competing in the smallest class, it was, to say the least, quite nerve-racking. Marcus was dispatched to 'groom' for me, putting studs in the horse's feet, so I didn't fall completely on my arse, brushing him to look beautiful, tacking him up and getting me on in time for each phase of the competition.

Richard had sent him to help me and, by God, that's just what he did. I don't think I've ever been so grateful in my life. I put all thoughts of Marcus and Paul out of mind; that was a problem for another day.

By dressage time, Marcus had groomed, tacked and even put some hairy drawings of diamonds on Batman's backside to make him look extra special. He'd sent me into the lorry to put on my kit; buff breeches, white shirt, tweed jacket and stock. So, I stopped short of the stock. Everything else I could cope with, but the stock? Consider this: one long bit of material, with a few curves along the way, plus a randomly placed hole, and you have to make it look like a twisted knot in a way that is actually not really possible without a degree in origami. I tried a few times but, as the minutes were running out for me to get on, I went to Marcus and had to ask him to tie it for me.

He did, and expertly.

It was time to get on. He gave me a 'leg up' but, in Marcus's case, it was very nearly a 'leg right over the other side', he threw me up that strongly. Fortunately, I gathered myself and managed to stay on board.

In the dressage warmup, Batman and I worked well. Marcus gave me some hints, like 'put your mobile phone away and concentrate on riding' and 'make sure you know your dressage test' (which saw my phone coming back out to check out the BE Dressage Tests app, that I'd found invaluable, so far). The steward who was looking after my section, was shouting numbers.

'Two, six, three. TWO, SIX, THREE!'

'That's you,' said Marcus. 'You ready?'

God, was I ready? Actually, now I wasn't so sure. My mind immediately went to my test again.

Down the centre line, track...oh hell, which way do I turn when I get to C? Is it left or right? My brain decided to give me a bit of a break and kicked itself into gear. *It's right*, I told myself, more confidently than I actually felt.

Once in the arena, I seemed to relax and that rubbed off onto Batman. My view was, we're here now, give it our best shot and if it goes wrong, then I'll become a waitress or I'll stick with my training job or something useful. It won't be the end of the world – just the end of the world-touring super yacht, for me.

In fact, the test was quite pleasing, evidenced by Marcus's grin and thumbs up as I left the arena. Unfortunately, that's about where the pleasingness (yes, this is my own made up word) ended for the dressage. Batman saw fairies or elves or some other mythical and entirely invisible creatures, to which he reacted what can only be described as extremely badly.

In one swift move, he leapt what felt like five foot in the air, twisted his body in a move that Rudolph Nureyev would have been proud of and deposited me on the grass. Why is it, when you fall off, the law of sod sees that you land on the site of your most recent injury? I was, to say the least, just ever so slightly, completely out of my mind with rage. Batman must have seen this in my contorted face, because he didn't hang around long enough to see what my reaction was going to be. Turning on his heels, with his reins flapping round his ears and his eyes wide, he pissed off with Marcus quickly in tow, abandoning me.

I picked myself up, dusted myself off, smiled at the now watching audience to show I was OK and headed back to the lorry park. If there were a chimney on top of my head, there would have been a plume of steam flowing into the atmosphere from my boiling temper.

Back at the lorry, Marcus was waiting for me.

'Is Batman OK?' I asked.

'Yep, he's back on board the horsebox, none the worse for his little jaunt around the park.'

'Good, because I'm going to bloody kill him.'

Marcus headed me off from climbing the lorry ramp and kicking the bloody creature in the shins and, instead, suggested we have a quick coffee before walking the cross-country course.

I'd calmed down by the time we got back from the cross country. I even went up the ramp and gave Batman a pat. I guess I was now thinking about the show jumping and didn't want to piss him off so close to what could soon become another disaster! Was this not all that was needed to fuel the self-righteousness of Sonia and Bridgett. They just wanted to see me flat on my face. It didn't help that my horse also seemed to have the same desire in life today.

So, ten minutes later, I was tacked and on my way to the show jumping. The collecting ring was quite busy. In fact, it looked like unorganised mayhem. Just what I needed with Batman in his current I-don't-like-the-whole-world mood.

He did warm up OK though. He seemed to be 'listening' to me. He took exception to a hairy pony that was coming towards us at one point, trying to turn round and run the other way, but apart from that, there was no indication he was up to any other mischief, which was a relief for me. I do sometimes wonder what on earth goes around in his head. He is a law unto himself and doesn't seem to follow any type of logical thought processes unless, of course, it involves his dinner, hay or treats, then the logic is quite simply get it and eat it as quickly as possible.

Our turn to jump came round soon enough. Marcus patted Batman on the butt and wished us good luck.

'Kick on,' he said. This seemed to be a favourite sentiment amongst the horsey community whenever you were about to do anything competitive.

I went into the show jumping arena. Faces seemed to be everywhere around the arena, all looking, judging. I tried to zone them out. They weren't in here doing this, I told myself; I was. I bet half of them wouldn't even dare get on a horse never mind jump it round an eighty-centimetre course, so why was I worried?

Truth is, I was worried, not because of them – they were just an excuse. I was worried because there were damn big jumps in there that I had to get my horse around and the result really mattered to me.

I've heard it said recently that a horse's behaviour, or rather its bad behaviour, will be directly proportionate to the number of people who are watching. Well, I can tell you, there were a hell of a lot of people watching at this point in time.

It all started so well. I got into the arena. Batman and I cantered round and the bell went - my signal that I had forty-five seconds to go through the start markers and jump the first fence. We approached the first fence. He was keen and, to be bloody honest, I was keen too. We jumped it and then it all just went quite significantly wrong! Whilst I thought I was steering us to fence two, Batman clearly thought otherwise, and immediately took hold of the bit in his mouth (which basically meant I had no damn brakes whatsoever) and decided to career at, what felt like, five hundred miles an hour around the outside of the show jumping arena.

Now, when things completely screw up in the show jumping arena, the thing to do is to retire gracefully. How do we do this? Well, I've been instructed expertly in my crash course for riding. If things screw up big time, put your hand in the air (doesn't actually matter which one) and this signals to the judge that you've had enough and will be taking no further part in the competition. It all sounds so simple, doesn't it?

During mine and Batman's five-hundred-mile-an-hour wall-of-death type demonstration of ourselves, I didn't actually feel comfortable letting go of any single part of my reins and, as such, found myself screeching at the top of my voice:

'I CAN'T TAKE MY HANDS OFF THE REINS LONG ENOUGH TO RAISE MY HAND BUT I AM ACTUALLY TRYING TO RETIRE!'

The judge, perhaps old and deaf, said over the shouty-loud-thing, 'That's a run-out for Fran and Blue Eyed Batman.'

I thought, *a bloody run-out*? *That's more of a complete royal bloody fly-past the whole damn course* (I was a touch neurotic by that point, hence the greater-than-normal volume of expletives). But, of course, I was dumbstruck now with fear as we tear-arsed round and round and round the arena.

'AND, I think that's going to be compulsory elimination for exceeding the time allowed,' called the judge. 'Sorry, Fran, that means no cross-country today for you.'

The steward opened the rope to the collecting ring and I steered Batman out. Marcus caught him on the way out, pulling him to an abrupt halt. There by the edge of the arena Gary was watching, his expression blank. Maybe I should just ask him out on a date and get it over with – go for dinner, be the completely useless individual that I am and just get him out of my system. I'd take that under further consideration.

Right now, all I could manage at that point was a slightly weak, 'Stupid idiot horse!'

Not only was he just a git and had just ruined any chance I had of actually contending in our first eventing competition, but he was seriously putting in jeopardy, the remainder of my business investment. The twenty-five thousand pounds I already had was amazing but, in reality, it simply wasn't enough. I NEEDED the other fifty.

It was time to rethink. I had to get on top of this situation. This damn horse was going to destroy everything for me. Stupid four-legged idiot, which it was. No matter what I did, for a while I'd feel in control and then BAM, the horse would just screw it all right up by doing something unpredictable. It was time now for me to take control; not just think I was in control but *really* take control. This four-legged overgrown dog was not going to win! I'm the one with the IQ of a hundred and sixty. I'm pretty sure he has an IQ similar to that of Dory the fish: I'm never eating carrots again...oh there's carrots! Perhaps more like: I'm never decking Fran again, oh, there's Fran on the deck!

I refused to speak to Batman once he was untacked, washed, rugged and finally on the lorry with a haynet.

Christ, if I'd screwed up that badly at work, I would simply have been fired. No kind person would have gently taken off my outer wear, bathed me personally, re-clothed me, put me to bed and then fed me, all for being an utter git! But, hey, I guess I'm not a damn event horse!

Chapter 51

My meeting with the first set of developers was set for ten in the morning. I was excited, to say the least. I'd done the mathematical algorithms to support the development of the software interface. Whilst developers are good at the logic of putting programs together, they don't always have the mathematical expertise to translate the complex learning formulae into computer instructions, so I thought I'd do it for them. I know, it's a contradiction in terms that I can do this complex stuff yet I can't put my pants on the right way round or boil an egg without decorating the kitchen in a nice shade of albumen with yolk; but life is full of paradoxes, as they say. I guess I'm one of them.

Armed with my laptop, I decided to set off in plenty of time so I wouldn't be late for the meeting. I arrived quite early – a whole week to be precise.

'I'm here for the meeting with Dr Andy Burns and his team at ten am in the conference room,' I told the receptionist.

'Really?' she asked me, frowning, scanning her computer screen.

'Yes, ten this morning.' I pulled my phone out and went straight to my calendar. That usual déjà vu feeling was settling on me like a pair of old and comfortable slippers as I opened today's date and found no appointment in there.

The reception started to fill up, as is typical when I screw up.

'Ah,' she said, eventually, with a smile. 'I see your mistake. You got the time right but the meeting is next week!' Her voice was that touch louder than it actually needed to be for me to hear her adequately. The result was that the rest of reception could also hear and consequently heads turned to look.

One day I will solve all my screw-ups with grace and maturity. Today was not that day.

'Well, it's here in my diary,' I said, in the same touch-too-loud voice she had used. 'There must have been a mix-up somewhere.' I was just keen on getting out of there without looking like the complete ass that I am! But, Miss-Bloody-Jobs-Worth-Receptionist clearly knew what I was doing.

'Oh, that's unusual, let me have a look.' She reached over the reception desk for me to hand her my phone.

'That won't be necessary,' I said, just a little more indignant than I intended, so added a wide cheesy smile to compensate. 'I'll see you next week.' At that, I turned and left quickly.

Perhaps it was meant to be. Reverting to a Plan B I didn't realise I even had, I decided to head straight to the stables and see Batman. At least he'd be happy to see me. Especially if I came complete with a pack of extra strong mints – they were just his absolute favourites. I guess they were to him, what Prosecco to me.

Chapter 52

As they say, there's no respite for the wicked and I must be particularly bloody bad. Gabby had already entered me into my next practise event. No point procrastinating about it, she told me. *Crack on whilst it's all fresh in your mind*, she insisted. What was fresh in my mind was the complete debacle that it was and the total screw up Batman and I made of it. I was neither inspired nor confident that I could make much of a better job next time.

Fear not, she told me. I had a week to prepare and she would be there to help and give me extra coaching. She was also planning to be at the event anyway, so would help me to warm up for each of the phases. I found that strangely comforting.

The week went way too quickly and the event was here. Gabby's help did make a difference though. She knows me so well now and helped keep me calm and helped keep me thinking!

Dressage was much better than the last time and, indeed, I successfully made it back to the lorry without falling off. The fairies must have decided to give this event a miss. My show jumping round was OK. Not the prettiest maybe, but I started, I finished and had only two fences down, so that was a proper result in my book. Just cross country to go and I'd have completed my first event.

So I saw a long stride into fence twelve. Unfortunately, Batman didn't see the same long stride. He saw an extra stride in there and took the executive decision, without notifying me in advance (as he so often does), that he was going to *stuff one in*, as they say. The result was that I jumped the fence without him. As we know, the bang of my air jacket inflating might scare a normal horse, but not Batman. In fact, he's positively used to it by now. I lay there on my back, held fast again by the inflated air jacket. This turtle-like position was becoming a bit of a habit - one that I was really keen to break. Batman stood there, reins around his neck, watching the floorshow from a safe distance. The fence judges ran over as I dusted myself off.

I wasn't ready to give up yet. First time out I'd only managed to make the show jumping and here I was now, on the cross country with only eight fences to go to complete my first entire event. It was within my grasp and I found that I really wanted to complete this competition.

'Give me my horse, I'm carrying on,' I said defiantly. At that moment, attention moved from me to Batman and we all turned to look at him as he stood patiently. There was just a fleeting instant as we all realised no-one actually had hold of him, but unfortunately that included Batman himself! His eyes widened in mischief, at which point he turned and just pissed right off, head high in the air. I watched him career off into the distance round the course, leaving me for dust.

An announcement soon came over the tannoy system notifying all that there was a loose horse on the course and that Fran McBride had been unseated. Unseated? More like unceremoniously dumped. It wasn't a big ask of him to jump the fence at the same time as me. I could see some commotion going on down in the far side of the course in the wooded area. Someone closed the gates and it looked like Batman was cornered in there with no route for escape. Batman, however, didn't like being cornered and found his jumping feet again because next I heard was the tannoy man asking for an event representative to hotfoot it up the road and catch the loose horse that had just jumped out of the event, over a hedge/barbed wire/ditch combination (which he jumped very well according to witnesses, I was later told). He was caught moseying down the A515 heading for Uttoxeter! Seems no one ever told Batman that horses are herd animals and, as such, instinct takes them back to where the other horses are, i.e. the lorry park. Fortunately, both rider and horse were none the worse for the experience. The groom, Marcus, however, was really quite knackered from joining the party trying to catch him! Seemed Marcus ran almost two kilometres in the search for Batman.

By the time we were reunited in the car park, around twenty minutes had passed. Since the time allowed for completing the cross country was in the region of seven minutes in total, we were without a doubt way over. Yet again, a competition came and went and I still hadn't completed. This was proving to be most tricky! I decided for my next event entry, I would bypass the middleman and put 999 down as my emergency contact.

Chapter 53

Recovered from my second failed event, I took heart that I was getting further each time. I realised what a bloody long way I had to go to get as far as being competent enough to actually win an event. I'd invested too much time, physical pain and mental torture in this process to quit though. Gabby decided I needed a bit of fun.

So now that I have this hacking down to an art, in as much as I can get out of the yard, round the roads and tracks and back in one piece, Gabby suggested that it would be a fun experience for me to go to the beach. I liked the sound of that. Last time I went to the beach was on a hen do. We had lots to drink, lots to eat and then even more to drink. It was a great day and we had a minibus there and back. However, it quickly became clear that this beach visit was going to be quite different. I suspected my mode of transport would be a horsebox and that the closest I'd come to alcohol might be a welcome glass of Prosecco when I got home.

We set off in two lorries, headed for Filey beach, near Scarborough on the North East coast. Sue had checked the tide times. That was a good job, really. Filey, I was told, has a five-mile stretch of beach that riders can use at any time of the year – when the tide is out, of course!

'We'll have a great time, galloping along the beach,' said Sue. Five miles seemed a long, long way for things to go wrong. If we add into that my complete and abject fear of water, it wasn't looking hopeful for me. I decided to take charge a little and took on the responsibility of checking it out and making sure I knew what to expect. I beavered away on Google Earth, looking at the street views from when we would arrive and park up to getting down to the beach. Preparation; a new concept to me, but Batman's unpredictable little ways were my incentive.

The car park looked good. There was plenty of space right at the end of a cul-de-sac with additional overflow space on the wide grass area at the back of the car park itself. The picture of the car park that was used on the Google Earth view, however, was clearly taken around six on a Sunday morning. When we turned up at ten-thirty on the Saturday morning following the schools chucking out for half-term on the Friday before, it looked (and sounded) like carnival central. The car park was full, the grass overflow was filling up and the place was swarming with children, families, prams, footballs and Frisbees. I felt like getting my mobile out and pre-booking my ambulance extraction!

My concern proved justified when we opened the back of the lorry and, as Batman's head popped out, his eyes also popped out at the vibrant scene playing out before him. When the trip was first mooted, my concern was the galloping along five miles of beach. It didn't occur to me that I might struggle to even get out of the car park. People in the car park seemed completely oblivious to my fear and made no attempt to tone down their activities to allow Batman and me to calm down a bit. Kids continued to scream, throw balls, bounce around and generally make a complete nuisance of themselves whilst I tried to work out how I was to get from the lorry to the other side of the car park without incident and, at the same time, remaining on the back of my horse. This, I felt, was going to be easier in theory than it was in practice. Batman looked unimpressed at all the commotion as I tacked up.

When I glanced at the others in my group, they were all busily tacking and getting ready with what seemed like no cares in the world. Were they just not seeing what I was seeing? Perhaps when I had their level of experience (although given my short timescale, that was unlikely to happen) I might be so blasé!

When I got on though, whilst he felt like he'd gotten taller by a few inches he was actually much better behaved than I could have hoped for. I think it was more that there was so much going on for him to look at that he was actually completely overwhelmed by everything. So, instead of spooking at anything, his fear of everything kept him where I wanted him: directly underneath me. We only nearly landed on one car bonnet and nearly squashed one loose child, so that was a good result.

Once out of the car park, the walk down to the beach whilst busy, was relatively uneventful. I was secretly just a little proud as people turned to watch us go by, some smiling and waving, some wanting to pat the horses. Once on the beach, we headed off to the right, which was much quieter than the main bit where the kids and families were headed. Still early in the day, the beach wasn't too busy.

We'd been out for over two hours so it was close to lunchtime when we arrived back at the main promenade to head back up to the lorries. Unfortunately, in the interim between heading out and heading back, the beach had filled significantly. There were two ways off the beach, one to the left towards the rocks that was much quieter in terms of family inhabitants and one a little further straight on that would take us up the main ramp back to the street above. That way, there were screaming children, children building sandcastles, parents sitting behind wind-breakers, flying kites, playing football, playing Frisbee and generally presenting a most bloody unreasonable set of obstacles that we had to traverse to get back to the lorries in one piece. But, that wasn't the worst of it. Since we'd left, some idiot in their ever-so-skewed wisdom had decided to bring a herd of damn donkeys – yes donkeys – down onto the beach, with their braying and their brightly coloured tack and bells!

Now, having grown up in my former years in a seaside town (Scarborough, to be precise), donkeys have been an integral part of my childhood seaside days out. I've been known to enjoy the odd tootle up and down the sand on the back of a donkey and never would I have thought that they would have been the source of very clear and urgent terror for me; with their big long cuddly ears, fluffy coats and their brow bands sporting names like 'Minstrel' and 'Buttons', but that's exactly what was going on right here.

Batman took one look at them and decided they were akin to a bunch of little, long-eared Satans and planted his feet. I kicked and kicked but he refused to move. He wasn't the only one either. Robbie was following suit, as were the other two behind us. It took us a good few minutes to persuade the horses to move at all. We decided, as a group, that the best course of action was to brave the mayhem that was the right-hand way rather than face the much quieter way that involved the satanic, life-threatening donkeys. I will never look at donkeys in the same light again. In fact, I've found that Batman has already had more than just a marginal effect on how I see the world around me. I can be wandering down the street at lunchtime, for example, and see a discarded plastic bag blowing in the wind. At one time, that would have invoked almost no reaction at all. Now, however, an occurrence like that would see a reaction more akin to: *what sort of completely selfish bastard drops a plastic bag like that with no regard to anyone else's safety?* The problem is, you understand, that Batman doesn't just see a plastic bag. He sees a monster that is out to eat him alive. It is of complete irrelevance to Batman that that monster is firstly, inanimate and as such has absolutely no eating capability at all and secondly, is roughly one hundred times smaller than he is so there's no possible way in which it would have the capacity to eat him anyway.

Chapter 54

After my first two rather unsuccessful competitive British Eventing outings, Gabby suggested that we needed a different approach. That approach was to load me, Batman and a shedload of others from the yard, plus their horses, into a set of lorries and head off to another event at the other side of the country. We'd stay over in the lorries and compete the next day. Marcus would come to help groom and Gabby would be in charge overall.

I wasn't sure I was loving this idea. Competing on a horse was bad enough without roughing it overnight in a bloody horsebox.

Had I been given Richard's own lorry to drive, that would have been a completely different matter. With its leather seating, pulley-out side panel for extra seating space, full shower room with toilet and double bed above the Luton, that might have been acceptable. But no, I got the clapped-out Ford Cargo HGV lorry that was 'mine' for the duration and had frankly not only seen better days but had seen a good number of not-so-better days.

It did, though, have a functional living area with a seat, table and hob. In the absence of a fridge, wine would need to be kept cold in a cool bag. The sleeping area on the Luton had just about ten inches of head room, if that. Big Katie was to share the lorry with me but as she was working, she would follow us down in the car and join us a little later.

On the way it pissed down. And, guess what? The lorry leaks! I had to throw the rest of my Costa extra hot, large latte out the window, marginally missing an overtaking car, and use the paper cup to catch the drips. The passing driver shook his fist at me. I made a mental note to remember to have my middle finger ready on standby when driving the lorry. If Richard was testing my strength of character, he was doing a bloody good job of it! Whilst my strength of character might not be as rigid as he might like, the strength of my desire to flatten Richard was pretty invincible.

When we arrived, we parked up, unloaded the horses and got them settled in their stables. We'd walk the courses tomorrow, so for tonight there wasn't much else to do but eat some supper and drink some wine. Oh, and learn my dressage test. I hadn't done that yet, which was very remiss of me. I decided to learn it at bedtime so Gabby didn't realise I was quite this unprepared. She didn't like unpreparedness, especially in me. My dressage test was scheduled for nine-thirty in the morning so I planned an early night and placed a mental restriction on myself on the amount Prosecco allowed.

We met up a little later in Liv's lorry, which was parked a bit further down the line from mine, to eat together and have a few drinks. Big Katie arrived in time to eat. We had a large bowl of chilli each. It was actually good fun. Liv was clearly recovering well from Mark's departure. We had a good laugh and plenty to drink – I clearly had forgotten my earlier mental restriction on consumption. So much so that I managed to completely miss my footing on the lorry steps and do a rather poor impression of a diving swallow. This particular swallow, however, was afflicted with a serious case of expletives.

'You OK, Fran?' called Liv from the lorry, clearly having heard my crash landing.

'Ahm awl gud,' I called back, not actually sure if I was or I wasn't.

Clearly extremely worn out from the lengthy drive (absolutely nothing to do with the copious amounts of alcohol consumed), my mishaps didn't end there. I managed to fall into a hedge as I tripped over, well, it was essentially my own feet, though I tried to convince Katie it was a divot in the ground.

Katie told me the next day that she did actually consider leaving me there but then realised she might have to own up to knowing me in the morning so decided instead to pull me out and assist me back to the lorry.

My bed for the night was the Luton and Big Katie was sleeping on the seat that folded down into a makeshift bed. Once up on the Luton, my head had barely hit the pillow and I must have been out cold. My big mistake was not going for a wee before bed. All that Prosecco had to go somewhere (other than my head, that is) and the Prosecco was seeking that somewhere to go at around four in the morning. I was pretty drowsy when I awoke, bursting for the loo. I soon found out that it's not ideal, when sleeping on a lorry Luton, to forget you are a good six feet off the ground when standing down from your bed. The result was a crash landing, for a second time that night, on the floor with a rather sharp 'ouch'.

I'm not sure whether Katie just slept through the minor commotion or just chose to ignore me. I think it might have been the latter but I can't be certain.

When morning came, my head felt thick and I wished I had just heeded myself on the early-night-with-not-much-wine front but, to be honest, no one ever seems to listen to me so why the hell should I? Suitably kaylied (otherwise known as in a state of high inebriation), in addition to forgetting my bedtime toileting, I also managed to forget to learn my dressage test, too. Oops!

App out on my phone, I cracked on trying to learn it through the fog that was purporting to be my mind. It was difficult, I can tell you.

Turns out that a hangover is my ideal competing state. Too concerned with making sure I didn't simply puke all over Batman's mane in the dressage, I seemed to relax completely – in honesty, I don't think I had the bodily capability to even clench my butt cheeks never mind get tense with nerves.

Proper result! I was so pleased, I called Paul.

'You won't believe this, I got a twenty-nine dressage.'

'And that means what?'

'Well, you start an event with a score of zero and the aim is to stay as close to zero as possible. The more penalties you get, the higher your score and the worse you're doing. Anyway, anything less than thirty for the dressage is really very good.'

'Well done! I'm impressed. Does that mean you win?' At that point, my short-lived elation soon faded when I remembered I still had two pretty decent jumping phases to go and with a hangover to boot. 'Afraid not, I still have to jump and I'll get more penalty points for making mistakes and getting things wrong. This is something I'm pretty damn good at.'

'Good luck, sis, or break a leg, or whatever you horsey folks do for luck.'

'It won't be breaking a leg, that's for sure, but thanks.'

I almost, and I stress *almost*, wanted to phone Mother too, but I felt her lack of understanding around the scoring added to her general distaste for me even being involved with horses and would simply end up dampening my currently quite-high spirits, so I decided against it.

Again, the hangover worked in my favour. Batman was amenable and didn't spook, sod off, buck, rear or otherwise try to cause me any general and unnecessary pain and suffering. As a result, I did my first clear round show jumping and my first clear round cross country which meant I had gone 'double clear', as they say in the eventing world. I did, though, go way too slow cross country, exceeding the optimum time by a good thirty seconds. This added eighteen extra time penalties onto my dressage mark, leaving me with a final score of forty-seven which saw me well short of even being within the top ten and getting a rosette, never mind winning. I had to look on this positively. I was progressing. This was a huge improvement on our last disastrous outing.

'Well done, Fran,' said Gabby, when I was done. 'Bloody good result! You can go back to the yard this time with your head held high.' Whilst surprised, her comment was welcome and somewhat unexpected. It also reinforced how badly I'd screwed up last time.

She added: 'This is it now. Next time out it's the real deal, the one you need to win! Just two weeks.'

It was time. Though I was now thinking it was doable.

Chapter 55

Successful event now under my belt it was time for attempt #2 to meet with the developers. It was the same receptionist and I'm pretty damn sure she was smirking to herself when I walked into the building. I chose (unusually) to be the adult (in reality, not exactly sure I know what being an adult actually involves) and ignored her smug look.

To get into the meeting area, there was a suitably placed security Perspex double-glassy-barrier type construction that blocked the way. I was quite desperate for a wee so asked the receptionist for the ladies.

'Through there, and to the left.' She pointed past the barrier to the door to the corridor leading to the 'beyond' that I couldn't see.

The double-glassy-barrier thing opened like magic and through I went. I was, indeed, quite bursting when I got there and was almost doubled up in a kind of crab-like-hold-it-in-desperately walk whilst trying to look normal. This resulted in my bottom half doing a sort of independent tango whilst my top half was erect, still and smiling. Anyway, crisis averted, wee done and underwear intact, I returned to reception to await my meeting.

A guy just in front of me walked through the double-Perspex-glassy-barrier thing using his pass, so I instinctively followed him. If the receptionist had a) forgotten all about the last debacle when I arrived for attempt #1 of the meeting and b) thought I was a credible business person, then I screwed those up in one fell swoop. As I followed Mr Man-With-The-Pass, the glassy-barrier-perspexy gates decided to close right about the time my lower thighs were about to pass. The result saw me arse over tit over the top of the glassy-perspexy barriers and sprawled on my face. It was a real big plus though, that for such an important meeting, despite landing on my face with my glasses strewn across the floor, my clothes were on the right way out AND the right way round (I double checked before I left home!).

When I finally got into the meeting room, it was warm and I rolled up my sweater sleeves, revealing the bruise that emerged from one of my many unintentional, involuntary dismounts from Batman.

I could see Dr Burns looking and followed his gaze, lifting my arm up a bit like a trophy. I did look a bit like a battered wife, to be fair.

'I fell off,' I said, in explanation.

He looked at me with that sort of quizzical, I-don't-know-what-the-hell-you're-talking-about expression on his face.

'Fell off what?' he asked.

Silly me. So overtaken with the whole riding situation I found myself in, I was beginning to forget there was a whole society out there whose every waking moment and movement is not governed in some way by a big, hulking four-legged creature that takes all your time, energy and life force.

'My horse,' I said, and I just couldn't help the faintest feeling of pride when I spoke of Batman in this way.

Dr. Burns nodded his understanding.

'I didn't realise you rode,' he said.

'Neither did I,' I said, chortling neurotically. The looks on Dr. Burns and his team's faces suggested a need for some type of explanation.

'Long story,' I said. 'I've not been riding long. It's a new experience for me, so it's early days.'

'Good for you,' he said.

We got down to business. A plan started to take shape to produce the software for my app. I shared my algorithms with them; they were super impressed. I inwardly beamed. It felt good for my work to be appreciated in knowledgeable circles. It was good to feel like a respected and intelligent human being again rather than the village idiot, which is what I felt like most of the time I was at the yard. We agreed a date for the prototype to be ready. It would take some Skype calls in the interim to review progress but it felt good to have a plan.

Forty thousand pounds would be the overall development cost and they wanted twenty thousand up front. It doesn't take a genius to work out that that left me with just five thousand of my current investment. I felt exposed thinking about this. I actually liked having twenty-five thousand pounds in my business account – to be honest, who wouldn't? Whilst spending the money was, indeed, essential as well as its actual purpose, it was proving difficult.

I asked Dr. Burns to email me their bank details and promised to transfer the money by close-of-play the next day.

As I was leaving, one of the developers asked 'Is your top on inside out?'

Any normal person would think he was joking but this was me. It most certainly wouldn't be the first time. Whilst I was sure I'd double-checked every item of clothing as I'd put it on, seems I'd missed one crucial item

– my jumper. To be fair to myself, I hadn't missed it, I'd checked the label was in the right place and still managed to get it wrong. I think there might come a time in my life when I can put myself forward as a sensible and responsible adult human being. That time will be signified by the fact I can firstly, dress myself correctly (especially when it really matters, like when I'm trying to present a professional image) and secondly, I'll tell you when I can remember what the hell I was going to write at this point (I got distracted by *First Dates* on TV!). In the moment - that's where I need to be.

Chapter 56

The final two weeks passed way too quickly. The day was here. It was my event: BE80T competition at Bears Grove College. To be fair, I was absolutely crapping myself. I'd just arrived at the yard with all my gear on, over trousers, to keep me clean whilst I muck out and get ready to load up in the lorry.

Marcus arrived at the yard plenty early and I was extremely grateful for that, because he is often so very late.

Marcus took one look at the plaits I'd done in Batman's mane the night before and promptly set about taking them out and redoing them. In honesty, my plaiting left much to be desired. I've heard it said on the yard that crap plaits look like golf balls but mine went a step further and looked more like a bunch of Rambutan fruit (google image it if you don't know what they look like and you'll see – a bit like extra hairy testicles to be honest, and definitely not neat plaits). I guess, that could just have been my general inexperience, though.

I finished my stable, made sure my tack was loaded, along with my other riding kit and Marcus loaded Batman on the back of the lorry. We were fit and ready to go.

First stop, as you might imagine, was the services on the M62 to pick up two cups of fresh coffee. Functioning, in my opinion, was not possible without a shot of coffee.

Marcus's coffee went straight down in about two gulps after which he went into his default position of sound asleep, head resting on the passenger door, mouth hanging open, snoring loudly. He stopped short at drool escaping and dripping down his front, for which I was grateful. And he should have been grateful too, because it would have made a super social media post.

So, I drove, following satnav to Bears Grove College. The trip was quite easy. As I came within spitting distance, my heart started going ten to the dozen and I found myself desperate for the loo. It seems that arriving at a competition has an effect on my physiology that I can't control but that, if I'm not careful, could become debilitating. Debilitated is a state I don't like; it signals simple loss of control. If I were to lose control today, that would be the end of the remaining and substantial fifty thousand pounds. Richard has been explicit about it. Winning today is non-negotiable if I am to win the remainder of my investment. So, that's it. It's all or nothing. The reality was sinking in fast. I had worked many months for this and it was all going to boil down to, not just my performance today, but Batman's too. I couldn't do this alone. I couldn't make Batman do this either. We had to work together – today was about a partnership. I realised this. There would be no kicking his shins today (not that I had actually done that yet, but I had wanted to do it several times).

Once in the lorry park, we were directed to our spot for the day. The place was filling up with a steady stream of competitors, with lorries lined up in rows. We parked, pulled down the ramp and Marcus busied himself getting buckets, sponges, sweat scrapers and the grooming kit out. He lined them all up neatly down the side of the lorry on the ground, ready for use. Watching him work away there, I was supremely grateful I had him to help me. A moment later, Sue and Liv rolled up.

'Hey, how's it going?' asked Sue. They were dressed up warm against the autumn chill. 'We wanted to be here for you.' Sue gave me a knowing look. She knew just what today meant. Liv, whilst a good friend now, still didn't know the real reason I was competing today, but I was very thankful for her support nonetheless. 'We'll leave you and Marcus to it for now but we'll be there for each phase and we'll be proper rooting for you.'

'Thanks guys, I really appreciate it.'

As they headed off toward the trade stands, my heart sank just a tad when I saw the little dumpy figure of my mother walking across the lorry park heading right in our direction. And why wouldn't she be here? Didn't I chastise her for not supporting me in our last conversation? She looked just a touch ridiculous in a skirt and ankle welly boots.

'Fran. I've come to cheer you on,' she told me. 'Please don't fall off or screw this up so badly you make us look like idiots.' That was such a 'my Mother' thing to say.

'Mum, they don't do cheering at events. Just watch quietly, please. 'And,' I added, 'don't get in the way.' I ignored the screwing-up comment completely. She looked a touch indignant but didn't argue.

'Why don't you head off up to the trade stands by the show jumping arena and get a coffee? Sue and Liv are there somewhere. I'll see you a bit later.'

Marcus pulled a piece of paper and a pen from the lorry cab and scribbled some notes. He handed the paper to Mother.

'These are Fran's times.' She took the sheet but looked a touch confused. 'The first time is for Fran's dressage test, the second for her show jumping and the third for her cross-country. Follow Sue and Liv and you won't miss a thing.' She tootled off and I was relieved...well, as relieved as I could be when I was about to compete in the biggest and most important competition of my life.

Marcus smiled at me. I sensed he knew the nerves I was feeling.

I wondered if Richard would show up today to watch or whether he'd just rely on seeing the results afterwards to see if his gamble had paid off or not. I wasn't quite sure which I preferred. If he arrived here and hung around with us, would it put me under added pressure? I wasn't actually sure how much more pressure I could feel. I was doing a good enough job of stressing myself out.

Marcus sent me off to pay my start fee and get my number. Our plan for today was dressage first, then I had a two-hour break before my show jumping round, so I could walk the cross-country course then so I'd know where Batman and I would be going. I'd then warm up and jump my show jumping round, then get ready for cross country. Marcus would do all the grooming and tacking up. All I had to do was get myself ready for each phase. I wished I had a bottle of Prosecco with me but I was quite sure the only effect it would have would be to make me care a little less and the only part of my riding ability it might improve is the falling off part. I wasn't keen on that today.

When I got back to the lorry Paul was there, deep in what looked like close conversation with Marcus. It seemed that everyone was keen to support or, indeed, watch me fall on my face, today. With the exception of Sue and Liv, I wasn't sure it was a welcome intrusion though. I needed to be focussed and didn't need these distractions.

Ready and on board Batman, we headed off for the dressage warm up. This was just my third ever event in history and it was all feeling extremely tense at the moment. I needed to keep my head, if this was to work out. Batman seemed to have developed a sixth, seventh and one-hundredth sense about when I was feeling nervous or wussy or scared. And, in such situations, instead of helping me out and making me feel better, he took the approach of follow my leader. At any other time, Batman likes to take any opportunity to try to get one-up and think he's the boss.

I took some deep breaths and really calmed my thoughts down. Time to focus on just one thing at a time. The thing at the moment was my dressage – nothing else. Tempting though it was to allow my little mind to wander and see me falling off in the show jumping, I pushed those thoughts away and stuck with dressage.

The collecting ring was busy. We warmed up well, with Marcus interjecting at points, as he did at my first event, with some useful comments to make things better; like steer out of the way that horse and avoid running that trainer down: all helpful direction from one who knows. Then it was time. I was in the second of five arenas. I'd practised this before, I'd done dressage tests.

So, as I said at the outset of my tale, here I am, warmed up, all my show best on, ready to go into the arena. My heart is beating ten-to-the-dozen, as they say.

After all, there's more to this than just winning a competition.

'Come on Batman,' I tell him. 'This one needs to be the best.' His ears come back towards me, like he's listening. That's good enough for me. And off we go. The test goes OK. It's hard to tell afterwards really. I don't think we did much wrong. Batman felt good and I tried really hard to sit up with a 'look at me' posture. Marcus tells me it looked good. Unlike my dressage test at my first event that, if you remember, was a real bloody dog's dinner, this was OK. I'm smiling, at least for a few moments. That is until I remember that the next thing I have to do is show jump – then I start to tremble just a little.

We head back to the lorry, Marcus untacks Batman and loads him back up. We have two hours before my jump time. We head off out to walk the cross-country course. Gabby had decided that it wasn't a good idea for me to walk the course the day before. In my very limited experience, I'd found an ability that saw the jumps growing in my mind overnight, so she thought it best that I keep them in proper perspective. Well, after walking it, I'm not quite sure that has worked because they look massive to me!

Richard had instructed Gabby not to be here. 'This is your big challenge, Fran. You have to be able to do it without having Gabby there as your crutch. Marcus can help as a groom, but you must compete on your own,' he'd told me back at the yard. Initially I was horrified. Actually, I probably still am horrified but the nerves are now at full throttle so they are cancelling out anything else.

'Just how big can an eighty-centimetre jump be, for goodness' sake?' asks Marcus. 'Get a grip!'

Get a bloody grip? The way I'm feeling about the rest of this competition, I wouldn't have minded getting a grip – a grip of Richard's neck, in fact. If he was here right now...

'Hi there,' says a familiar voice from inside the back of the lorry.

'Richard. You came! Great to see you,' I lie.

OK, so that was actually just bravado, I wasn't actually going wring his neck now, was I? I needed him for the rest of my investment.

'How's it going?' he asks. 'I got stuck in traffic so I missed your dressage. Sorry about that.'

'That's OK,' I say. 'It's going good, so far. Dressage wasn't a car wreck so that's a very good start. The cross country is bloody mahoosive in my opinion, but Marcus thinks it's fine, so I guess it is fine – I just need to get my head around it.'

Richard chats with Marcus whilst he tacks up Batman again, this time in his jumping saddle. I'm instructed to go into the lorry and get my jacket, hat and number bib on.

We head to the show-jumping warm up. I have Marcus with me. I can see Richard, my Mum, Paul and then the girls from the yard. They're scattered around the edge of the arena, all there to watch me. Off to the left of the arena, I see Gary. My heart is pounding so hard and my stomach is in nauseating knots.

'You're alright, you know,' Marcus says, drawing my attention away from the ring and the watching faces. 'Let's get you and Batman warmed up. You can do this.'

I warm up well and now that I'm jumping, I feel a little more relaxed. Well, maybe not relaxed but at least feeling a little less like I'm about to throw up all over Batman's mane.

Two more practice fences jumped and they call my number. It's my turn to jump.

'You're ready for this, Fran,' says Marcus. 'Go in there and show me everything I've taught you.' He smiles. I smile back but I think it materialises a touch more like a grimace.

As I canter round in the arena, the bell goes to indicate I can start to jump. Over fence one, two, they're staying up. I almost want to hold my breath but I don't. Fence three, four and then, over five, I hear a clatter. I think a pole has fallen. I put it out of my mind. I've got three more fences to jump and I have to stay focussed. And then I hear the commentator. I'm expecting him to announce that I've had four faults for a knock down.

'And that's a lovely clear round for Fran McBride and Blue-Eyed Batman.'

I can't believe it.

'Good boy, GOOD BOY!' I pat him wildly all the way out of the arena.

'Well done, Fran,' says Marcus, feeding a well-deserved treat to batman.

Back at the lorry, it's a quick change to get ready for cross-country. My elation over my clear show jumping round is soon set aside as the challenge of the cross-country course sets in. The air is cool and I'm glad I've got long sleeves on. I can hear Richard, Marcus and Paul chatting.

'Fran, dear,' I hear the dreaded voice of doom, calling to me from outside the lorry. 'Fran, you in there?' I pop my head out the door.

'Hi Mum.'

'I watched your jumping. I think under the circumstances you did very well. Not quite as stylish as the proper riders but you didn't knock any down so that's good.' She doesn't wait for me to respond. 'Is it time for coffee yet?'

I roll my eyes.

'No, I've still got cross country to go yet,' I say slowly, trying to retain my patience.

'Mrs McBride,' says Marcus, 'Fran needs to focus and avoid any distraction. The cross country is the most challenging phase of this competition.'

'Pardon me,' she says, her voice thick with sarcasm. 'I don't mean to get in the way.'

'That's not a problem, Mrs McBride, you're not in the way. Fran just needs to be on the ball right now.'

'I'll go and find somewhere to watch then, shall I?'

'Mum, I'll come with you,' said Paul, he looked up at me and winked.

The coast clearing of critical eyes, I come out of the lorry, suited and booted for cross country. The butterflies in my stomach are fluttering in a hurricane.

Warming up for cross-country doesn't take too long.

'It's time,' Marcus says to me. 'I'll come to the start with you.'

We walk the short few strides over to the white-railed start box. The starter is standing with his stop-clock, watching it intently, and is counting me down from twenty seconds.

'Keep your shoulders up and remember to kick,' instructs Marcus. 'Ride safely out there.' I intend to heed that advice.

'Three, two, one..., good luck,' says the starter and I'm off. Batman and I speed out onto the cross country course and I feel the wind whizzing past me. We jump the first, the second, the third. I feel a smile creep over my face. Scary yes, but absolutely wonderful too!

I am approaching the trakehner jump. It's a wide wooden pole sat diagonally over a ditch. I'm nervous of this one. I know that Batman is good with ditches but he senses when I'm not one-hundred percent about anything and on walking the course I wasn't loving the trakehner. Travelling at around twenty-five miles per hour, rapidly approaching the dreaded jump, my brain quickly assesses the situation: Give up, don't ride the fence like I should, get a massive twenty-penalties for a cross-country refusal added to my score and definitely lose the investment, or kick like hell and get over the trakehner first time. Before I even know what I've decided, my legs are in gear kicking like hell. The jump is coming up fast, Batman's ears are pricked, he's picked up the jump. I can feel it, he's locked on and is going to jump it. There is just a split fraction of a second at take off where he just dwells a touch, but our partnership is now so solid that I react immediately with an extra kick and we're over.

As I gallop on to finish the course, I feel like we're flying. I feel like I'm free and it feels fabulous.

Marcus, Richard, Paul, Liv and Sue are there at the finish line and they clap and cheer for Batman and me. It feels awesome.

I jump off Batman and Marcus takes over to get him back to the lorry, cooled down and back on board with a haynet.

'You were clear. What a great round,' said Liv. 'I'm so pleased for you.'

'Thanks. Where's Mum?'

'We left her with a coffee. She felt it was too far to walk up here to cross-country finish.' I feel just a touch disappointed. I'd have liked her to have seen how good my cross-country riding has become. 'We'll go find her while you and Batman get sorted and meet back by the scoreboard,' said Sue. With that, I hurry off after Batman and Marcus.

I don't want to look at the scoreboard, yet I can't look away. My dressage score was good. Not brilliant, but it was good. It puts me in the top ten out of forty. That's good. Adding up the scores, it looks like at least six could go ahead of me. They still have cross-country scores to go up. My time penalties would be crucial and then it was out of my hands. It will be dependent on how those other six have fared out on the cross-country phase. The likelihood, though, of them all falling behind me is really pretty damn slim. The sinking realisation that I am within probably less than an hour of failing, having worked my arse off for more than eight months at this challenge, is now dawning on me. My heart is feeling heavy as the lady with the clipboard comes mooching into the score tent to put up some more scores. My time penalties are confirmed as five. So I had been over the optimum time. Even so, for such a novice at eventing, that was a pretty bloody good round. My final score is a very respectable thirty-eight but I know in my heart of hearts that it's not a winning score. The course is tough and is causing problems but it won't be enough of a problem to save my fifty thousand pounds. Of the six remaining scores in my section, one had jumping penalties on the cross country which took that competitor behind me, three had time faults but not enough for me to trouble their placings and the last two went clear with no time faults.

It's confirmed then, it's clear as day; I am in sixth place. I feel the sting of tears and I breathe deeply to fight them back. I will not cry here in public. I tried the best I could, I worked hard with the horse I was given and we did well but it just wasn't good enough in the end. So yes, I'll get the honour of attending the prize giving in all my posh gear and I'll go home with a rosette, and I know that's a real achievement, but it's not the achievement I needed. I've failed the task, the challenge is over and my months of pain and struggle have been for just about nothing. I'm going to have to find Richard, face up to him and concede defeat.

'Poor you,' says Mum, standing behind me as I take in the scores. 'I could have told you it would end in tears.'

'Thanks for that, Mum, that's helpful,' I say with sarcasm. 'Why don't you go, join Paul and get us a coffee?' To be honest, I just want to get rid of her for now; she's bringing me down. Her negative attitude is doing my head. Why can't she see that I've actually done really well. OK, so it's not the win that I need but, of anyone, she should be singing my praises and boosting me back up.

As I leave the score tent, I can see Richard, Marcus and Paul hovering by the coffee stall. Marcus and Paul are looking just a little too comfortable with each other, but right now I don't think I care too much. I sneak away back to the lorry. I just want some time to reflect on the whole situation I now find myself in: half a product developed, no money to take it any further, all to take part in this stupid challenge and end up stuck in the same crap job.

What the actual hell had I been thinking in the first place? Am I really that delusional that I thought I could do this? I want to blame Richard for putting me in this position but, to be honest, I did a good enough job of it for myself. I head straight back to the lorry and into the back to Batman who, now his job is done, is munching happily on his net. And to be fair, he did his job well today. I pull a few Polos from my pocket and feed them to him, one-by-one.

'Well, my man, we did what we set out to do. We're here, you and me; probably the most badly matched partnership in the equestrian world – maybe even the entire world. We didn't win, but we made a good show of ourselves. Thank you, Batman. You could have been the out-and-out arse of a horse I've seen on many occasions these last few months, but you weren't.'

In fact, when the chips were down, he was there for me, this quirky, mild-mannered horse that I realised had become my friend.

I don't notice Richard and Marcus have followed close behind, with Mum and Paul in tow.

'Sixth!' says Richard. 'An excellent result. Surpassed all my expectations, to be honest.'

I look at him with a scowl.

'You didn't even think I could win?' I feel cross.

'Well, even you, with no knowledge at all, knew it was a big ask.'

'Yes, but I cracked on and had a good go because you let me think it was possible.'

'And succeeded! Against all the odds.'

'Not enough – sixth, as we both know, isn't a win.'

'But it is a win for you and Batman. Maybe not in the event placing sense of the word, but what else would you call a result like that?'

I can't help the smile that breaks across my face as I understand what he is saying.

He continues, 'the big question is; what to do with Batman now that the challenge is over.'

My smile fades. I knew the time was going to come and, to be honest, when I started out on this quest, I couldn't wait for it to be over, but the truth is; through all our very few ups and very many downs, I'd actually grown quite fond of him and was not looking forward to him no longer being a part of my daily life. My concern over the remainder of the money had faded with my smile.

'I won't beat about the bush – do you want to keep him?'

My smile is back, and that is all the answer that was needed.

'Sis, I knew you could do this. Marcus had every confidence.'

'And, you two are just friends?'

'Yep. I plan to call Mike and straighten things out.'

Mum, tagging slowly behind, joins us.

'Perhaps you'll give up on all this rubbish now,' she says smugly. 'You were never going to win.'

Before I can respond, Richard jumps in.

'Fran has shown grit, determination and unbelievable strength of character to complete the challenge I set down for her. Not only is she a winner in my book, but she deserves every single penny of the investment.' I'm grateful to Richard for his words. Mum, however, looks less grateful, but I think the penny is finally dropping that I am actually capable of just a little more in life than she gives me credit for.

Epilogue

Competition over, entire challenge over, we agreed to meet at the pub that night for a celebratory drink. The whole yard was invited, but most wouldn't come. Some people just don't like to see others succeed. That aside, those of us that were there were all on good form and ready for a typical horsey night out. The Prosecco was flowing freely. And Gary showed up – not that I'm interested, of course.

'Great result,' he said. 'I saw you jump.'

I did a double take.

'Why didn't you come over and say hi?'

'Didn't want to put you off at all – you fell off last time you saw me at a competition.'

He wasn't wrong.

'Can't stay, though. Just wanted to say, well done!'

And, he was off. Just as well I'm definitely not interested and just as well I didn't ask him out on a date just to get it out of my system. Maybe that will come.

I pulled Richard aside. I told him that I just don't get it. I get that he's really rich and can afford what he's done with me. I get that investing in my business makes sense (of course it does!) and he stands to see a significant return on his investment. I even get that it could seem a bit of fun to watch a bumbling idiot like me try to learn to ride, and the money, to him, is really just a small fork of shavings in the muck heap. However, when I add it all up and look at the evidence, in my view, it just doesn't stack up. You just wouldn't spend that kind of money for no good reason.

'I'm in love with Sue,' he told me. My jaw dropped wide! 'I wanted to impress her. It was her suggestion to get you involved in horses. She said you needed an interest outside of your business obsession.' My jaw fell just a little further than I even knew it could. Sue! She was behind this. I guess I should have known. No random millionaire was going to set me up like this. I didn't know whether to be happy or cross.

'She cares very much about you,' he continued. 'She told me you hadn't just gone the extra mile but an extra ten miles, when her marriage split. You were her rock and helped get her through. She wanted to repay you.'

Hmmm, now let me think this through. Your best friend wants to make your life better so sets you up to take on a huge challenge of learning to ride: In which, you are likely to hit the deck, at least more than once, you are forced to compete and you have to give up every damn second of your spare time looking after and pandering to a four-legged creature that, most of the time, is only concerned with either eating, crapping or sleeping and that's repayment for a good deed?

Given that I realised I was going to miss Batman when this is all over, I think maybe, on balance, she did good.

'I see. So you did all of this for me, because you're in love with Sue?'

'She just never really noticed me, not in that way. Then this opportunity came along. We went for a drink and discussed how we could work this best so you got your investment and a life outside of business. For the first time since she had arrived at the yard, she *really* noticed me. It's early days, but we're moving in the right direction and not just because I've helped you; Sue's not like that.'

'You don't need to tell me that. I know her well.' At least, I thought I did – I wouldn't have expected this from her, though. In a way, I was a little down that the whole experience was over. The challenge was done. My business was progressing. But now I know I have new challenges ahead. The only difference is that now I'm setting the goals, all of them, myself. And do you know what? Most of them include Batman along the way. I've taken over the livery, I'm paying for my lessons with Gabby. I must like working with her, now I can choose to pay or not, as I see fit.

And, on the business front, Richard is taking more of a management interest. We're trailblazing ahead and *Liberty*, my super yacht, is most definitely on the horizon. Perhaps that horizon is on Mars but now it's potentially viable – at least with something akin to a Meerkat radio super telescope! So, watch this space for more news of the adventures on Planet Fran.